JUSTICE
FOR SOME

REID CHERNER

A POST HILL PRESS BOOK
ISBN: 978-1-68261-405-1
ISBN (eBook): 978-1-68261-406-8

Justice for Some

Cover art by Christian Bentulan

Post Hill Press
New York • Nashville
posthillpress.com
Published in the United States of America

DEDICATION AND ACKNOWLEDGMENTS

No author writes alone and this book certainly proves that.

Every family member and friend has a piece of this book. My father, Stanley, died decades before this was written but I thought of him every day when I wrote it. My mother, Irma, maybe the best writer in the family, was my first editor and continues to think everything I do is award-worthy.

Nothing gets done in my house without my wife Sara's approval. She also edits me on a daily basis and remains the one person I most want to impress. Our children Quinn and Hannah are why we get up every day with joy, and my brothers Randy and Joe teach me something new each time we get together.

As for this book, in particular, two people are responsible for getting this into print. My lifetime friend Rachel Shuster is among the three greatest editors in print history and she gave me no free passes in editing the many versions of this book. Debra Englander then held my hand and guided me through the process and nothing happens without her doing that.

CHAPTER 1

The only promise I make is this: the dog does not die in this story. Now, I might be lying, but what kind of rat bastard lies about a dog's safety?

I will lie a lot, but—and you can trust me on this—the dog remains unharmed.

Still, if you prefer your stories without death, then turn this off now. People will die before you finish.

I can't promise I won't be one of them.

Why should you care what happens?

I don't have an answer. But either I'm dead and you are the only one who has seen this or you found it and were intrigued enough to continue.

How you found it and what you decide to do with it is your story.

This one is mine. My promise is the dog; your promise of trust is a bargain I'm making on faith.

I didn't live with my grandmother but you could say she raised me. She was a presence in my house, and while my parents worked she took care of my three sisters and me.

(A brief interlude to say my sisters won't be involved in this story.)

They lead their own extraordinary lives. Sophie is a doctor, Zora is a teacher, and Harper is a pilot of small aircraft.

I would kill to protect them. Those watching this know the irony of that statement.

There is my first lie.

I said they would not be a part of this story and they already are.

I'm not going to apologize for untruths or this would be just one big apology.

My parents read *Goodnight Moon* and *Pat the Bunny* and the George and Martha books to me.

My grandmother read from Raymond Chandler.

Before my first birthday she finished *The Lady in the Lake* and all the Philip Marlowe novels were done in a few years.

I was probably the only 5-year-old to say a neighbor "was so ugly, even the tide wouldn't take her out." That wasn't really Marlowe but we ascribed all witty banter to Chandler.

If there were a "Bad Chandler" writing contest, we would have won.

Here is another one we got from a cop movie. "He had more collars than a Chinese laundry."

Once, when we were talking about an alcoholic neighbor, my grandmother pulled this one out.

"He's an occasional drinker, the kind of guy who goes out for a beer and wakes up in Singapore with a full beard."

That is real Chandler.

Later, when I read Marlowe for myself, we set about reading all 90 books written by Elmore Leonard. I am trying to channel Leonard here now.

It was Leonard who said, first you write and then you go back and take out all the boring stuff. Best advice I've heard on any subject.

But if you want to keep this between us and Raymond Chandler, then go with the notion that you should throw up into your typewriter every morning. Clean up at noon.

If you ask, "What kind of grandmother reads Chandler and Leonard to a baby?" I would answer, "The best kind."

But maybe it will help to relate this story. I entered a contest asking you to write a story in 55 words. I wrote several. None of course better than Hemingway's "For sale: Baby shoes. Never worn."

Here is one I wrote about my grandmother. It was called "Enough."

She was old and only wanted a quiet bus ride.
They were young and only wanted her money.
As they laughed, she feebly opened her purse.
She looked up. There was no mercy.
Two quick shots. They were dead.
The last thing they saw was her wrist tattoo.
The last words they heard: "Never again."

It isn't the funniest story I could have told and I'm a funny guy. But it is true and moves my narrative along.

Second drafts are for those reviewed in *The New York Times* Sunday book section.

I don't want this to come out wrong. My grandmother was a stone-cold killer, but not defined by that. We aren't just lawyers or mothers or racecar drivers.

While assassin seems like a defining career, you have to let yourself be open to that person having other qualities. Baking a chocolate cake, driver to basketball practice, and in a pinch, substitute at a parent-teacher conference.

This is getting grim so here's one that always makes me laugh.

Two cannibals are eating a clown when one says to the other, "Does this taste funny to you?"

I am getting loopy so let me share a 55-word story my grandmother wrote for the same contest.

She titled her story "Perfect Father."

As he waited at the station all he could think about was getting back to his children.

He would burst through the door and shower them with presents.

They would give him hugs and kisses.

The train arrived.

"Men to the left. Women to the right," he shouted. "Follow the signs to the showers."

My grandmother met as many of those men as she could. Women too. But never lost sight they were more than they presented to her. You have to admire that kind of compassion.

She enjoyed her work and when she got too old to be effective, she searched for a partner. But she needed someone she could trust, who could expand the business, and most important, someone who would never talk about it.

Until now, he never has.

CHAPTER 2

It may be true if not accurate that Secretariat's run in the Belmont Stakes changed Roza Grundstein's life.

She never thought she would cry again. She was a bit of a freak that way. There were never tears of frustration and, despite burying a husband and many friends, she never welled up.

So, imagine her surprise on that 1973 June day when Secretariat made the turn for home and she blinked away a tear.

When jockey Ron Turcotte looked under his arm to check his margin on the field, there were lines in her makeup. By the time the colt finished 31 lengths ahead and broadcaster Chic Anderson had screamed he was running "like a tremendous machine," she was sobbing.

In a world of cruelty and ugliness, Roza was overwhelmed by unspeakable beauty.

She sat for 15 minutes before trusting herself to put the teakettle on.

She picked up the phone and called her son.

"Samuel, did you see it?" she brayed when he answered.

"Mama?" he said, not quite recognizing his mother's voice.

"Did you see it?" she said with a laugh. "Did you see the horse?"

"The Belmont, mama? You watched the race?" he asked.

"I did. I did," she said. "It was the most magnificent thing I've ever seen, Samuel. It was beautiful. It was so beautiful."

As an adult Samuel was ready for almost anything his mother could throw at him. But the woman on the phone was one he had never met.

"Mama, are you okay? You sound so, so different," he said.

"Samuel, I want to go to the races," she said, giggling just like a schoolgirl.

"Now, mama?" he asked in confusion.

She chuckled. "No, son. Not now, but soon. Will you take me?"

"Of course," he said.

"You are a good boy, Sammy," she said, using a diminutive discarded decades ago. "I've always loved you and even when I couldn't show it, I've always loved you. You didn't get any prize for a mother, but I wanted you to know I tried my best."

"I know you did, Mom. I love you too."

"How is Hersh?" she asked.

"He's taking a nap. The girls are at the park."

"He seems like a sweet boy. He reminds me so much of you," she said.

"Mama, are you sure you are okay?"

"I am, Samuel, I am. I just want to spend some time at the track one day. I want it so much."

"Okay, then let's do it. We can make a day of it."

That was the day Roza brought over *The Lady in the Lake* to her son's home and read to Hersh.

CHAPTER 3

Hugo Yardley knotted his tie, gave his hair a hand comb, grabbed his briefcase, and strode into the kitchen.

"You leaving already?" asked his wife.

"Have a client who wanted to meet before the office officially opens," he said, grabbing a piece of toast. "When you have a client who has this kind of money, you cater to every whim."

"Well," said his wife, already bored with the business conversation, "don't forget the Boyles are coming for bridge tonight."

"Already have it written in my diary," Hugo said.

Yardley, who lived in the United States for decades, could let his European upbringing slip into conversation. He would say "lift" instead of elevator. His secretary would change "organise" to "organize" in memos.

"Could you do me a favor tonight and not talk about the election? You know how you and Charles get when you talk politics."

Hugo smiled. "Me?"

She laughed.

The Yardleys and Boyles were friends because the wives volunteered at the soup kitchen. Hugo and Charles would probably never have gotten together.

The Boyles did not run in the financial circles of the Yardleys.

The wealth Hugo brought from Europe started his investment career and had grown so exponentially in 50 years that Hugo could be described as filthy rich.

Not that he or his wife flaunted it. His wife worked as a department store buyer, and both were generous. Hugo especially.

He funded the support of rain forests and roads in other countries, but maximized his efforts in the United States. He was a "President's Circle" giver to his local theater, the Red Cross, the United Jewish

Appeal, and the "Feed the Hungry" program. He endowed scholarships at the local prep school and his alma mater Michigan, and to show he had no Ivy envy, gave endowments at Harvard and Princeton.

He contributed because he could and not because he was guilty about bilking clients. Hugo was not Bernie Madoff but he wasn't Caesar's wife either.

If you put on a $3,000 suit, trimmed your hair and fingernails, and spoke with an almost detectable accent, people trusted you with their money.

If you were what Hugo called "mature women," you trusted him with *all* your money.

He wasn't greedy. He would be called a skimmer and almost any audit would miss what he was doing. If caught by a good enough accountant he would be contrite, offer to reimburse at a good interest rate, and say how embarrassed he was at his mistake.

It helped while he was skimming that he was making money for his clients.

When you get 22 percent on your return, no one looks to find if the profit was really 24 percent.

He didn't need the money. But he couldn't help himself. The game was boring if you played by all the rules.

"You did hear me say bridge, right?" his wife repeated.

"Bridge and no politics," said Hugo with a laugh. "Should be loads of fun."

"Please don't be late. It makes us look like we think our time is more important than anyone else's."

Hugo looked around the 17-room apartment he bought for cash and resisted the retort sitting on his tongue. His wife knew what he was thinking and swatted him with a dish towel.

"Hugo, sometimes I think you value money over everything else."

"You are right, honey. So today I'm going to give it all away. I'm going to give up this apartment and the house we have in Italy and the condo at the beach. I'm going to give away the sports car you drive to work. And in an effort to help clothe the world I'm going to invite some people in here to pick over the designer clothes you have in your walk-in."

His wife laughed, kissed him on the cheek, and pushed him out the door.

Few people knew it but Hugo owned the building where he worked. It was just another investment kept hidden, because while it helped to be known as a rich man, it didn't always work to be a really rich man.

As he walked into his office, Dennis was already there. Hugo preferred male secretaries, or, as they preferred to be called, "assistants." Dennis was a particularly good one. He seemed to have no life outside of Yardley Investments.

"Morning, Dennis. Did you sleep here?"

"No sir, I did not," said Dennis.

Of his many qualities, Dennis wasn't blessed with a sense of humor.

So, Hugo told him a joke every morning.

"Three guys are up on an 18-story building. One says there is a draft between the building they are on and the adjourning building.

"One guy doesn't believe him, so the first guy jumps off the building, starts to go straight down and then floats back up.

"The other guy thinks it is the greatest thing he's ever seen, so he too jumps. And he plummets to his death.

"The third guy looks at the first guy and says, "You are one mean drunk, Superman."

For Hugo, the enjoyment was his assistant's confusion of whether to laugh.

Hugo patted Dennis on the shoulder and told him to let him know when the client came in.

Minutes after settling himself into his chair, Hugo swiveled around and looked out his window. He loved the view and was almost sorry when his buzzer went off signaling the client had arrived.

But an extended view was a reward for making money and Hugo estimated he'd need about 30 minutes before he was rewarded.

CHAPTER 4

Hugo could smell money and he smiled as the elderly woman walked in. She was on a cane but not overly dependant on it. She had gray curly hair and while not fat, she charitably could be called portly. She wore thick glasses and had a slight palsy in her left hand. Nothing showy but she looked like money with a tailored suit.

Profit was in the air.

"Okay, Mrs. McKay. I've gotten all your documents you sent to Dennis. It appears you have about $4.5 million to invest."

"Give or take the money I'm going to spend parking in this building."

Hugo's eyebrows shot up before realizing his client was having fun with him, and he barked out a laugh.

"There will be no parking charge for clients of your caliber, Mrs. McKay. We'll call it a perk."

"Well, we are off to a good start, aren't we, Mr. Yardley? I've made a profit already."

Hugo smiled but with a little less zest. He was not used to not taking the initiative.

"Could you tell me how you would like to invest this money?"

"Well," she said. "Most of the money isn't going to go to me in the end. I don't have enough time to spend what I have right now. So, I'd like to manage enough of it conservatively so there will always be something to draw from, but we can take some risks so those who inherit the wealth will have a bigger piece of the pie."

Hugo smiled. "I think we can handle that. I'll put together a portfolio and next week we can get serious about where you want the funds to go."

"Sounds like a plan," she said with a smile.

"Okay, then," he said. "Today we can set up the account. All I need is a user name and a password for the online file we can set up."

"User name could be Mrs. McKay."

"Simple and easy to remember."

"The password will be A16845."

"Not so easy to remember," said Hugo. "Perhaps you'd like something more memorable so you don't have to write it down or so you won't forget. At our age, it is easy to forget."

Mrs. McKay smiled and slowly rolled up her sleeve and looked at her wrist. "Not so hard to remember."

She then reached into her purse, pulled out a revolver loaded with a silencer and shot Hugo Yardley twice in the head.

Quickly making sure he would never get up, she swiveled his chair so he was looking out the window and his back was to the door.

She walked out and handed a package to Dennis.

"Mr. Yardley asked if you would deliver this across town. He needs about 45 minutes to create some other documents and then he'll be ready for you."

"Sure," said Dennis.

"I've got another appointment in this building so I'll see you next week," she said. "I'm just going to slip in the restroom down the hall and be off. It was nice meeting you."

As Dennis pushed the elevator button, Mrs. McKay went into the ladies' room. It took just minutes to slip off her wig and brush back the flaming red hair underneath. She removed the bridge forcing her teeth outward and wiped away the heavy makeup and much of the cloying perfume.

She removed the padding that added 30 pounds.

The lifts in her shoes were next and the tailored suit was replaced with a white shirt, button-down sweater vest, flannel pants, and running shoes.

The woman who walked out of the building bore some resemblance to the woman who walked in, but you'd have to know her to tell.

She walked east and wondered whether the morning papers would have her letter she had just sent out with Dennis.

Mrs. McKay was not a braggart but sometimes she felt a need to explain herself, and Hugo Yardley was about to be unmasked.

CHAPTER 5

The death of a prominent financier and benefactor was always news but the headline is what made you want to read the story.

KILLER OF HUGO YARDLEY
CLAIMS PHILANTHROPIST HAD NAZI TIES

The story had a small lede with the news of Yardley's death and mentioned a letter had come into the newspaper from someone claiming responsibility for the murder.

The reporter contacted police, who admitted the letter writer knew too many facts to be making a false claim. In exchange for the letter, the police allowed the paper to print the story.

Not too surprisingly, the letter trumped the news.

The letter was accompanied by a sheaf of documents the paper also ran. The documents, which the letter writer said would support the claims of the letter, had yet to be verified.

The letter was short, clean and pulled no punches.

I have killed Hugo Yardley. My only regret is I could not bring him back to life so I could kill him again.

The obituaries will certainly list his charities, his family, and his amazing financial success. Some friend might even mention his sense of humor and appreciation of a good joke.

What it won't mention is as a teenager, Hugo Yardley was a murderer and responsible for thousands of deaths in the camps during the war.

But of course, if you research Hugo Yardley, you will find no proof. However, if you look up Henrik Klemmer you will find a man responsible for misery and death.

I am sure his family and friends will denounce this letter or say a mistake has been made.

Let us be clear about one thing. You can argue whether death equals death. You can argue whether vigilantes are ever justified and you can argue whether time equals healing.

What you can't argue is Hugo Yardley aka Henrik Klemmer was a murderer. I didn't find out about him and then kill him. I researched him for many years. Then I stalked him. Then I hunted him, and then I shot him twice in the head.

I thought I would want him to know what I was doing but in the end, I couldn't stand being in the room with him, so I ended it quickly. You have to give me points for an iota of decency.

If anyone is going to take the time to track me down, let me end this by saying Klemmer is among the worst murderers I've known, but he's not the first I've sent to Hell. But he will be my last.

Emotionally and mentally it isn't hard for me to do what I've done but physically time has taken a toll. I lived a life without credit; for since this is my swan song, I thought of taking a bow before I left the stage.

CHAPTER 6

It had been years since Hersh used an alarm clock. He awakened one minute before his scheduled time. But if that failed, Clemenza would not.

"Hey, buddy," he said. "Is it time to go out?"

The dog looked at him like he was an idiot.

"Don't you want to sleep in today?"

The dog lowered his head, pushing his roommate out of bed.

"Okay, boss man," Hersh laughed. "Let me get my pants and shoes and we're gone."

Clemenza loved to run and knew the rules allowing him to be without a leash. First, they stopped at the end of the driveway so Hersh could get the paper.

Usually he flipped to the sports pages to get the scores, but today he stared at the first page. Hersh got down on one knee and showed him what he was looking at.

"Guess who?" he said.

Hersh then threw the paper on the stoop and the two of them took off on their two-mile run. Clemenza sometimes let his friend win but usually he was sitting at the finish line when Hersh came trudging up.

"You are one mean drunk, Superman," Hersh said. But then he reached into his pocket and produced a bone Clemenza grabbed and wrestled with.

Hersh and Clemenza also worked together. It could be debated who was the boss.

When he worked with the parents of clients, Hersh would describe Clemenza as the alpha dog and rarely said, "No pun intended."

Clemenza got a wide berth from adults. They rarely asked questions about him and never reached out to pet him or talk to him.

But of course, the bigger the dog, the less afraid children were.

Hersh, who set up the appointments, was the face of the organization. Clemenza was the heart.

Talking to a parent of an abused child was easy when you had an 80-pound therapist who was all action and no talk.

Mute children damaged by others talked a blue streak to Clemenza, and parents cried hearing giggling as their kids wrestled on the floor with an animal closer-looking to a bear than anything else.

Clemenza was blessed with the ability to treat children differently. A session with a child sexually abused was different than one who came from a home of physical abuse. A deaf child got something different than a Downs Syndrome client who came to bond.

Hersh taught them math, English, and problem solving. He was their therapist but it took clients longer to bond with him than his partner.

Children opened up as a dog laid by their side. When they faltered, Clemenza pushed them to go on. He would rest his head in their laps or poke his nose into their stomachs or chests. Sometimes they would be laughing as they told Hersh of their nightmares.

Hersh's radar was good, not perfect. Clemenza was a whole other story.

Sometimes, when Hersh wrote down information, he was thinking more about the next question. That is when he'd get a nudge and his pen skittered across the page.

He'd laugh, give Clemenza a head rub and gently rebuke him for the interruption. Then he would look again at his new clients. If they were annoyed, he'd know he was dealing with amateurs overwhelmed or ill-prepared for their parenting tasks.

The frightening ones laughed with Hersh and applauded the cuteness of his dog. They were the sociopaths who had gone undetected by neighbors, police, and professionals like Hersh.

Clemenza never tipped his hand. Few could imagine the carnage the dog could create. Clients were ignorant that a word and a gesture from Hersh would turn a living room into a Roman coliseum.

But Clemenza preferred the higher road and the result was a child ultimately would be removed from the home and the state would take care of the parents.

Clemenza and Hersh had built a reputation as go-to therapy guys. It was why they were sitting in the kitchen having tea and a bowl of water with the Murphys.

"This is Clemenza," said Hersh.

"Do either of you want something to eat?" asked Gina Murphy.

"What do you have?" asked Hersh.

Gina Murphy laughed.

"I'm usually more behaved but Clemenza is a glutton and never turns down food," said Hersh. "I'm really speaking for him."

"And what does he eat?" asked Gina.

"Well, he'd be happy with a piece of chicken over there. And so as not to make him feel bad, I'll always have some," said Hersh.

Gina got up squeezing the hand of her husband, Roger, who wasn't as amused as his wife. While she sliced the chicken, he stepped to the visitors.

Clemenza yawned and Hersh relaxed. He pegged Roger as a worried grandfather and not the root of the problem they were hired to fix. But it never hurt to have affirmation.

"So how does this work and how much will it cost?" said Roger.

"Roger!" said Gina.

Hersh held up a hand.

"Both excellent questions. Let me take the most important one first. The way it works is, we will meet with Jack. I'll talk to him and he can play with Clemenza. I'll give him some short tests and figure out exactly how we'll proceed."

"And what if Jack doesn't respond?" Gina asked.

"He'll respond. Whether he responds positively is the worry."

"And how often does it happen?" she asked.

"More than we like," admitted Hersh. "But I can promise you this, Jack will not be worse when we are finished. If we can't help him in any substantial way, we also will not hurt him."

"And the cost?" asked Roger again.

"Zero," said Hersh.

"Zero?" said Roger and Gina at the same time.

"Well, maybe not zero," said Hersh. "I have many wealthy clients and frankly, I overcharge for therapy. But since I've worked miracles, no one complains. And because I overcharge them I can do pro bono work. But I tell my clients this: if and when you hit it big, then you make a donation to help another family."

"Are you for real?" asked Roger. "There has to be a catch."

"Well," said Hersh. "You do have to sign a document giving me your soul when you die."

Roger looked puzzled but Gina laughed.

"He's putting you on, honey."

"And he's thinks this is funny?" said Roger with a trace of annoyance.

Hersh crossed his legs and took a piece of chicken off the plate and handed it to Clemenza.

He looked at the Murphys and smiled.

"Roger," he said as he held up a finger indicating he wanted to be heard without interruption. "I've seen kids who were so abused, my first thought was, death was better than the hell they were living. I've visited children where I remained motionless because any movement would remind them of the horrors they lived. You think the worst thing that ever happened in life was what is happening to Jack. I don't want to minimize your pain but you cannot imagine the damage inflicted out there. Everyone thinks they can and trust me, you cannot."

The room grew still and Hersh knew he had to dial it back, but not before he got his whole point across.

"Mr. Murphy, I am not married and I have few friends. I am not a person who can live with other people. My burden is way too much for me to carry but I'm not going to unload it on anyone, much less a loved one. So, do I make jokes and do I find things funny others may not? I do. And I do it for one reason. Do you know what that reason is?"

"So, you can help people?" said Roger.

His wife looked at him and slowly shook her head.

"No, Roger. He does it so at the end of the day he doesn't go home and blow his brains out."

Hersh reached down and patted his partner on the head. He then looked up at Gina Murphy and smiled.

CHAPTER 7

When he was 8 years old, Hersh was the target of a bully. He was afraid to go to school. But what made Hersh different than most kids was he didn't suffer in silence. He told his parents.

And he didn't object when they scheduled a conference with the principal.

Hersh wasn't a child who believed grown-ups had all the answers. So, he wasn't surprised when the visit with Dr. Gentry was a bust.

"Well, I've talked to Greg's parents and they assure me he hasn't been bullying your son," said the principal.

"So, you are saying my son is lying," said Hersh's mother.

"No, I am saying sometimes boys will be boys and sometimes one boy will be more sensitive than the other."

Hersh's mother stared at the principal.

"The fact Greg's parents built a gym at the school has nothing to do with it, then?" said Hersh's father.

The principal's eyebrows shot up.

"I am insulted you think I would put a student's welfare in jeopardy," said Dr. Gentry. "Just because Greg's parents have been generous to this school has no bearing on this, and maybe this isn't the school for your son."

Hersh's parents looked at each other. His father was about to speak when his wife put her hand on his elbow to stop him. She smiled at the principal.

"Dr. Gentry, I hope you take this in the spirit it is intended. In everyone's life they make a decision they think is a smart one. Or, in your case, one in which they think it is worth prostituting themselves."

"I beg your pardon," said the principal.

"I'm not delivering this like I need to," said Hersh's mom. "I'm saying everyone makes decisions they think are good ones. It is only later they realize it was the worst decision of their lives."

"And why will this be a "worst decision?" asked the principal, as she used air quotes.

"Because, now, Dr. Gentry, you get to meet my mother-in-law. And I mean this with no sarcasm or malice. May God have mercy on your soul."

CHAPTER 8

In her memoir, *H Is for Hawk*, Helen Macdonald writes about the prey and predator.

"I'm starting to believe in what Barry Lopez has called 'the conversation of death', something he saw in the exchange of glances between caribou and hunting wolves, a wordless negotiation ends up with them working out whether they will become hunter and hunted, or passers-by."

Dr. Gentry would know the feeling when she sat across Hersh's grandmother. It was glances more than words. Roza was a good talker but a masterful listener.

She'd tell her grandson many people could hear but few could listen. And it was off-putting the way Roza listened. Some people make you nervous just sitting and staring.

When Roza tilted her head 90 degrees, it was chilling without anyone knowing why. It speeded up that chilliness for the person who was the object of the gaze.

"I'm hoping Hersh understands we all need to get along," said the principal. "And I include Greg. I hope you don't think I'm not laying some of the blame on both boys. For some reason, they don't like each other. Who knows why? I'm sure when you were growing up there were girls in your school who you didn't like and vice versa."

Here the principal let out a nervous chuckle.

"There were certainly girls who didn't get along with me when I was young. I just left them alone and they left me alone. Hersh and Greg just need to avoid each other. I'm sure it will all work itself out. Kids are so resilient."

The principal might have continued to babble if Hersh's grandmother hadn't smiled and risen from her chair. Even at 8 years old her smile froze Hersh. No one confused it for mirth.

"Mrs. Gentry…"

"Doctor."

"I'm sorry?"

"It is Dr. Gentry."

"Ah. Well, then doctor, let me thank you for your time. I believe you've illuminated us," said Roza.

Hersh felt bad for the principal, who had the idea she was the winner here.

"I am so happy you came in. It is good to get things straight and I am always happy to educate those who come in. After all, it is the business we are in."

Hersh didn't know what to expect. He could see how well his grandmother was holding her temper. It would not have surprised him to see her go over to the desk and accost his principal. He prayed she would not.

And she didn't. She smiled again.

"It is like Jack McCoy said on *Law & Order*," said Roza. " 'If you are going to play stickball in Canarsie, you better know Brooklyn rules.' "

"I don't know what you mean," said the principal.

"It means we've been schooled. It means when you can't reason with a bully you figure another way around the problem."

"I am going to object to you referring to Greg as a bully."

"Yep," said Roza. "I would imagine you would. Only I wasn't talking about him."

Hersh and his grandmother walked out of the office and out of the school.

He had no idea how he and his grandmother won, but he knew she did. He didn't let his 8-year-old mind worry about it, and he didn't worry when his grandmother explained things to him.

"Hersh," she said. "The battle is long and it won't get better right away. You are going to have to take a couple for the team."

He nodded and that afternoon took the first one. The black eye was courtesy of a blindside punch from Greg. His parents were livid but his grandmother was not. She took him for ice cream and then signed him up for boxing lessons.

By the time he was 12 he had also taken instruction in several disciplines in the martial arts. He became a distance runner in his teens. He lived through the Greg years and the two never had a showdown. He would leave the school when his parents moved.

Shortly before he left the school Dr. Gentry was killed in a car accident. Hersh wanted to ask and knew it was better if he didn't.

Greg had spurred the physical training but Roza never had to explain it was never about one bully. There were Gregs everywhere protected by the Dr. Gentrys. When handed a fact, don't argue the fact, make it irrelevant.

Still, had it not been for Greg, Hersh might have led a different life. He might have gotten out of his formative years without the survival instincts. He might have married and had children. He would have had a "normal" job where he didn't take on the weight of the world.

But when you know how to kill a person in a dozen ways it doesn't matter whether you use the skill or not. It gets into your DNA and it sets you on a path not often taken.

Roza knew with her youngest grandchild the training didn't get into his DNA. It was already there. She was the one who awoke it from its dormancy. She had unleashed it and it was her greatest accomplishment. And she never forgave herself.

CHAPTER 9

Betty Thompson turned to her left when talking to people. She had done this so long, she wasn't conscious anymore of the tic.

It didn't fool people for long. Soon their eyes drifted to the side of her face looking like it had been caught in a French fry vat. It was tragically true. Her father had thrown grease at her mother. She ducked. The 4-year-old Betty didn't.

If her mother felt guilty, it didn't show. Her father was just a mean man. Drunk or sober.

Now 16, Betty, a genetic dice roll loser, was lucky to have found Matty Grimes at her high school.

A counselor in the best sense, Grimes put Betty into advanced classes and was there when kids called her "Frenchy" or the thousand other nicknames they thought clever.

The one thing Matty Grimes couldn't do was talk Betty into counseling.

"I know you have my best interests at heart, Mrs. Grimes, but I don't see the need to talk to someone about my horrible childhood. Once was enough."

"It might help."

"Mrs. Grimes, everyone has trouble. Mine was bad but I'm here and you're here, and look how far I've come."

"Betty, what you've done is extraordinary," said the counselor. "You are on track to attend a great academic school. And as much as I would like you to talk to someone, I've reconciled myself to it not happening. So, I'll not waste time to push you somewhere you have no intention of going."

"So, I win?" Betty said with a big grin.

Matty Grimes laughed. "Yes, you win. Again."

"So why have you called me down here? I know you, Mrs. Grimes. There is no way I'm here to accept surrender terms. You've got something else, don't you?

"Ah, Betty, I am afraid I'm not as stealthy as you think."

"Well, I am an expert in human nature, as you know," said Betty.

"I'm afraid I'm going to ask you to do something harder than going to a therapist."

"Not sure there are harder things," said Betty, with another laugh.

But Matty Grimes did not laugh.

"Giving back is harder," she said.

"Giving back?"

Mrs. Grimes began to cry and it was Betty who comforted her mentor, the woman who had stared down her parents when they thought Betty "was getting bigger than herself" to want to take advanced classes. She would eventually escape this town because of Mrs. Grimes.

"Mrs. Grimes, it is okay. I'm okay and I'm going to continue to be okay."

"I know you will. And I'm not crying for you or because of you."

"Then what?"

"I'm crying for the others," said the counselor.

"What others?"

"Come with me."

CHAPTER 10

Early mornings were stress-free zones for Hersh. He woke at 5:30, put on sweat pants, a hoodie, long black athletic socks and then anklets so his running shoes would be snug.

He'd jog a mile and then run six. Often with Clemenza but sometimes not. It freed his mind and he thought about everything but the day ahead. That kind of thinking would return him to his bed with the covers over his head.

After his run, he unfolded the paper, pulled out the sports, and started with the box scores.

No longer the fanatic he was in his youth he still followed a couple of players. A-Rod. Josh Hamilton. Andrew McCutcheon.

Since the papers eliminated horse racing results and odds he spent less time but still dawdled over the entertainment pages. He loved gossip, advice columns, and especially the comics.

He saved "Big Nate," "Doonesbury," "Baby Blues," "Zits," and "Pearls Before Swine" for last. He would bet himself which one would be the funniest of the day. Often it would be the advice columns getting him to laugh out loud.

"There are a lot sick people out there," he said to himself.

The hour in his studio before attacking the day was sacred. He never answered the phone and people knew better than to reach him before 9 a.m.

Hersh didn't look up from his paper so he didn't see the 250-pound bald man walk into his studio. But he sensed him. When he looked up he couldn't help but stare at the hoop earring and arms muscular and tattooed.

Even if he weren't carrying a gun, this was a guy who scared tough guys. He was one of the few who looked less threatening by carrying a weapon.

The man starred at Hersh, who still didn't look up. But he did speak.

"Two things," said Hersh.

"Yeah," said the man.

"First, you can never be buried in a Jewish cemetery."

"Yeah, I know. What is the second?"

"It was your turn to buy the doughnuts."

"You eat doughnuts, you are doing to die," said the visitor.

"Francis, if you keep speaking the King's English people won't know how tough of a guy you really are."

Most people got to call Frankie Dolan "Francis" just one time.

"Yeah, well, fuck you."

"A very Kaufmanesque response by you," said Hersh.

"You done with the comics?"

"I am," said Hersh, pushing the paper his friend's way.

"Who was the winner today?"

"Zits."

"Jeremy is pretty funny."

"Read and let me know what you think."

Dolan picked up the paper. He started with a low chuckle in his throat and he broke out into a full laugh. And Frankie Dolan's laugh was among the scariest events in history.

He was a frightening figure at all times but when he got a goofy grin he scared the crap out of anyone who didn't know him.

Dolan opened the door and let Clemenza in. The dog leaped up on the visitor and soon the two were wrestling. Clemenza did his best to bite the man on the face and Frankie did his best to pretend he couldn't stop him.

"I don't know which one of you is the most like a child," said Hersh.

Frankie got Clemenza on his back and started to scratch his stomach. The dog surrendered and the two played for a while before Clemenza knew it was work time and trotted into the playroom.

"You know I only come here for the mutt."

"That's why anyone comes here," said Hersh.

"Well, I also come here for the coffee."

"We don't have coffee here."

"Well, I must have been misinformed."

"What are you, Bogart now?" said Hersh.

"Makes you Captain Renault."

"So, you are looking for a beautiful friendship then?"

"No. I'm looking for coffee but I know better than to expect it in this rat hole so I brought my own.

"So, you avoid doughnuts but drink coffee?"

"I need the caffeine."

"Hey, did you hear about the antenna who got married?"

"Oh, God, please, not now."

"Yeah, the wedding was okay but the reception was excellent."

"You know, I could just come here and drink coffee and we don't have to talk?" said Dolan.

"What and get out of show business?"

"You know you are not funny?"

The two would have kept up the banter but were aware they were not alone. They eyed a teenaged girl approaching with horror in her eyes.

"You've got a visitor," said Frankie.

"Thank you, Captain Obvious."

Hersh looked at the young girl.

"Can we help you?"

"Um, I'm Betty. Mrs. Grimes sent me over."

"Oh, Betty. Great. Welcome. I'm Hersh and this dazzling urbanite is Frankie. We met on the internet."

Betty was nonplussed but jumped from a loud crash behind her. She looked to see an 80-pound dog bounding toward her.

Before she could react, the dog had his paws on her shoulder and licked the side of her face.

"Meet Clemenza and since he's already accepted you, we don't need to do too much more interviewing."

Betty heard laughter and was surprised to realize it was coming from her. Like Frankie she was soon wrestling on the ground.

Then Clemenza sprang up, ran to Hersh, accepted a biscuit and laid down to work on it.

"So, Betty, what brings you here to Chez Hersh?"

"Oh, God," said Dolan. "She came for the waters."

Betty stood with her mouth open as the men started to giggle.

CHAPTER 11

Since the day Secretariat won in 1973, Roza barely went a week without visiting the racetrack.

It became her sanctuary. She came at dawn to watch the horses work. She stood at the rail drinking tea and watching horse after horse.

The quality of the breed didn't matter to her. It was the syncopation that entranced and freed her.

She loved walking the backside. The smell of grass and manure had a restorative effect, although it was more the horses themselves. She was physically afraid of them, of course. No animal this powerful and single-minded failed to summon a little fright in any well-thinking human.

Sometimes she would never go trackside. She watched trainers and grooms getting horses ready to run and then watch them come back, either with the unbridled joy of winning or the rictus of an agonizing day. Or the worst, those who came back shaking empty reins, meaning a horse had been lost to another trainer's claim or to the trackside ambulance.

The day in 1973 awakened something else in Roza. It opened her gambling gene full throttle. Roza was a cautious but big bettor. She didn't bet all the time but with both fists when she did.

If you weren't putting yourself on the line, it had no meaning. But she didn't leave her zone of safety. She might bet a sporting event but never entered a casino. She knew nothing about blackjack or roulette.

Horses she knew and loved the challenge of looking at *The Racing Form* and deciphering the mathematical puzzle of past performances. She used the Beyer Speed Figures but was more intrigued by the performances of horses that had run that day's distances on that day's track.

She loved George Clooney's speech in *Ocean's Eleven*.

Because the house always wins. Play long enough, you never change the stakes. The house takes you. Unless, when that perfect hand comes along, you bet and you bet big, then you take the house.

She found truth there. So, there were days when Roza never bet a penny. But she took notes and watched for trends.

Sometimes the racing gods gifted her. Opening the *Form*, it would be like a horse was circled and the page screamed, "Winner, winner!!!"

Then Roza would step to the window and instruct the teller to hit the number until he got RSI.

Picking a favorite racetrack was like picking a favorite grandchild. Roza had both and her favorite track was the one she was sitting in.

There was nothing like a Saratoga summer. A walk to get the newspapers and then another to the track was followed by a huge breakfast and then hanging on the rail.

Roza wasn't a social animal but there wasn't a trackside conversation she didn't enjoy. She picked the brains of everyone and was free with information. Bettors competed but there was a fraternity. It was hard to keep a winner quiet.

Feeling a buzzing in her pocket, Roza picked up her phone and stared and smiled.

"I've got winners," she said in greeting.

"Every degenerate gambler says that same thing at the beginning of every day," said Hersh.

"Which means you want part of the action."

"Did you think I was calling to see how my beloved grandmother was feeling? I'm only staying in touch because I'm in your will.

"Yeah, I called my lawyer. You're out. I'm giving it all to my new lover."

"God, do you think any other person speaks to their grandchildren like you do?"

"There are probably not too many grandmothers who generate money for you like I do."

"Fair enough."

"So, how wet do you want your beak to be today?"

"10."

"Spread it around?"

"Well, take $8,000 for your syndicate but can you give me $1,500 on Revolver and a $500 straight box on Revolver and Planet Hollyweird."

"Will do as long as you aren't betting names again. I can't stand that type of nonsense."

"Planet Hollyweird can't beat Revolver but he's also the only other horse to run on this track and among the three the only one to have won at the distance on any track."

Roza chuckled.

"Looking forward to your adding to my account. The kids could use it."

"How are things there?"

"Well, Frankie here's eating all my doughnuts."

"And how is he?"

"Still scaring widows and orphans."

"You know I won't have you say anything bad about my boy. He's just misunderstood."

"Misunderstood like a rectal exam."

"I knew he was a little cutie when you brought him home in second grade."

"Only because I took a thorn from his paw."

"Oh, you're a riot, Alice," said his grandmother.

"Frankie says he wants $2 to show on the favorite in the feature."

"Tell him it is a done deal."

"Okay, I'll let you run but I'll leave you with an oldie but goodie. An A-Flat walks into a bar and orders a beer. The bartender says, 'Sorry, we don't serve minors.' "

"Now I may not bet for you."

"You're only hurting the kids."

"Tru dat," she said and hung up.

CHAPTER 12

Betty didn't know what to expect when Mrs. Grimes had sent her out.

She figured on another type of therapy. She never faulted Mrs. G because she saved her. But it was hard for even her counselor to understand how damaged she was. More therapy wasn't going to help. A hypnotist who could erase her memories would have been a better bet.

But these two were a surprise. One looked like a college professor and the other was too scary even for a motorcycle gang. And here they were giggling like schoolboys who put a tack on the teacher's seat.

"Mrs. Grimes thought I could help," she said.

Frankie looked at Hersh and said, "You know why I like Mrs. Grimes?"

"Because she didn't report you for blowing out Mr. Kingman's tires in the parking lot?"

"The bastard deserved worse and she knew it."

"Then my well-rounded friend, tell me why you like Mrs. Grimes."

"Because she sends us Bettys and never Veronicas."

Hersh cocked his head and grinned.

"You, my friend, are a philosopher," said Hersh. "Somewhere in your murderous and larcenous body beats the heart of a real thinker."

"You know what I'm thinking now?"

"Don't tell me but I'm getting a picture of me, my head and a platter."

"You can read minds."

"Would it help if I offered to buy you the next tattoo?"

"Do you think I'm cheap?"

Frankie looked over at Betty and smiled. "You'll find quickly I'm the smarts of this outfit, and this waste of muscle and bone is around merely to be the front. He's a moron but harmless."

Hersh laughed and told Betty to take a seat at the worktable.

"Betty, I'm assuming Mrs. G sent you over to give us a hand."

"Well, she didn't specify."

"Did she give you the 'time to give back' speech?" asked Frankie.

Betty's mouth dropped open.

"We've all heard it," said Frankie. "Makes me want to cry how gullible we all are when we hear it."

"Still," said Hersh, "it is Mrs. G."

"Love me some Mrs. G," said Frankie.

Betty looked from one man to the other. Her confusion had only grown since she stepped in the room. These guys were more like Abbott and Costello than counselors.

"What is it you guys do here?" she asked.

"We facilitate," said Frankie.

"Excuse me," said Betty.

"Yeah, he learned the word yesterday so he's throwing it around."

Betty looked at Hersh.

"But my friend is correct. We facilitate. We work with children and we make their lives better."

"How?" Betty asked.

"However, we can," said Frankie.

Hersh walked over and laid a notebook in Betty's lap.

"These are our clients. Betty, if you choose to work with us we must tell you up front you are going to go home each day with a broken heart. At least once a day you're going to want to kill someone and at least once a month you're going to want to kill yourself."

"Been there," muttered Betty.

The two men exchanged glances. "This is different. You wanted to kill yourself because life labeled you worthless. You'll want to end your life now because of how despairing it will be when you realize how helpless you are to help all of these kids."

"So why do you do it?" she asked.

"Because," said Hersh, "every now and then you win the lottery. You reach a child, you make a difference, one person's life is changed and you're the instrument of re-invention. The fact you are here tells me

Mrs. G won't go home tonight, unscrew the cap on the vodka bottle and swallow a fistful of pills with a jelly glass of liquid."

"And what if I still want to kill myself?" Betty asked.

"Then," said Frankie, "we'll put a pillow over your head ourselves and bury you in the back with some of the other interns Mrs. G sent us."

That put the two men into a fit of giggles again.

CHAPTER 13

Roza was there when Hersh entered the restaurant, having taken an earlier plane.

When she had funds to distribute she was never late. She didn't see Hersh enter, giving him a chance to study her. She had aged and the tremor had accelerated.

Of course, with Roza, it was possible the tremor was for affectation. He would not put it past her.

She had taught him to be unpredictable even to those you trusted.

But affectation or not, Roza had slowed. You didn't live the life she did, do things she did and not have them drag like a parachute. Hersh knew it was a big reason for this meeting.

"Saw in the papers you've been busy," he said.

"Ah, my obnoxious and know-it-all grandson," she said.

He kissed her cheek and said, "And in Yiddish I think 'obnoxious' translates to 'favorite,' does it not?"

"Obnoxious translates to obnoxious. So, sit down and let this business begin."

"Okay. Are you ready?"

"Please do not waste my time."

"Subject?"

"Golf."

Hersh smiled.

"Police enter a man's apartment and they find him sitting on a chair with a golf club in his hands and a dead man on the floor.

"The police asked what happened and the man says, 'He broke in and tried to rob me so I hit him seven times with this 4-iron.'

"The cop says, 'You hit him seven times?'"

"And the man says, 'Why don't you put me down for a 5?'"

Roza takes a sip of her tea and looks at her grandson. "You know that's a pretty good golf joke."

"Best I ever heard."

"Okay then. I called you here because I'm retiring from the active end of the business."

"It had to come some day."

"I can't physically do it anymore."

"Quite an admission."

"I shouldn't have done the last one but it was like a drug."

"The first taste is free."

"It isn't like in the books," Roza said. "Marlowe and Spade never got older. They just kept solving crimes and cracking wise."

"Now all you can do is crack wise."

"If I thought those bastards were still out there I might feel different but I've got mine and now I'm leaving the business to you."

Having expected this didn't make it any easier. His grandmother always said, "Many can hold the gun but few can pull the trigger." She didn't mean it euphemistically.

"It is good you are leaving. The crap with *The New York Times* was show-offy."

"I spent 50 years in the shadows."

"You figured it deserved a curtain call."

"I achieved greatness."

"Others might differ."

"For them I have a Kaufmanesque response."

CHAPTER 14

This far in you have met the dog and get an idea of how I got here. I knew I might screw up. I had two things working against me. I wasn't my grandmother and the law of big numbers says we couldn't get away with this forever.

But I won't live at the Temple of Regret. I won't dwell on how my career was shortened.

The goal was a curtain call but absent that I'm going to download every joke in my arsenal. Consider this the entertainment portion of the program.

When comedians say, "I died up there," it might be accurate in this case.

Not every Jew will laugh at this but trust me, no Gentile is going to find it funny. I just hope I don't hurt myself laughing at the end.

A ship locates a man who has lived on a deserted island for 20 years. The captain docks on the island and strides up. He sees the man and over the shoulder of the castaway is a beautiful building. He says to the man, "What is the building?" And the castaway says, "Is my synagogue. I built it myself." The captain asks, "Do you pray there?" and the man says, "I go every day. It is a magnificent place and I found God there waiting for me." The captain looks over the man's other shoulder and sees another spectacular building. So, he says to the man, "And what is that building?" And the stowaway says, "Oh, that is the other synagogue here." The captain asks, "Did you build that one too?" When the castaway nods yes, the captain says, "So I guess you also pray there." The castaway spits on the ground and says, "I never go near the place."

Hey, I know you're out there. I can hear your breathing. Oh, wait, it's me breathing and not strongly.

My grandmother was right about Marlowe and the others. They got shot, hit over the head, drove cars off the road and went into scary places protected by nothing more than a good-looking hat and a heater. Somehow, they were able to get out snappy dialogue and the girl at the end.

Here I sit in a scary place with no gun, I've lost my hat and it was a woman who put me in this position. They won't be writing books about me.

So, this will have to do.

CHAPTER 15

Eddie Doss turned on the charm when he opened the door to the police officer.

The goal was not to let him in. While Mary wasn't about to contradict him, the welt above her eye was harder to dismiss. It wasn't the first time a neighbor called 911.

Eddie figured it was the hag in 116. Like he couldn't have called the cops on her damn mutt. He had plans and the dog wouldn't bother Eddie much longer.

"Mr. Doss. We got a call there was a disturbance at the house," said the officer.

"You sure they meant this apartment?" said Eddie.

"Yes sir. They gave this address."

"Well, no problems here."

"Yeah, I believe you Mr. Doss but procedure says I have to check it out. May I come in?"

Eddie sighed and figured he'd get this over.

"Be my guest, officer."

"My name is Pete. I need to know if you are alone."

"Why, no Pete. I'm with my wife and daughter."

Pete walked into the apartment and looked around. It wasn't spotless but he had seen worse.

"May I talk to them?"

"Mary, Kathy, can you please come out and talk to Officer Pete."

Two females emerged from a bedroom and Pete could tell both were scared. They were too practiced to give much away. But the young girl was clutching at her doll like a talisman.

The older woman had a cut above her eye.

There was nothing special about Eddie Doss. There was nothing special about this apartment or this visit by the police.

"Ma'am, miss. I'm Pete. A neighbor said they heard noises and wanted me to make sure nobody was in trouble."

"No trouble here," said Mary Doss. "Can I get you a cup of coffee?"

"You know," said Pete, "I'd love it but first I just need to ask some questions. The first is about your eye."

He gave Mary credit; she never looked at her husband. She might live in fear but wasn't stupid enough to make things harder.

The daughter was more open but even she had seen this movie. She began to primp her doll's hair.

"What a pretty doll," said Pete. "What is her name?"

"Just Doll," said the little girl.

"I love the name," he said with a smile. "Does she have her own room or do you guys share one?"

"We share one."

"What kind of car does she drive?"

The little girl laughed. "She doesn't have a car."

"Oh, so what kind of car do you drive?"

"I'm not old enough to drive."

"What? How old are you? Twenty-five?"

The little girl giggled and hid behind her mother's leg.

"Ma'am, if you could just tell me about your eye for my report."

"Oh, sorry," said Mary. "I hit myself with a frying pan. Well, not hit myself. I opened a cabinet and it fell out."

"Ouch," said Pete, who admired the inventiveness.

"I'm embarrassed to say but maybe the neighbors heard me cursing," she said. "It really hurt."

"I can imagine."

"Are we done, Officer?" asked Eddie.

"Pretty much. I'll fill out the report, have you sign it and I'll be on my way. But I would love coffee if the offer is still on the table."

Mary nodded and disappeared with her daughter.

Sitting on a chair, Pete took out his iPad and began typing. "We can get you to sign this electronically."

Eddie Doss smiled at the officer.

"I'm sorry you had to come out for nothing."

"All part of the job, sir."

"Don't you guys usually travel in pairs?"

"Excuse me?"

"Well, you're not the first policeman in the neighborhood and usually you guys have partners."

"Yeah, they are sending some of us solo. They figure we can get to twice as many calls."

"I see."

"Besides, I'm really here to deliver a message."

"A message?" asked Eddie.

"Yes, sir."

"A message from who?"

"A message from me."

Eddie looked at the police officer with bemusement.

But his eyes grew wide as the cop pulled his gun and laid it on the table and his baton next to it.

"What is this about, Officer?" said Eddie with a short nervous laugh.

"You actually don't have to call me 'officer.' "

"What is this about then?" said Eddie, now with a hint of annoyance. "You are in my home and now it is time you left."

"I'm leaving but like I said, I'm here to leave a message."

"From who?"

"From whom."

"What the hell?"

"Just because you are a sick bastard doesn't mean you can't speak the proper English."

Eddie started to get up but stopped when the officer picked up his gun.

"Okay. Let me just say what I was paid to come here to say and then I need to speak to your wife and then we'll never see each other again."

Eddie sat, clenched his fists but he didn't interrupt. He needed this to be over.

"My employer wants you to know he's watching," the officer said with a two-fingers-to-the-eyes gesture. "He wanted to ask me which you prefer, the gun or the stick. Because if you touch your wife or child again you are going to get one or the other."

"Hey, wait a minute…"

"Please shut up and listen. We know you bat your family around. You're a sick man and you need help but don't have the motivation. So here is the carrot. If you straighten up, then you'll never see me again. Here is the stick, if you'll excuse the pun. If you continue, you'll get another visit. The length of the visit will depend on your choice of gun or baton."

Eddie was on his feet and moving toward the visitor. Instead of meeting him halfway the visitor leaned back and crossed his legs.

"I see you are having trouble making up your mind, so why don't I leave and you can talk to Larry Dody and ask him for advice."

For the first time Eddie knew he wasn't looking at a policeman.

"Let me think about it," said Eddie.

"It is all we ask," said the cop. "We think everyone is on the same page. But we'll be watching. You need a new toothbrush, Eddie. The purple one is getting ragged.

The cop stood and walked into the kitchen. He accepted the coffee from Mary and sat down.

"Did you hear?"

"Yes."

"We don't have much faith in Eddie but stranger things have happened. So, I am going to give you a number. If you call it, we pick you up and take you to a safe house. Then we'll get you to another town."

Mary rubbed the top of her daughter's head and looked up slack-jawed. "Why?"

"Why you?" the stranger asked.

Mary nodded.

"You've got an angel out there. Your daughter's age probably had something to do with it. And of course, Eddie being Eddie."

"What do we have to do?"

"Nothing except call. After we set you up we no longer have contact. Works best that way. You need to forget about us. It goes without saying you need to stay quiet about us."

Mary then stunned the visitor, making him want to laugh and cry.

"God bless you, Rick."

He smiled and flashed on Bogart and Bergman standing on a tarmac. He then pivoted and walked out.

CHAPTER 16

Roza and her sister would not have lasted an hour if not identical. Sometimes she believed her sister was the luckier one. Shoshana had not made it out so she carried her for 75 years.

Although she didn't suffer nightmares, there wasn't a day Roza didn't live out those days in captivity. She thought of the experiments and thankful because of her age it was medical curiosities and not sexual ones. She had seen the women return from sessions with soldiers with the light gone from their eyes.

It was like watching the dead return. Roza became a surrogate for every prisoner who lost a child. She was given extra rations and held warm by women who only wanted to feel maternal again.

The curse was watching all her surrogate mothers die. At first it was hard as she became attached. But soon she treated it like business and making it to the next day.

The women understood and encouraged her to be hard. They took no offense but made her promise they would not be forgotten.

She made good on the promise by doing what they had done. You can't save everyone but you can save someone. First she saved herself and then started a list.

When she weakened, she ran a slide show of all those who kept her alive and it recharged her.

But the journey was over and soon she would join those women. And she believed she would. How else could she have lived all these years if she didn't believe? They would be sitting in peace and marvel at what they endured.

This life was not her reward. For years she had done what was necessary. She didn't have regrets about it.

Her regret was Hersh. She had been chosen. He had been drafted and the difference was large. She never wished for a different life but wasn't ignorant of how things could have been different for her grandson.

She feared he would collapse from the burden she unloaded on him. She feared his shoulders, thus far so sturdy, would give it up and call it a day.

There was not a day she didn't recognize she was using him like she used the women in the camp. They kept her alive and so would he after she was gone. Even if just the two of them were aware of the legacy.

They had been circumspect and she had been clever.

When the good guys caught the killers on TV, Roza wondered how they got caught. Could Columbo or Christopher Foyle, Jane Tennyson or Lennie Briscoe have caught her?

Being lucky was good. Being patient and smart was better. Careful was best of all. Now at the end she was proud of herself.

Hersh rarely asked about what happens at the end but she said she stood a chance.

"If there is a trial for heaven and hell and God is an understanding jurist then I think I'll be acquitted."

"If not?"

"Then I'll lose all respect."

CHAPTER 17

Betty was surprised on Monday to find no children at the clinic. Even Clemenza was passed out like a Saturday night drunk.

She saw Hersh and Frankie pouring over a map. Hersh punched Frankie in the shoulder. If she had just met them she might have suspected them to be gay.

Actually, she didn't know about Hersh, who never seemed to be interested in any of the sexes, but she knew Frankie's type.

At first, she was surprised he chose the bossy ones.

If they wanted to see a chick flick and go to the ballet, he was always ready. He never raised his voice and seemed to be amused by being led by the nose.

Hersh laughed when she asked.

"Women adore him because he can protect them and he's quite the gentleman. Don't ever tell him I said this but he's smarter than almost anyone I know. He can discuss books and politics. But ..."

"But?" she repeated.

"Look at him again. He also can beat a man to death. If you are going to take him down, you better come at him with more than a kind word and a gun."

"And that is why women boss him around?"

"It is a game," said Hersh. "He knows and they know if he says enough there will be no crossing the line. It ends where he says it ends. But anything before the line is fair game, and when you rule your world the way Frankie does any change of pace is good."

"He's a conundrum all right," said Betty.

"Conundrum?" said Hersh. "Look at the brains on Brad."

Betty colored and Hersh reached for her hand.

"We took a vote this morning and it was 2-0."

"What kind of vote?"

"A partnership vote."

"Partners for what?"

"Partners in us. Welcome aboard."

"What does it mean?"

"Well, today it means a field trip," Hersh said as Frankie came through the door holding a picnic basket.

"Road trip!!!" Frankie yelled.

Hersh rolled his eyes and looked at Betty. "And you are going to be the parental chaperone for this child."

"Where are we going?"

"The amusement park."

Betty looked at two grown men antsy as schoolboys.

"Frankie loves roller coasters. It calms him down."

"What about the kids?"

"They need a break from us," said Frankie. "Hersh can be a little intense."

They grabbed Betty by each hand and escorted her out of the building. She knew this trip was probably more about her than them but they'd get to that in time.

Besides, who couldn't use more roller coasters in their lives?

Betty was a bit dizzy and took a pass when Frankie wanted to take his eighth ride on "Superman."

"Let me sit out this dance," she said.

Hersh laughed and said, "I'm with Betty. We have enough tickets for you, Frankie, so go run in line and enjoy yourself. We'll talk business while you take a turn."

Frankie wanted to protest but wanted to take another turn more, so he pivoted away. Betty and Hersh were amused at the reaction Frankie got from others in the line. Teenagers were awed and parents taken aback by his excitement.

Hersh cleared his throat and Betty looked over.

"Okay. Let's talk shop."

"Ready."

"We'll see," said Hersh as some nervousness creeped in his voice.

Betty waited him out.

"It probably won't surprise you," Hersh started, "to know the work Frankie and I do is not restricted to the children."

"I had suspicions," she said. "Some things are hard to miss. Like when you come back from somewhere and go into a room and don't come out for an hour. You go in looking totally tense and come out looking somewhat less so."

Hersh smiled and said, "We deal in so much violence, the two of us."

"Yes. I see the children every day and marvel at the two of you."

He looked up and smiled again. This was a sadder version. "Ah, yes, the children. Yeah, we deal with them too."

Betty looked into his face and realized he wasn't sure he wanted to take the next step, and she was unsure whether she could handle hearing it.

He took a long breath and pointed into the distance, where Frankie sat in a car at the top of the track. He was holding his hands in the air and screaming.

"Are you ready?" he said.

"I don't know."

"We don't have to take this step. We can stop right now."

"No, we can't," she said.

"Yeah, I knew it from the day you walked in. Mrs. G probably knew it before then."

"Mrs. G?"

"Yeah, she is a recruiter."

"A recruiter?"

"How much do you know about Mrs. G?"

"I know she saved my life and she's the best counselor ever."

"Do you think she's the first to understand you?"

It was exactly how Betty felt.

"Do you know why?" he asked.

"Because she is good at what she does," said Betty.

"She is but there are a lot of people who are good at their jobs who couldn't ever reach you."

"Because she's really, really good at her job," said Betty with a smile.

He smiled back and then said, "When you went through the nightmare of your life did you think no child had ever experienced that kind of hell?"

"I did," said Betty.

"Could you imagine anything worse?"

"Not at the time."

"Because you didn't know any better?"

"Yes."

"Mrs. G knew better. Mrs. G is an OG."

Betty began to weep. All this time she didn't see the woman's pain and now it made her feel selfish.

"What happened with Mrs. G?"

"Nothing you haven't seen. The particulars aren't important. I'm sure your mind can wrap around the general idea. But here is the key part. Mrs. G isn't a victim. She wouldn't let herself be. She gathered herself and said, 'Where do I go from here?' And she went and she's continued to go."

"How did she do it?"

"She studied her victim. Which wasn't hard because he was part of her family. She made herself stay in the room with him. She didn't know what she would do with the information she collected but it helped to collect it. The first step was making peace with what happened and then figuring out if she wanted to do anything about it."

"Did she?"

"Not for many years. And then one day she was having lunch with Frankie and me and she told us something that amused her about the villain in her life."

"What was it"?

"The man she thought of as a monster loved going to amusement parks. He had a fondness for roller coasters. She couldn't believe a man like that could enjoy himself that way."

"What did she do with the information?"

"She had already done it. She told Frankie and me."

"What did you do?"

"I didn't do anything."

"Frankie?"

"Well, that is interesting."

"Interesting how?"

"Well, Frankie was in the same car with him when he suffered a fatal heart attack. The ride seemed to be too much for him."

Betty paused and looked over at the ride and the big man screaming in delight.

"Natural causes then?"

"Nothing Frankie does is natural."

"Kind of a peaceful end, though."

Hersh studied her and shook his head. "Everybody screams on the roller coaster."

When Frankie joined them later he knew things had changed.

Betty sat a bit apart, fiddling with the straw in her drink and looking at the roller coaster. They left her alone and studied the map of the park.

At some point she had joined them and they let her ease into the conversation.

"Would you guys answer a question honestly?"

They nodded yes but didn't speak.

"What happens if I don't want to continue to work with you?"

"Then," said Frankie "we take you on a roller coaster ride."

Betty looked up in time to find the two of them giggling again.

CHAPTER 18

There are things you believe and things you know, and Hersh knew his grandmother was livid. Usually a model of self-control, she was in a blind rage directed at him.

The few who had seen her like this didn't ever tell anyone. They couldn't.

They were in her library and Hersh tried to deflect the anger by staring at the thousands of books. Though they were alone it didn't hurt that the books absorbed the sound.

It infuriated Roza more when Hersh didn't utter a word in defense. He was waiting for her anger to crest.

She knew she should be proud. It took years to teach him to be this calm.

While she blew a gasket, he was figuring a way out. Roza wanted to slap and hug him at the same time.

Truly upsetting was the knowledge he was no longer the student. He made a decision without consulting her. It was like being the founding CEO and watching the next generation nudge you aside.

No storm can blow forever and she calmed, as he counted on. It was okay to come up and assess the damage.

"A man walks out of his house…"

"Not the time, Hersh."

"Always the time, Grandmother. So, sit and listen. I had to listen to you."

She sat back clenching and unclenching her fists.

"A man walks out of his house and trips over a snail. He picks up the snail and throws it as far as he can. Two years later the man gets a knock at the door. He opens it and looks down to see the snail, which looks at the man and says, 'Now, what the hell was that all about?'"

She didn't want to laugh but she couldn't help but smile. She didn't agree with what Hersh had done but she knew he thought he had made the right decision.

"So," said Hersh. "What the hell was that all about?"

"I worry," she said.

"We worry. But we also prepare."

"Bringing a teenage girl into this is risky."

Hersh snorted. "You are probably right. Who would ever think a teenager, much less a teenage girl, would know how to handle herself after years of abuse and horror? It just boggles the mind. Teenage girls are just so scatterbrained. All they are thinking about are boys, shopping at the mall and texting."

"It was different then," she said.

"Of course it was different. It will be different tomorrow."

Hersh stopped and looked at his grandmother and then made a face indicating he had figured it out.

"Wait a minute, wait just a minute," he said. "You are saying your pain was special. You are saying only you were mature enough to handle what needed to be done."

"Hersh, you know I am not saying that."

"Convince me."

"Convince you? Why you little shit. Do you really think you can turn this on me? I'm the one who needs you to convince me. Don't forget …"

"Please don't tell me you use to change my diapers."

"Well I did."

"Pretty soon I'll be returning the favor."

"You really are a cruel bastard."

"No, I'm not."

Her face softened.

"No. You are not."

They didn't speak for a minute. One of them would have to break and she decided it should be her.

"So, genius. Tell me why this girl."

"You know your 'trust but verify?' "

"Yes."

"Well, sometimes you have to just trust."

"God, I certainly didn't teach you that."

"No, I learned it on my own. When I was in second grade I met a boy so mean everyone stayed out of his way. There wasn't a teacher who thought he'd make it past sixth grade before committing a felony. The chances living past being a teenager were longer than horses you bet on. One day he threatened to beat me up. Before it happened, you walked up. He started to run but you told him to stop and shockingly he did."

Roza smiled at the memory.

"You took him home with us. You told him to take a bath. You took his clothes and washed them. When he was dressed, he ate with us. We had never seen anyone with his appetite. When we drove him home you told him to see you the next day."

"It seems like yesterday," said Roza.

"He came to our house the next day and I asked how come you were so kind. Why you fed him and why you weren't afraid of him."

"What did I tell you?

"You told me some people in the world stay thrown away unless someone takes them off the trash heap. You said you have to know who is worth making an effort for. I said, how do you know?"

"I said," whispered Roza, "you have to trust."

"You have to trust," repeated Hersh.

"I curse your memory sometimes."

"Well, then, you are really going to throw some expletives at this next memory," Hersh said.

"Oh, God. Please tell me it wasn't something else I said."

"You said it is a fool who spends time ranting at things they can't change. You know when someone raises their voice in displeasure you have them."

"I'm getting old, aren't I?" she said.

"You got a minute while I print invitations to this pity party?"

"You are a little bastard."

"Sometimes I wish I had a grandmother who baked cookies and gave warm hugs.

"You do. On your mother's side."

"I love her."

"She didn't make you rich."

"In money or experience?"

"Both."

"I have you to thank. I also want to thank you for 30 years of sleeping with one eye open, a lifetime of solitude and the worry I'm either going to be exposed or worse, beaten by someone smarter or tougher than me."

"And you blame me for that."

"No, I thank you. I wouldn't change a single minute. I've given up so much and never regretted a thing. My days are 24 hours long and if I ever stopped off I would die like an alcoholic going cold turkey."

"Well, as long as you're happy," she said. "Now, tell me your plans for this girl."

CHAPTER 19

I've been on the road to hell for so long I don't remember the first step anymore. But it wasn't a step paved with good intentions.

Even if I got a mulligan for most of the things I've done, my name was sealed for eternity for Betty. My grandmother knew what price I would pay.

But in my defense, I'm not sure what I did wasn't the thing to save her. Mrs. G sent us a drowning child.

You can say I'm rationalizing but video your own damn story if you want to criticize.

I'm won't apologize for what happened and I can be sure the work goes on. Frankie might not have had the touch to control things but with Betty, I believe in the future.

Future? Do you get the irony of me using that word? It is strange at this hour that I'm thinking about the day in the diner, but who can predict what the mind will do in extremis? Maybe I figure I can alter the things that happened if I remember them differently.

But things didn't start to go wrong then. In fact, it might have been our finest hour. When Roza had us back off, it was a reminder we weren't a group without conscience. We didn't commit whatever actions we wanted to.

I'm not saying we're in the running for sainthood or others would have done the same as us. We're not ignorant of the fact we broke all the laws and not just the ones in the legal system.

When you finish this, you won't think better of me and you still won't forgive us. There are few wired like *us*. And we're not productive members of society.

Or is this just another sad action of self-justification?

Well, you can't say I'm not paying for it. This hurts like a bastard, and truth be told I'm feeling a little sorry for myself. I'm asking God whether this a good use of his time.

When I close my eyes, I see all the people. I see the good ones I thought I was helping but even more the bad ones. I see the light go out of their eyes, and they will haunt me.

All you can do is put on the big boy pants when the time comes. So, I can't forget, I can't regret what I did for love.

Of course, that is from *A Chorus Line.* You didn't think I'd pass up a chance to throw it out? Even if you don't like me I want you to say I was a complicated guy.

Is that too much to ask? You don't need to name a street after me and you don't even have to like me but please don't dismiss me as someone easy to fathom.

My grandmother said I was smarter than Einstein. She says only a few people understood Einstein but no one understood me.

Take my word on this, when you think it is the end, many things come to mind and they are not always things you think they'd be.

For instance, it is the Jewish high holidays and I'm thinking I have a legitimate reason for missing services. I was never good for sitting in synagogue. I was always too jumpy and much of the service didn't speak to me.

We shouldn't get started on the notion of me pounding my chest while we all renounce sins from the past year. To swipe the slate clean you had to make amends with those you harmed.

Now how in the world would I do that? Although in a funny way I might be getting closer to accomplishing it. I won't know until I know, but there it is.

I am going to rest now but I feel I've left you in a bad place, so let me add this. "A man walks into a bar with a chunk of asphalt under his arm. He says to the bartender, 'I'll have a beer and one for the road.'"

Thank you for coming and please tip your waitress.

CHAPTER 20

When they napped, the children liked when Clemenza slept beside them. He guaranteed no one would turn dreams into nightmares.

Clemenza knew the time to curl up and just collapse on the floor. The kids dragged blankets to the mats where Clemenza slept and would drift off.

After lunch was story time and Hersh liked to read from the children's books he enjoyed as a youngster: *Mike Mulligan and His Steam Shovel* and *The Story of Ferdinand* and anything by Beverly Cleary. But also, the *George and Martha* books. Plus, anything with Viola Swamp in them got the kids squealing.

Children laughed hardest when Frankie read. His falsetto for the parts of girls and women had them shrieking. But Frankie was also lyrical in his reading of different parts and he mesmerized his audience with his pitches.

Betty was another favorite. Her reading was soothing, a big plus in the room, especially with the younger clients.

Hersh was looked on as silly and goofy for his faces and weird noises. He was the clown except when he did magic, which enthralled them.

Today, they would get Betty. When Frankie walked through the door he was in no shape to read. The kids and perhaps even Betty may not have noticed but Hersh saw his friend was reeling. Two hours in the meditation room was the final proof.

Climbing the stairs Hersh knew this wasn't going to be an easy day. The violent second grader had been tamed but there was a lot of anger still in Frankie.

When unleashed, even Hersh couldn't reach him, and often Frankie would have to sleep it off. Only Roza could have a soothing effect, and it wasn't guaranteed.

Reaching the meditation room, Hersh wanted to laugh when he saw his friend actually meditating.

He waited for him to finish. Hersh didn't want to bring the big man out of his trance a second before he was ready.

When Frankie looked up, Hersh froze. What he saw was new. He saw fear.

"I've screwed up," said Frankie.

"Will I read about it in the papers?"

"Yes."

The two men were silent. Hersh, because Frankie was ready to tell the story and Frankie because he was working up the nerve to let it out.

Hersh knew if Frankie sat the story might be bad but not as devastating as if he stood.

Frankie stood.

Then he sat down with a slow smile. "Just messing with you there."

"Asshat," said Hersh, clearly relieved.

"Yeah, but a funny asshat."

"Tell the story."

"Ben Cartwright is dead."

"When?" asked Hersh.

Frankie looked at his watch and Hersh continued with another question.

"Where?"

"His office."

"I'm assuming you were there."

Frankie snorted.

"Gallows humor," said Hersh.

"Funny choice of words," said Frankie.

"Ah," said Hersh.

"Yeah, he accidently hanged himself."

"Well, accidents happen," said Hersh, knowing Frankie hadn't gotten to the bad part of the story.

"He had a couple of other accidents."

"Such as?"

"He accidently broke his left kneecap."

"Falling down?"

"Hammer."

"Ouch."

"And a slip with a knife."

Hersh involuntarily looked down at his lap and cringed thinking about the ultimate indignity.

"Clumsy guy."

"Have to give him credit. He held out as long as he could."

"But he ended up talking."

"He did."

"And you are sure he confessed the truth and wasn't telling you something to make the accidents stop."

"I'm convinced."

"Okay."

"Doesn't excuse it."

"No, it doesn't. But it does explain it."

"You know I'm not a finesse guy."

This time Hersh snorted and patted his friend's shoulder. They sat in silence for a second time. Almost without knowing it, Hersh reached for Frankie's hand. The men sat companionably and even when Frankie began to speak, he didn't let go of Hersh's hand.

"I know we agreed not to go forward," said Frankie, referring to the New York diner vote. "And it wasn't my intention to go against the rules."

"But you did," said Hersh.

"I did."

"Because you couldn't let it go."

"I couldn't let it go."

"You didn't come to me for help because why?"

"Because I didn't think it would end this way."

"And?"

"I knew you would talk me out of it."

"You knew because I am a superior intellect and you hang on my words as if they are diamonds."

"Well, there is that. And the fact sometimes you're a real pussy."

"There is that."

"I followed him to Benny's Bar, where he approached a young woman."

"How young?"

"Legal."

"So, you figured this was not the night to catch him."

"Yeah."

"But it changed."

"I sat at the next table having a beer. Really, I was about to ask for the check. I just really wanted to see him up close."

"But he did something."

Frankie shook his head.

"He said something?"

Frankie nodded.

"The two of them were having a pretty normal conversation. She plays softball for her company. He says maybe his team played hers. I can see how well it is going. She's had maybe a half a beer too many. She's doing the lean in indicating she's interested."

"The old lean in," says Hersh. "The deal-closer."

"Yep. I'm about to call it a night because I don't have to hear the rest. I've heard this tune."

"But?" says Hersh.

"But. He doesn't go that way. Well, he does go that way but with a twist."

"Not a good twist?" asks Hersh.

"He asks how old her daughter is."

"Oh," says Hersh.

Again, they go quiet.

"So, what happens next?" asks Hersh.

"They leave."

"Without you?"

"Yeah. He's a stalker who will drag this out for weeks. The ugly stuff won't come for some time. He's smart and he's patient."

"A dangerous combination."

"The worst."

"But you decide you won't give him a few weeks."

"My thinking."

"So, you sit and wait."

"Got some reading done on Philip Kerr's "Berlin Trilogy."

"Nothing like Bernie Gunther to while away the time."

"Finished *A German Requiem*."

"My favorite of the three," says Hersh.

"Me too."

"But probably not something putting you in a mellow mood."

"Funny you would say that. I was being contemplative at the moment I saw him leave her house. I would have probably gone home if he didn't come out at that moment."

"Bad luck for him."

"I looked up in the upstairs window and I saw the daughter. She must have awakened as he left the house. She was in her pajamas and holding onto a doll."

"You stopped being contemplative."

"I did."

"You followed him to his house."

"I already knew where it was."

"So, you were in the house when he showed up."

"No. I skipped the house and went to his office."

"Where you stayed until he showed up?"

"Exactly. But I didn't expect him to show up that night. I don't know who was more surprised. He found me sleeping and demanded to know why I was in his office."

"What did you tell him?"

"I didn't like his tone."

"His response?"

"He was calling security."

"Oh, boy."

"I knew security was gone because I had scouted out the building. They don't stay all night."

"How come he wasn't scared? He walks into his office and sees a man who looks like you."

"Because he's arrogant."

"Can be a fatal flaw."

"When I told him I knew there was no security, he got more arrogant. He reached into his desk and pulled out a hammer and told me he would teach me not to break into his office."

Hersh could only wonder at the missteps people took.

"So now you have the weapon and you threaten him."

"Not really. Oh, I had the weapon but I just said I wanted to talk to him about his sickness. Of course, he said, 'What are you talking about?'

"But in the end, he understood why you were there."

"Yes."

"But he didn't understand quick enough."

"He did."

Hersh got a sick feeling and when he looked at Frankie he knew he was right.

"He talked about it?"

"He bragged about it."

"Oh, God."

"In detail."

"Didn't he know you would take unkindly to it?"

"It was like he thought he had this ring of protection."

"When did he know he was wrong?"

"I think the crack of his kneecap might have been a warning."

Hersh listened as Frankie described the escalating violence and the final confession.

Hersh realized had he been in the room he would not have talked him down. He might have left when things got too ugly but returned for the cleanup.

Frankie's crime wasn't what he had done. The crime was performing it under the worst circumstances. It should have happened elsewhere and the victim should be a missing person not found by the cleaning crew in the morning.

None of that was a concern now. Frankie wasn't talking to Hersh as his confessor; he was talking to him as his partner.

"Roza has to be told," said Hersh.

Frankie nodded and hanged his head.

"Hey, cheer up. Maybe she'll see the humor in it."

CHAPTER 21

They found Roza on the track backside trying to get a couple of winners.

She often talked with trainers but was more disposed to sneak in a word with the grooms. They lived with the horses and knew the idiosyncrasies of these thousand-pound animals. Then she moved onto the exercise riders, who told her how their horses were moving that day.

In a fraternity closed to outsiders, Roza was a welcome visitor. She laughed with the trainers, spoke Spanish with the help, and was quick with a joke. Most of all, she listened.

She would listen to a groom's story for an hour to elicit 60 seconds of inside dope. She was treated like racing royalty.

As much as they loved seeing her in the morning, the help really liked when she returned at the end of a race day. It meant she'd done well and they'd done better.

It was not unusual for his grandmother to dispense thousands of dollars on a good day. When Roza bet the mortgage, it meant others would be able to pay their rent.

Even if she lost she came around and handed out envelopes with modest amounts to say, "Thanks for the effort."

When Frankie and Hersh reached her, she was scribbling in a notebook and underlining *The Racing Form.*

"We are all going to get well today, gentleman," she said without looking up. "You know, this is the favorite part of my day. Even if I don't bet a penny. Dogs and horses are proof God exists even to someone like me, who questioned His decisions."

She realized she was carrying on a monologue and let out a slow smile.

"Which one of you screwed up?"

Frankie pursed his lips and hung his head.

"Bad?" she said.

"God, it is hard to believe you two aren't twins," said Frankie, pointing to Hersh. "It is bad."

The two patiently told the story. When they finished, Roza stood and threw out her coffee cup. She watched a string of horses make their way to the track.

"You know what I feel like?" she asked. "I feel like breakfast trackside. Do you guys want to join me where we can talk about the great events?"

Trudging toward the track apron they were stopped by dozens of Roza's well-wishers.

She ordered, toast, bacon, eggs, and pancakes. They had coffee. Then she opened up the *Form* again and said, "Money in the third, fourth, and ninth races today."

Frankie and Hersh knew not to rush it. What the old lady was going to do would happen and trying to make it come sooner wasn't going to help. In fact, they knew part of the punishment was the wait.

"So," she finally said. "Frankie has broken protocol."

"Yes ma'am," he said.

She paused as the waiter came with her food. After he departed she began to eat and then pointed her fork at the big man.

"Are you going to be okay," she asked.

"I'm living with it but yes, I'm going to be okay."

"Okay," said Roza. "Cool."

The two men looked at her.

"Nothing else?" asked Hersh.

"What is it you want me to say?" responded his grandmother.

Hersh put his hand to her brow like he was checking for a temperature and then pinched himself.

"What did you do with my grandmother?"

"Oh, you're a riot, Alice," she said.

Then she grabbed each man by the hand and squeezed. "What we agreed to so many years ago was just untenable. It was a miracle none of us went off the reservation before. I shudder to think what might have happened if Frankie had continued to bottle up his rage. I was less worried about him than I was about you."

"Me?" said Hersh.

"Yeah, you. Frankie and I have a bond. As much as I love you, there is no way you could fathom the extra weight we lug around. But I knew when he decided to shed it, whether on a one-time thing or as a habit, the right people would pay the price."

Frankie nodded but didn't add anything.

"But you, son," she said, pointing her fork once again. "You are the dangerous one. Because when you blow you won't be so well-aimed. There is always a chance you'll suffer a crisis of conscience and then we're all running for the hills looking for a safe house and new identities."

"So, my reading *The Way of the Samurai* was a wasted effort?"

"Joke all you want, funny boy, but Frankie and me are ready for the end. We've been bluffing and tap-dancing and denying but we know how this ends."

"So, what happened?" Hersh asked.

"You happened and I got the shock of my life," she told him. "I loved my husband and my children. I love all my grandchildren. But the moment I picked you up, I knew I was a goner. When you looked up at me I saw both my mother and father in your eyes and God help me but you made me want to stick around because it was a second chance for them."

She paused for just a moment as she stared out into the vista.

"They never made it out of the camps, as you know, and my rage began there. It was so easy in the beginning. There were so many of those bastards running around. In the first 20 years, it was like picking apples. There was great confusion and police tactics weren't sophisticated. There was no *CSI Germany* or *Criminal Minds Poland.*

"It was the Wild West and even a young girl and then a young woman could get away with things. Who would suspect a young me? As it got harder, I got smarter. But I had the fallback position. I didn't give a damn if I got caught. But I do give a damn if you do."

"So where do we go from here?" Hersh asked.

"We just go. Look, my race has been run. See what I did there?" she said with a chuckle. "Whatever happens I've done everything I wanted. The past years just reserved my spot in hell. Now it is up to you guys, and from all appearances, our new young friend."

"What does it mean?" asked Frankie.

"It means the work continues and I hope that Hersh is a distance runner and not a sprinter."

She held up a hand. "Please don't take it as a criticism. I know the toll this exacts. We are all too smart, too careful, and above all too vicious to be stopped. But there is a reason I skipped a generation in my partnership. I really do love your father but he wasn't ever going to be able to do this. He had a different path. Who knows how a sweet boy like him ever came out of someone like me. He's like my mother. Hersh, you are so much like me it keeps me up at night. But there is a streak of your father and I thank God for it. But it is also what might end all of it for you."

"So, I repeat," Hersh said. "What do we do now?"

"Well," answered his grandmother. "For the next few hours we win a crap load of money and make a lot of people happy."

CHAPTER 22

Marian Webber would never tell anyone about her feelings. At first, she had jerry-rigged the dating site so she could meet him and get close.

She knew what men saw when they first looked. And most of them missed the 167 IQ.

There were plenty of people in jail cells wondering how a prom queen caught them.

So when the assignment came to tag and bag yet another man, she knew what plan to follow.

But this guy's profile read like he deserved a medal, not handcuffs. He had the aura of a miracle worker.

She would bring him down because she was good at her job. And in the interim, she would not hesitate to steer all the damaged children she came across his way.

"Robert, who is this guy?" she asked her supervisor after she finished his file. "I mean, what the hell?"

Robert Gregory laced his hands behind his head.

"Pretty impressive, huh?"

"Damned impressive."

"I've talked to parents of children he's helped and they would lay down their lives for him."

"As would I if those were my kids."

"Marian," her boss said. "Just because you save lives doesn't mean you have *carte blanche* to take them."

"And we're sure of this."

"Pretty sure."

"Pretty sure may not be good enough. If we run this guy off and we're wrong, we won't be able to remove the stink. We'll all be going down."

"The reason why you are on the case."

"What is the time frame?"

"None."

"None?"

"Marian, what I am about to say never leaves this room."

She nodded.

"This guy is a mass killer. We're pretty sure of it. We think his bald-headed friend is just as culpable."

"I can believe it."

"But."

"But?"

"Look, the people we think he's made disappear, and I really do mean disappear, are not the salt of the earth. The really bad ones speak for themselves but even the ones who look shiny don't end up to be that way."

"Sounds like a man with a code."

"He's got a code and part of me admires him for it but I can't excuse homicide."

"So why the no timetable?"

He looked at her and wrinkled his brow.

"Those sons of bitches."

He released a slow smile. "You catch on quick."

"They don't care how long it takes because he's erasing people from the board they think need to be gone."

Robert put his finger to the side of his nose and said, "In case we're being recorded I want to say I have no idea what you are talking about."

She sat across from her boss and imagined how all of this could go wrong. Of course, she thought it before every assignment. That is why the tough cases came her way.

She wasn't foolish enough to not believe her looks were also why she was summoned. A personal touch would take precedent over a comprehensive computer search.

"Can I assume I'll be putting on the full-court charm?"

"Assume away."

"You know, some of the things you make me do are things we arrest other people for."

Her boss laughed a non-funny laugh and said, "But you're a prostitute for the good guys. You use your feminine wiles for truth, justice, and the American way."

"If I called HR right now you'd be packing your stuff up in boxes by lunchtime," she said.

"So true. But I'm guilty of so much more and harassing you would be such a minor crime in my HR jacket."

She nodded while moving a pad and paper from her purse.

"You have to be the last agent who writes stuff down," he said.

"Saving it all for my memoir," she said, and then after a beat, "or my trial."

"You know, you might end up liking this guy. Reports say he's funny, good-looking, and treats people with great respect."

"Please don't tell my mother. She's wondering when she'll have grandchildren and even as a good Catholic she's started to think marriage doesn't have to be part of the package"

"We won't ask you to marry him or get pregnant," he said. "Even for us that is over the line."

"Robert, I hope we don't regret this one."

"Regrets, I've got a few but then again too few to mention."

She removed herself from his office because he had a full day ahead. She needed to become a redhead and do major research on this guy.

CHAPTER 23

Alarms went off for Betty and Frankie when Hersh came into work whistling.

It wasn't until they were eating that Betty and Frankie found out why their colleague was fairly skipping about.

"Hey," Hersh said apropos of nothing, "did I tell you guys I have a date tonight?"

There was silence at the table. Betty had been with them for months and this was the first time she had known him to be interested in the opposite sex. At least she assumed it was the opposite sex.

Frankie was equally nonplussed but didn't remain speechless for long. "Whoa, dude, I thought you was gay."

"Hardee har, har," said Hersh. "You really are immature, you know?"

"Not exactly an AP bulletin, you know?" Frankie said with a smile, indicating he wasn't done. "Seriously, guy. Do you even know anything about going on a date? I mean, you have to make conversation and hold doors and work up to kissing her at the door."

"I've been on dates, you know."

"What, Cathy Kramer and the senior prom? We know how that worked out."

Betty decided to be the mature one here and get actual information. "Does she have a name?" she asked.

"Marian," said Hersh.

"First name Maid?" rejoined Frankie.

"What are you, three years old?" said his friend.

"Is she a librarian in River City?"

Frankie couldn't control himself and was breathless from laughter when he said, "And will she play your 76 trombones?"

Hersh appealed to Betty but even she was laughing, and so he pretended to sulk.

"I don't really know much about her," he said. "It is a blind date and I arranged it through the internet on one of those dating sites."

Betty was often surprised when Hersh did normal things and he never seemed embarrassed. He would say he "loved Barry Manilow's music" and was never trying to be ironic or funny. He didn't care about what people thought. She really liked the goofy guy who came to work. It was the same guy who totally let go with the kids.

"Well, I think it is great Hersh is actually going to get out of this place for a night," said Betty.

"Why, thank you Betty. I'm glad there is one mature person on this staff."

"Can you just do one thing, though?" she asked.

"What is it?"

"Can you watch for telltale signs of corruption? You know, the minute your son leaves the house, does he rebuckle his knickerbockers below the knee? Is there a nicotine stain on his index finger? A dime novel hidden in the corncrib? Is he starting to memorize jokes from *Captain Billy's Whiz-Bang*? If so, my friends, ya got trouble."

Frankie was laughing so hard he had to spit out his sandwich but he really broke up when Betty started to dance around the kitchen and raising her hands to the ceiling as she sung "Ya Got Trouble" from *The Music Man*.

How a teenager even knew a Broadway tune was a mystery to Hersh but he started giggling himself.

But if the truth were known, Hersh was really looking forward to his date.

There was a tipping point and he was perilously close to it. If Roza had taught him anything it was to be playing chess while those around you played checkers. You didn't have to be too many moves ahead, you just had to be ahead.

CHAPTER 24

Marian was a stunning redhead. Not much of a surprise since she was also a beautiful blonde and brunette. But even she had to admit going red was a spectacular move.

She felt earthy and risk-taking. It was no surprise when heads turned on her walk from the salon to the car. The next stop was to get a new wardrobe.

Thankfully, the Bureau picked up the tab. Being a chameleon was only exciting if you had the wallet for it.

This was not an expensive makeover, though. She didn't need to be buying Carolina Herrera for this assignment. Everything she needed would be off the rack and on sale.

She was trying to impress a guy not impressed by high-priced restaurants and high-end clothes. This was probably the closest to her style. That is, if she still had a style after dressing up, and down, for years.

The nearer the truth, the more at ease Marian would be in her assignment. She hated the lies because she had to memorize so much more.

She had never blown an undercover assignment but sometimes she felt one sentence away. If this didn't work with the new guy it wouldn't be because she said or did something.

Her research said she should be honest. She didn't have to go into detail but for once she could let it be known she was with law enforcement. It would allow her a certain amount of freedom and the ability to carry a gun. It was when she was the most natural.

She figured he would be interested in her work and hopefully would open him up about his.

Part of her worried this would be the guy who saw through her and called her on it. But then she remembered he was a man and that always worked in her favor.

CHAPTER 25

Hersh recognized his date by the flower pinned on the left side of her hair.

They shook hands and he began to fiddle with the menu.

"How did you pick this place?" Marian asked.

"Price," said Hersh.

"Just in case it doesn't work you don't want to have spent too much money."

"Exactly."

She nodded and smiled. He smiled back to show he was joking.

She was a little surprised by how dressed up he was.

He wore a sports coat and a white shirt with a green tie. Looking close she saw it was decorated with frogs. But it was expensive and expertly knotted. His style was missing from her reports.

Her mother always said look at a man's shoes and it will tell you how he treats himself. He followed her gaze and chuckled.

"Bass Weejuns. Freshly polished and recently given new soles," he said. "I treat myself pretty good."

She colored before laughing at herself. Not too smooth for an agent but maybe just right for a person on a first date.

"Do you go out on a lot of computer dates?

"My first," he said.

"Oh, wow. This could be a complete disaster."

"So true but then we'd have nowhere to go but up. And at least it will be a story around the water cooler."

The waiter interrupted again when he served the drinks and took their order and it gave Marian another brief recess to study her date. She didn't find him unattractive and he appeared to be pleasant. The test would be how forthcoming he was.

"Well," she said, hoping to start things off by revealing something about herself. "I'm on a lot of computer dates. The rate of success is not exactly staggering."

She left off the part about it being part of what she did for a living.

"Well," he said, interrupting her interior monologue, "it isn't like we've staked a whole lot of equity into this. At the very least we'll have a good meal and hopefully things won't go so terribly wrong where we'll have to call a referee."

"We can only hope," she said.

"Do you ever read 'Date Lab' in *The Washington Post*?" he asked.

"I don't. Should I?"

"A few years ago," he said, "they had the greatest or worst opening for a blind date ever. *The Post* pays for a meal for two people on a blind date and they first meet in a restaurant. So, a woman is sitting at a booth when her date comes in. She didn't know until then he was confined to a wheelchair."

"Awkward," Marian says.

"A little bit. He wheels over and she says, 'I'm betting you didn't have too much trouble getting a parking space.' "

The peals of laughter surprise them.

"You made it up," she said.

"You can't make that up," he said.

"Oh my God."

"Yeah, I figure either it ends the date or it is so honest and refreshing he enjoyed it more than you and I are right now."

"That," she said, "is so classic. I have nothing to add to it or top it."

"Human nature just fascinates me. I think it I would have proposed marriage right there. You aren't going to find a better partner to go through all the crap with."

"I would probably need a little more information," she said.

"Sometimes you have to take a leap."

It was the last thing said before the waiter brought the food. She wasn't surprised he went for steak. He was pleased she ordered a meal a human might eat if she didn't think she were being judged.

After she drained her wine glass she decided to dive in.

"I understand you are a therapist of some kind," she said.

Of course, she knew to the tiniest detail what kind of therapist he was. Her research had revealed his numerous degrees and she even knew about the extracurricular activities. He was an expert in several martial arts and he took ballet or a few years and was in an improv comedy group.

As she forked up her eggplant, she tested the waters by asking what kind of therapy it was.

"Well, it has a medical name but my partner and I just call it total therapy," he said. "When you work with children they aren't interested in the science of it. They just want to be better."

Marian was relieved she had gotten a talker. She was an expert in extracting information but it was a joy to not work at it.

He wasn't going to tell her in his spare time he killed people but she'd be thrilled to end this dinner with a baseline of information. Perhaps she could trade some nuggets about herself. The only difference was his would be true.

"So, it isn't asking questions trying to get them to reveal their feelings?"

He smiled. "No. We're not that type of therapy."

"I'm intrigued," she said.

"I love my work but since this is a first date I should let you know not everything I do is suitable for dinner conversation."

Startled, she looked up and then quickly realized he wasn't talking about his after-hours activity.

"How so?"

"Well, we deal with children with severe problems."

"Like learning issues?"

"Like learning which adults they can trust not to severely damage them."

She regretted pushing it so she tried to pull back a bit.

"Sorry about being so nosy," she said.

"Oh, don't worry about. Frankie and I are an open book when it comes to our work," he said. "We don't ever want the children to think what happened is something to be ashamed of."

"Is Frankie your partner?" she asked.

He got a big grin on his face and said, "No, Clemenza is my partner. Frankie is our protector."

She knew who Frankie was but had no idea about Clemenza. How could she have not found out he had another partner?

She waited for dessert to ease back into the conversation.

"Is Clemenza also a therapist?

"Clemenza is the greatest therapist in history. There are cases I spend weeks trying to reach and Clemenza gets them in 30 seconds."

"How?"

"I think it's his cold nose. But Frankie says the wagging tail is hypnotic."

She roared with laughter. "Your partner is a dog?"

He reached into his wallet and pulled out a picture. The man in the photo stood 6-foot-4, bald and heavily illustrated. He would have dominated any other photo he was in. But Marian moved past him when she saw the animal in his lap. She couldn't take her eyes off the dog.

He was staring into the camera and although she knew it wasn't true she believed he was staring at her. And even stranger, he seemed to indicate if she took a misstep with Hersh she would have to answer to him.

The man in the photo was truly frightening and she could believe he stopped most arguments by just staring at his combatant. If you came at him, you better have a stick in one hand and a gun in the other and even that might not be enough.

But given the choice she would have faced him rather than the dog.

CHAPTER 26

Say I'm stupid about women. Or, incredibly naïve, if I'm feeling charitable with myself.

Don't paint me as a person who hates women. If a man had gotten me into this place, I wouldn't have hated men.

When you do stupid things, you look at the common denominator. That is, I. I don't want my last moments taken up by bitter recriminations.

Besides, I lived a matriarchal-led life. My grandmother, my mother, and my sisters were major influences on me.

There are so many things I wish I had done. I wish I had bought Apple, Microsoft, and Google. I wish I had been old enough to attend Negro League games. I wish I had kissed Pammy Stelkowski at the eighth-grade dance. I should have eaten more chocolate cake, and I should have seen fewer French films.

So, those are what I'll obsess over. I could rue the blind date but there were so many exits, I could have gotten off the bad road I was on.

Somewhere, Frankie is throwing darts at my picture. He has to be pissed after cautioning me on many occasions.

The only good thing is I won't have to see his look of disappointment and won't hear the name-calling.

My hope is Frankie has taken his money, gotten on his bike, and disappeared. If I thought this manifesto would lead to finding him, I would have cut my throat an hour ago.

If I had lost him, I would have been heartbroken so I'm sure he's in a funk. But I would never confuse sorrow for inaction. Frankie will miss me but doesn't need me. His life will be lonely at times but not bereft of good things.

Will he carry the business? I doubt it. Frankie was loyal to Roza and me but never had the passion or familial connection I possessed.

So, don't think you'll find him by studying the latest crime statistics. If you think Clemenza will give him away, well, good luck. Not even witness protection and a lifetime of steak bones will get that dog to hunt.

See what I did there? I made a joke through my pain. There is no reason why we can't laugh a little through this.

I don't blame anyone and I'm not bitter. Nothing that happened blinded me to the fact of what I did. Of course, I felt justified, but what person of action doesn't? Given time to think through my entire history doesn't leave me with regrets. But I'm not so stupid as to think everyone will share my view.

Certainly, victim's families will not see them as the scum-sucking blowfish they are but as fathers and brothers (and in total truth-telling here, some sisters and mothers). To them I'm Lucifer. I accept the weight.

I'm not a gladiator who wanted to be carried out on my shield. I would have preferred to die in an old-age home with my family and friends around me.

My self-importance notwithstanding, a couple more times at the plate would have been sweet.

Right now, you think I'm going soft. But maybe I'm like James Cagney in *Angels with Dirty Faces.* Heeding the pleas of Pat O'Brien, being led to the death chamber, Cagney pretends to be a coward so the kids who idolized him will turn from a life of crime.

It led to one of the greatest lines in cinema history when O'Brien, a priest named Father Jerry but also an uncaught delinquent with Cagney's character in their youth, says after the execution:

"All right fellas ... Let's go and say a prayer for a boy who couldn't run as fast as I could."

God, I loved that movie. It brings up another great moment between my grandmother and me. One more Chandleresque utterance even if it was Cagney as Rocky Sullivan.

"You'll slap me? You slap me in a dream, you better wake up and apologize."

Man, they don't write dialogue like that anymore. I mean, you have to be carrying a 45-caliber gat in one hand, smoking a cigarette in the other, and have a doll on your lap to carry it off.

Timing can be a bitch. I'm Cagney. I got caught. For all the Pat O'Briens out there I can only say, God bless you, sirs and madams. Play on. There will be no "why me?" from here on. I know exactly why me. I played the hand and while a full house doesn't win every deal you have to play it like it does.

I got beat by four queens.

Don't you draw the queen of diamonds, boy
She'll beat you if she's able
You know the queen of hearts is always your best bet
Now it seems to me, some fine things
Have been laid upon your table
But you only want the ones that you can't get

My God, I'm starting to sing to myself. The hourglass has to be empty now.

Mother of mercy, is this the end of Rico?

Please stop me before I do an entire floor show. First Cagney and now Edward G. Robinson. I must be losing oxygen.

If I had the strength I'd do a little soft-shoe off the stage but as I said before, "I'm dying up here."

Right now, I'm going to rest.

CHAPTER 27

If anyone honored family, it was Roza. She knew how fleeting it could be. So she remembered birthdays and took her granddaughters to lunch and shopping.

She never missed a graduation, wedding, or anniversary. She was there with a check or a coffee cake or a shoulder to lean on. They didn't know it, but she would leave them an incredible amount of money.

She laundered enough cash to make it all clean and the government would never know where it originated. The cash she would leave to Hersh. He knew what to do with it.

Roza looked at her hands and thought about all they had done. She didn't flinch from the knowledge but neither was she gloating. The price she paid was steep but early on it was "in for a penny, in for a pound" for her.

She never believed it wouldn't end somewhere.

Shockingly, it ended in retirement but she knew at any time it all could catch up to her and she'd be in front of some magistrate explaining it all.

A ringing phone broke her out of her reverie.

"Where are you?"

"And good morning to you, Grandmother. I can only hope you are enjoying a lovely day."

"Back at you," she said. "Now, can I know where you are?

"At the clinic. Just called to tell you I had a date last night."

"With a woman?"

"Yes. Now you can cross one worry off your list."

"I would love you no matter what," she said.

"So they all say."

"You forget I've seen real persecution of gays. Not the minor stuff of discrimination."

"Way to play the trump card way early."

"It must have been a good date."

"What makes you think so?"

"Because the amount of cheek you are giving me says you're in a great mood."

"It was nice. She was nice. I was nice."

"Was she Jewish?"

"She said she was."

"What does that mean?"

"Well, I didn't give her the paper bag test."

"Are you actually making a racial joke?" she asked.

"No, I'm making a grandmother joke."

"And yet your audience is not laughing."

"Because you have no sense of humor."

"We'll dispose of the referendum on whether you are funny. Does this woman have a name?"

"Marian."

"Is she the only person in the world without a last name?"

"You are not getting it."

"Why not," she asked.

"Because you'll run her name through every database and you are going to draw up a family tree and find a distant relative lived in Europe during the war and the distant relative rousted people out of their homes and put them on trains or in ghettos."

"I hate being predictable."

"You're not. It is why we aren't talking through a sheet of Plexiglas where you instruct me to buy you cartons of cigarettes for you to barter with."

"Are you saying you would visit me in prison?"

"Of course I would. I would visit you on the rare days you weren't in lockdown for violence against an inmate who tried to coerce you."

"I'd be a badass inmate."

"You'd have your own gang and the warden would come to you for favors."

"You make it sound appetizing."

"Please don't go to jail. I couldn't stand the family stain."

"I'll do my best."

"I do want to thank you for changing the tenor of this phone call from upbeat to downtrodden."

"It is what I do."

This was her way of not asking too many questions about his life away from her. As much as she could she would give him the freedom to pursue a normal life.

Both appreciated the charade.

"Anyway," he said. "What about lunch today?"

"Business or pleasure?"

"Business."

"The thing with Frankie."

"Among other things."

This time they met in the bleachers. Roza was among the flock of foreigners who loved baseball.

Football was too violent for her. Even she laughed at the absurdity. And basketball was too fast. For action, she loved horse racing and for game study there was nothing better than nine innings.

Whenever there was a day game at the minor-league park Roza would sit in the stands and keep score. She passed that on to her grandson. They had animated discussions on ways to fill out a card and each borrowed from the other.

The stadium also gave them anonymity. On a weekday afternoon, they could sit in the outfield and no one would bother them.

And they could have a hot dog.

"Why don't we dispense of business first," he said.

"Eat the frog first thing in the morning."

"Exactly."

"I checked into the Frankie caper."

"Is that what we're calling it?" he said.

"Massacre was taken."

"What did you find out?"

"It is a five-alarm fire."

"No surprise."

"My people say they are looking for multiple suspects."

"Yeah, Frankie can multitask."

"We have that going for us."

"Your people have an idea of what the police are thinking?"

"Not police. Feds."

This stopped him for a second. Why on earth would a federal agency be interested in a single pedophile? It was bad news. The database would be more sophisticated and the search more prolonged. The overworked police would shelve a cold case. The feds just kept spending more tax dollars and took this stuff personally.

There would be no juking the feds. If they wanted to put their talons into a case it was going to be a long slog to get out from under it.

"What in the *Wide, Wide World of Sports* is going on?"

"Seems like our friend wore a badge."

"How did we not know?"

"Undercover."

"Please tell me they knew he was a sick bastard."

"They did but he closed cases for them. He wasn't shy about infiltrating the bad guys."

"But he was a bad guy," Hersh said and then got a bad feeling in his stomach. "Oh, God, please tell me the pedophile thing wasn't a cover for him. Tell me he was a sick bastard and deserved what he got."

He looked pleadingly up at his grandmother.

"No worries there. He was sick. They knew it. He was moved around so he wouldn't have time to set up roots and find a victim. We have that going for us. They are going to have to tread lightly.

"So, we got a break because the feds were covering for a guy who they should have taken off the streets in the first place. It is too twisted for color TV."

"Gives you a headache just thinking about it," Roza said. "But we live in a glass house, honey, and we can't be throwing too many boulders."

Hersh knew she was not just right but a hundred percent right. There was no way he could dispute the facts. They were among the sickest people out there. Einstein may have been right about God not playing dice with the universe but the same couldn't be said for him.

"I'll agree. But I can't say I'm happy about it. There are crimes and there are crimes against humanity and you can't close a blind eye."

"We don't," Roza said.

"Look, I'm not saying all of them should be treated the way we treat them. Some struggle with who they are. So, I'm not advocating we round them up. It would be even hypocritical by my standards. But they do need to be moved from temptation. If they need help I'm all for it. But our guy was beyond help."

"We can debate that on a different day. Right now, we have to stay out of the lane when the feds come down the track."

"Any thoughts?"

"We do nothing for right now. They have no DNA or trace evidence. Frankie is good. They don't even think there was a cleanup. That is how good our boy was. "

"He's a pro."

"But so are they. We're good and they are good. You remember Wilfred Brimley talking to Paul Newman in *Absence of Malice*?

Hersh smiled.

" 'You're a smart man, Mr. Gallagher. I'm pretty smart myself. Don't get too smart.' "

"Exactly."

"I shouldn't have given you my Netflix account password."

"Like I couldn't have hacked it on my own."

With information passed, they watched the game. He was also a minor-league enthusiast and a day in the sun was what he craved.

"One more thing," she said.

"There always is, Lieutenant Columbo."

"Thank God he isn't on the case."

"You know he's a fictional character."

"If you say so."

Roza pulled out a set of car keys. She dangled them in front of her grandson and then put them in his hands.

"Getaway car?"

"What is wrong with you?" she said.

"You have me at a disadvantage."

"Don't I always."

"Is this going to be 20 questions?"

"They are for Betty."

"You bought Betty a car?"

"You got a problem?"

"Of course not. I think it is an incredibly generous thing to do. Please tell me you aren't going to get mushy on me."

"She deserves good things."

"Agreed."

She said something to herself but Hersh heard it.

"She reminds me of my sister."

He reached out and put his arm around his grandmother. He gave her time to compose herself.

"What will she be driving?"

"Corvette convertible."

"You have got to be shitting me?" he said.

"Of course, I'm kidding you. Geez, you're an idiot. It is a Ford Taurus. But I loaded it up with goodies."

"She'll go bat crazy over it."

"I want her to have some freedom. She couldn't be in better hands with you and Frankie."

"And Clemenza."

"Goes without saying," Roza agreed. "But she also needs some time away. She needs to be a young woman."

"I won't argue," he said.

"Please take this the right way, sweetheart. I don't want her to become you."

"Again, I won't argue."

"At the end of day, she needs to be able to ride into the sunset and not look back."

"Who rides into the sunset in a Ford Taurus?"

"The people who can," she said.

As they left each noticed the car a block away. They didn't comment but knew the other was aware. He kissed his grandmother and drove away. She headed the opposite way. Later they could compare notes.

CHAPTER 28

Marian watched them drive away.

She could fall for a man who hung out with his grandmother. And she had to admit the first date had been surprisingly fun.

He let her know he was interested. But done it so gently she wasn't aware until he walked her to her car and seen her off.

She wasn't used to not getting hit on. Some were smooth, and some so clumsy it was almost funny, but all made the attempt.

He hadn't. He must be gay, she thought, making fun of herself.

There was no pretending to be interested in what he was saying. A terrific conversationalist, he seemed interested in her. When he asked for her number she asked him about a second date.

Then she had gone to her apartment wondering why he had not pressed the issue.

Now she was shadowing him and it was creepy. But you don't do a job halfway.

She had felt bad a lot on assignment but always did the work and caught a lot of bad people. When information was wrong, she walked away and chalked it up to experience.

There was nothing wrong in casting a wide net and throwing back the minnows.

So she told herself.

CHAPTER 29

Mrs. Grimes picked Tuesday to visit Betty. It was the primary reason but she also wanted to talk to Hersh.

She hardly recognized her. She found a confident and happy woman taking the place of the scared child she sent over.

Betty was chattering away about work, her new car, and most shockingly, about the weekend trips to pursue her new hobby, photography. Betty was snapping away while she talked.

Mrs. Grimes saw a photo of Betty and Clemenza up on the wall, where Betty's scars were prominent in full digital glory.

If the teacher had doubts of giving Hersh another case, the picture erased them.

After lunch, a meal prepared by Betty, she took a walk with her and barely said a word as Betty carried the conversation.

She had known Frankie and Hersh for so long and she loved them. They had done so much good but she wasn't unaware of the downside.

The absence of guilt made her uncomfortable but it got easier each time.

She used to say "this far and no farther." Now she didn't even entertain the charade.

Mrs. G had become a movie buff and like her friends she began to quote from them and to see her life played out in scenes.

She handed Hersh a file with a history and a photo. He glanced at it and wrote something in a notebook. Mrs. G knew he was writing in code and the notebook would never come back on them. Still, she felt trepidation when he wrote something down.

"You know who I've become?" she asked Hersh.

"Who?"

"I'm Ernst Janning."

Hersh roared with laughter.

"You don't look like Burt Lancaster."

"Nevertheless."

"Mrs. G, as many times as I've watched *Judgment at Nuremberg* I've never thought of you. While I believe you could be anything you set your mind to, I can't see you as a Nazi doctor."

"Nicest thing anyone has ever said to me," she told him.

Hersh could clearly see she was laboring to deal with it all.

"Lancaster was so great," said Hersh.

"Remember the scene at the end with him and Spencer Tracy when he tries to justify his actions?"

"Sure," says Hersh. "He says, 'Those millions of people…I never knew it would come to that. You must believe it!'"

She looks at Hersh with a sad smile.

"And Tracy's character, the judge at Nuremberg, just blows up his shit."

Hersh roars with laughter again.

"I was so thunderstruck when Tracy looks at Lancaster with no sympathy at all and tells him, 'Herr Janning, it came to that the first time you sentenced a man to death you knew to be innocent.' "

"Tracy lost Marlene Dietrich because of it," says Hersh.

"What are we losing, Hersh?"

"A little sleep for me."

"Only sleep?"

"Mrs. G, I don't think about it."

"If you did?"

"It would bring me to my knees."

"Are we going to hell?"

"I've earned a place there long ago. Your place in heaven has been reserved."

"How could you know?"

"Because the good you do has gotten you an invitation."

"And the bad?"

"What bad?"

"I give you names."

"When I was a kid I used to watch the *Lone Ranger* and *Roy Rogers*. I'd watch them shoot the gun out of the hands of the bad guys. I mean the really bad guys. Even early on I couldn't understand. I wasn't bloodthirsty, just couldn't understand showing compassion for people who didn't have the morals of a peanut."

"That is all it took for you?"

"In a shorthanded way, yes."

"I don't believe you."

"Because you can't stand to think of me and Frankie as anything other than your students. You're a good person, Mrs. G, but if you are Burt Lancaster, then I'm Paul Newman in *Hombre*."

"He was so handsome," she said.

"Yes, he was. But I meant I had the moral sense of John Russell. There is the great scene when Richard Boone comes to parlay with Newman's character. Boone has been hunting the stagecoach party and kidnapped a passenger. He has tried to kill them all and denied them water. After he makes his demands to Newman, Newman says to him, 'Hey, I got a question. How are you planning to get back down that hill?' Then he shoots Boone's character."

Mrs. G marvels at how he does the voices of Richard Boone and Paul Newman. And how he shows the shock on Boone's face and calm on Newman's when he pulls the trigger.

"You don't mosey up to people you are trying to kill and expect them to meekly go along and not take the advantages they were given," Hersh explained. "It is the genius of Elmore Leonard. His characters acted like real people."

"On an intellectual level, I'm in agreement," she said. "But we don't always live on an intellectual level. Those are real people in hotels and alleys and cars and wherever you do your work."

He kissed her cheek. Then he squeezed her elbow and led her into a chair.

"Mrs. G, if this is getting too much, I want you to stop. I would not respect or trust you if this didn't bother you. I'm in a dirty business and covered in guilt. But I don't want you to go down a road you can't return from. Do you understand me?"

She nodded and said to him, "I've only got one question for you."

"Yes?" he asked.

"How am I going to get back down that hill?"

CHAPTER 30

Marian was reading reports when Jack Comstock came in. He slapped down a newspaper and told her to start reading.

A woman had been found in a hotel room with arms and legs shackled. She had a rope around her neck tied in a way that she'd strangle if she moved.

When police, tipped off by a 911 call, opened a folder near the woman they found a history of a predator. She had abused several children, including her own. She burned and beat them. There were photos, a short bio, and hospital reports.

The woman claimed a frame-up but it unraveled a day later when the police got a package. They found a disc, and when they inserted it they wished they hadn't.

Her abuse was documented and the violence severe enough for one seasoned detective to vomit his lunch.

"I think our boy is at it again," said Comstock.

"It was his fingerprints," she said. "Except the woman was unharmed."

"What do you make of it?"

"Maybe it isn't him."

"Maybe he has a conscience?"

"Or maybe he made a deal with someone who has a conscience."

"Good or bad for us?"

"I wish I knew," she said.

Later, Marian read the story twice more. The answers were no clearer. But she held an advantage. She'd gauge firsthand in two hours.

When he called to confirm their date she almost jumped out of her skin. Had he known she was sizing him up? The timing of the call so spooked her he asked if anything was wrong.

She told him she was wrapped up in work but would love to meet for dinner. She set a time late enough to allow her to read his file again and get in a run. Nothing cleared her mind like exercise.

But it was not a good run. She never got in stride and never cleared herself of him completely.

She had confidence she would build a case no matter how she felt about him. If she chose her version of *The Thomas Crown Affair* she would be more Faye Dunaway than Rene Russo. Then she chuckled realizing the thief got away with it in both versions.

She'd have to pick another movie. But why was she even thinking on those terms? If the reports were true, this guy wasn't a charming thief. It wasn't artwork and diamonds for him.

When he stood up to meet her she had dressed to kill. She needed him to fall ever deeper under her spell.

Yet, she was underdressed standing next to him. He was wearing a suit costing a few thousand dollars. His white shirt was so crisp she heard the starch crack when he moved. His bow tie was a royal blue so deep she wondered if the color existed in nature. Once again, he wore handmade shoes. When they sat down she noticed he had bowed to one note of whimsy by wearing SpongeBob Squarepants socks.

"Love the socks," Marian said, hoping to regain balance.

"Found them at the bottom of the sea," he answered.

She knew the cartoon because she watched with her nieces. She figured the show played in his clinic but now she was starting to guess and it was something she didn't like to do.

He seemed to read her mind.

"I love cartoons. And I love socks. So, I pair my enthusiasms. Literally."

Part of her was scared but the other part was enjoying this challenge. It was good to be toe-to-toe with a pro.

"So, what did you do today?" she asked, hoping to land the first blow.

"Oh, it was a fruitful day, to say the least," he parried.

I'll bet it was, she thought.

"Oh?"

"Yes. My partner and I accepted some new clients. They come in so scared and so scarred we've got to figure out a plan."

"You probably don't like to talk about this."

"Oh, you'll find just the opposite," he said. "Anything about me is interesting to talk about. I'm the center of my own universe. My parents and sisters will give references on that."

"Are you parents alive?"

"Oh, yes. They live close. I see them quite often. My mom worries about me every day so the dinners are her chance to get it all out."

"Why does she worry?"

"Because she is a Jewish mother."

He asked her about work. Marian deflected well enough that by the time they were eating they were on safer ground.

Then she threw a Hail Mary. It came out and she couldn't take it back.

"Did you see the story today on the woman tied up in her hotel room?"

He answered without hesitation.

"I did. Weird and creepy."

"Weird?" she said.

"You can't imagine those people are out there. You want to believe they only exist in fiction. When they talked about what she had done, I cringed."

"Don't you deal with these types all of the time?"

"Each time I think this is an aberration. I'm with the last damaged child on earth and somehow the good guys have caught the bad guys."

"Sort of a Shangri-la thought for a man in your line of work," she said.

"You can't do the work if you think it is an assembly line. If I didn't fool myself into thinking there was an end to it, I'm not sure I'd be able to help the children we have."

"Okay. When you put it that way I can understand what you're saying. And of course, you live it. I'm just a back bencher lobbing verbal volleys."

"A lovely volley, though."

"You know, I wonder about the woman."

"You mean, how could there be these types of people in the world?"

"That too. But how does she get herself caught after so many years?"

"Great question."

She pressed down on the brakes.

"I'm so sorry for having brought this up. So, let me switch gears and ask what we're doing after dinner."

"I had no plans."

"Good. Because I would like to take you somewhere."

"A surprise?"

"One of my favorite places."

They took his car and he smiled when they turned into the zoo.

"Isn't it closed?"

"I know the director."

"I love a woman who has connections," he said.

"Any special exhibit?"

"I'm always up for the ape house," he said.

"Let's go ape," she said and colored. "My gosh, that was just so corny."

"I like corny," he said and kissed her. He was throwing a fastball. And she felt it. As a professional she had to watch herself but nothing was gained by living a nun's life.

Part of her genius was playing the part and nobody said not to enjoy it.

He reached with his thumb and wiped the corner of her lip.

"A little smear there."

"Do I need to freshen up?"

"I'm probably not the guy to answer that," he said, pointing behind him.

She looked where he gestured and broke into a wide grin. There were a group of apes looking at her with heads cocked.

She lost it when the biggest one pooched out his lips and nodded his head. Then another blew kisses.

"Nobody gets by with PDA these days," she said.

"There is a camera or an ape everywhere. Public displays of affection are the next endangered species," he answered.

"You think they tell each other that today they hope to see some human porn when they come into the cages?"

"Their version of Cinemax."

She grasped his hand and led him away.

"We can go over to the Tiger Den. Why should these guys be the only ones to gossip about us?"

"What do you think they are saying?" he asked.

"They are probably thinking that I am a little suspect because I'm a redhead but they really think you are a man slut."

"Always said apes were intuitive creatures."

"So, what now?"

"Well, we can pick your car up in the morning."

When the light filtered in the window, she stirred and wondered where she was before seeing him in deep sleep. She had no intention of slipping out with the morning light.

This might be a good time to scout out his place under the guise of finding a bathroom or a kitchen. She thought about last night and didn't have regrets. This was not her first rodeo but she was back punching a clock.

She was careful not to wake him but he was truly sleeping the sleep of the innocent. That gave her a little pause but didn't stop her.

Walking in the hallway she felt a pair of eyes. Slowly turning she saw the dog. He didn't move but didn't stop staring.

Her notes told her this was Clemenza. She was a dog lover but wasn't sure how to approach him. He was big enough to eat her but he was so cute she felt her feet move toward him.

He met her halfway and flopped down on the floor. She laughed and gave in to his demands of a stomach rub. He surprised her by pivoting and pinning her to the floor. She giggled when he wouldn't stop licking her.

"Cuckolded again by man's best friend," a voice above her said.

She looked at the bald-headed man and her position and his size made him look eight feet tall.

"I'm Frankie," he said.

"Marian."

"I would hope you are otherwise I'd have to call the police and report a break-in."

"You figure someone would break in to give your dog a belly rub?"

He scratched the dog under his chin and said, "He's just a friend of mine. The dog belongs to the man in the other room."

She had no idea how a man and a dog this size entered a house and she didn't hear either. That unnerved her more than being caught in a man's shirt and her underwear.

But he was treating this as an everyday incident. She had no idea whether that was true or not.

"Come on," he said. "The slug in the room is going to sleep another 37 minutes. I've got breakfast going and then we can walk this monster. Or he can walk us."

He handed her a pair of sweatpants that were big but not overly large.

Clemenza had no leash and went where he wanted. But never wandered far. If something intrigued him he rushed back and got them.

Clemenza took off after another dog and while he romped they walked wordlessly. Marian broke the silence.

"I assume you have a speech."

"Pardon?"

"A speech. I believe you brought me here to deliver a message. Is this where you tell me if I tell anybody anything about your operation you will kill me and my family?"

Marian had no idea why she said that. It wasn't the first time she had made the joke but there are some audiences you don't show your A-material to. Now all she could do is hold her ground.

But he laughed and continued to walk. He picked up a stick and drew patterns as they trudged along. When she thought this exercise was going to be a silent one he did speak.

"I've never tried online dating."

"No?"

"Too afraid."

She looked at him and got a look of mirth on her face.

He smiled back and said, "What, cut me do I not bleed? You might be surprised what a sensitive guy I can be."

"I would be surprised."

"I cry at the opening of an envelope."

"So I've stereotyped you. I feel like the worst person in the world."

"Like people thinking you're not as smart as you are."

She looked surprised but recovered by saying, "And how do you know I'm smart? Maybe you've just exercised some reverse stereotyping."

"No I haven't."

"Pretty sure of yourself."

"I don't know you. I know the guy sleeping. If you weren't whip-smart, a date with him would last 10 minutes. Long enough for a brush-off.

"So, he's dating me for my brains?"

Frankie laughed. "He's intrigued by your 'brings them to their knees beauty' but he stays for the conversation and challenge."

"Was that the message you were supposed to deliver?"

Most would have missed the anger on his face but gauging people was how she paid the bills. Inadvertently, she pushed a button.

The annoyance he next showed wasn't well hidden, nor did he want it to be. She reminded herself to tread softly and felt sympathy for anyone tripping this guy's wire.

"I'm probably not as smart as you are," he said. "I probably don't know a lot about the human anatomy. But even I know when you screw somebody you don't automatically download all their information. We can't pretend in one night you know more about the guy than somebody who has known him since second grade. Or you can shut the fuck up and let me say what I have to say."

Stunned and speechless that she had turned a harmless walk into the Maginot Line, she knew she had to fix it.

"We got off on the wrong foot, which is my fault," she said. "Please accept my apology."

He whistled and Clemenza came running. The three of them walked for a bit, and it was his turn to apologize.

"I don't know what comes over me," he said. "You'd think I'm a jealous lover. Maybe I am. Maybe I see you as a threat. I got my panties in a knot when I thought you were dismissing my friend. The only thing I can assure you is, Hersh will deliver his own messages. Not even a handsome hunk like me would dare think we could be his surrogates. A lack of communication will never be a problem."

When they got back Hersh was up and Marian was still dizzy. Having no one to talk this over with made it worse. She didn't have close friends and telling a colleague she was verbally slapped by the best friend of the suspect she had just slept with would have her packing up her boxes.

This was not Butch Cassidy giving the school teacher Etta a bike ride before returning her to the Sundance Kid.

This was going to be a long game but without knowing how she was already a touchdown behind.

CHAPTER 31

After their fourth date, Hersh asked Marian if she was interested in meeting the children.

She was taken aback by the offer.

"Don't they get nervous with strangers?"

"They do and it is one of the reasons why I like to bring in other people. They think the whole world is made up of monsters and they need to know it isn't true.

"How would you introduce me?"

"Well, we could go with 'friend.' "

"I'd love that," she said.

"Tuesday?"

"It is a date," she said with more happiness than she had expected.

On Tuesday, she pondered about what to wear before realizing how ridiculous she was. She had to settle her nerves before driving across town.

"Susan, this is my friend Marian," Hersh said as he introduced a 7-year-old.

"How do you do, Susan?" Marian said.

The little girl looked into her face and said, "You have pretty hair."

"Thank you," said Marian.

"Can I comb it?"

"Susan is our stylist here," Hersh said. "She'll give you any kind of hair style you want."

"Why don't I leave it up to Susan, then." said Marian. "What would you suggest?"

The little girl squinted her eyes at Marian and smiled. "A miracle worker." She then broke into giggles.

Hersh picked her up and threw her over his shoulder and said, "I forgot she's also the class clown."

He sat the little girl down and she walked over to the corner of the room and picked up a brush. She walked back to them and signaled for Marian to sit down.

"Really, I think I can do something with this," she said as she grabbed the hair. "But you have to stop putting chemicals on it."

Marian started to say something and then slumped in the chair.

"Yes ma'am," she said.

"But you are a pretty redhead. I can see why Hersh lusts after you."

"I also forgot to mention she's 7 going on 35. We let her watch too many noir movies."

Susan rolled her eyes at him and began brushing out Marian's hair. She stopped every few minutes to admire her work.

She finished by twisting and braiding a rat-tail for Marian. She picked up a mirror and showed off her work.

Marian smiled and said, "What do I owe you for this?"

Susan laughed but then looked at Hersh, who just shook his head. "What would you do with money?" he asked.

"I've got my eye on a sports car."

"Well, you've got nine more years to save up and by then there will be flying cars."

"No there won't."

"How do you know?"

"I asked Frankie the last time you told me that."

"Frankie knows more than me about cars?"

"Frankie knows more than you about everything. He knows more about everything than anybody."

"Even Roza?"

Susan furrowed her brow, then smiled at him.

"Well, Roza knows more if you count the stuff about women," she said. "But she doesn't know anything about motorcycles."

"What about Clemenza?"

Another furrowed brow.

"He knows dog stuff."

"So, I'm the dumbest person here."

"I guess so. But don't feel too bad. We still love you."

She jumped off her chair, waved at Marian and ran into the other room, where children were playing with Clemenza. Hersh also suspected she'd find Frankie there too.

"She has a crush on my partner."

"He's a charmer, all right."

"Yeah, I heard about the conversation."

"I don't think he likes me."

"If Frankie didn't like you, he has other ways than the unkind word.

"So, Frankie is the muscle of the organization?"

He looked over his teacup and answered with no hesitation.

"Frankie is the threat of muscle. It usually doesn't have to go past that."

"And the kids aren't afraid by that?"

"Kids know he's home base and safe anywhere near his orbit. A guy like Frankie who would take a bullet for them is cause for worship."

"You look at some of them and you can't even tell why they are here," she said. "If I had met Susan at one of my friend's homes I would have thought she was another precocious 7-year old."

"In many ways, she is one of the lucky ones," he said. "The damage to her was so early in life I'm not sure she totally understands why she is here. But sometimes these things stay tamped down and then suddenly these kids melt from the memories. Even if they can't put their finger on the exact incident."

"How do you prevent it?"

"We don't. Or can't. So, we pile on positive memories. Hopefully, by the time the bad stuff tries to come back up, the good stuff smothers it and makes it livable."

Marian tried to reconcile reports of this guy being an unrepentant murderer with the man sipping his tea.

"Still, it must be hard doing this day-to-day."

"If we didn't have outlets it would kill us."

"What kind of outlets."

"Roza goes to the race track and baseball games. Frankie rides his motorcycle, reads books, and attends martial arts classes. I dabble in the martial arts myself and some weekends I play the piano in a bar."

She looked up. "That last thing is a joke, right?"

"Nope. People put bread in my jar and say 'man, what are you doing here?' "

It was scary how much she didn't know. She covered her consternation by waving her arm across the room to include everything in it.

"How do you afford all of this? This is the most complete playhouse I've ever seen and the grounds it sits on is golden real estate."

"Well, we get donations of course," he said. "We all contribute. Roza is a generous benefactor."

She nodded but knew the cost of running this place went past donations and made a mental note.

She couldn't believe the rumor of a drug lord being ripped off for $7 million in cash. Urban legend had him backing up a truck and leaving with four loads of vacuum-sealed packs of money.

Asking around had gotten her odd looks. So, it was difficult to believe the guy in front of her had the stones to pull that off.

Spending any of that cash would have sent up a red flag and no one wants to sleep with one eye open for the drug cartel.

She chuckled to think she could believe this guy could murder people but would draw the line at drug dealing.

"Something funny?" he asked.

"Just me torturing my mind."

"Been there."

"Tell me about Susan."

"Well, there really isn't much more than Susan herself hasn't told you or shown you. We believe she's too young to really test but we suspect she's a genius. Sort of our *Good Will Hunting*.

"What kind of family life does she have?"

He looked down and when he looked up he was pained.

"She lives in a group home. A really great couple runs the home and they couldn't be more supportive but they have three kids of their own and five others they look after for us."

"What happened to her parents?"

"Her mother was lost to the streets. I see her sometimes but she has no interest in being a mom. I respect that. She doesn't try to reclaim

Susan and then abandon her for drugs or the next guy. She quit the parent game. I think her husband beat it out of her but maybe was never cut out for it in the first place."

"Did her father also disappear?"

"If only," he said. "He is what we're hoping she never remembers."

"What happens if she runs into him somewhere?"

He stared up at the ceiling and simply said, "She won't."

She blinked before saying, "Anything is possible."

"It is," he agreed. "But Susan is not worried about meeting her father."

"She isn't?"

"No."

"How come?"

"I told her it wouldn't happen."

"She believed you?"

He looked sheepish. "She did."

"Don't you worry you could be wrong?"

When he simply said "no," she was chilled.

CHAPTER 32

When Marian put a tail on Hersh she didn't expect he would expose nefarious activities.

But no harm, no foul. He would never know he was being watched by the best in the business. If he smoked them out the case was in deep trouble.

He led an almost boring life out of his clinic. He went to the track often to meet with his grandmother, whom Marian thought was rather sweet. She was a little taken aback when it was reported how much money they bet but gambling wasn't something they were investigating.

As he said, both Frankie and Hersh dabbled in the martial arts and she was not surprised both were quite adept. She mused as to why Frankie would need to become any more adept at taking care of himself but she admired the diligence.

When Hersh talked of Frankie being a reader she had let that pass, but now she knew what he meant. The big man looked almost comical reading the tomes he did, especially when he put on the tortoiseshell glasses that dominated his face.

There wasn't any genre he didn't read. He seemed to favor history but he was just as likely to be reading Candace Bushnell, Leo Tolstoy, John Irving, Stuart Woods, Hilary Mantel, Maeve Binchey, Reed Farrel Coleman, Robert Caro, Stephen King, David Halberstam, or Thomas Pynchon.

Hersh favored fiction. Both scribbled in their books and passed things onto each other. Sometimes they sat on a park bench and told jokes. The transcript showed some of the jokes to be really bad but they giggled for hours.

They were a magnet for children.

In minutes, they'd be surrounded by a passel of kids and quickly organize a game that got all involved.

If things broke down, they piled on Frankie. Hersh tried some magic tricks but Frankie would shout out the trick. Hersh would pretend he didn't know what was happening and the kids would roar with laughter when the trick didn't work.

There were gaps in the surveillance when the two went on a run.

A sting on Hersh was suggested but they'd get one chance and couldn't fail because they got too anxious.

He was too savvy for them to just put a case in front of him and think he would immediately go to the mattresses.

Christ, she had only been with him a brief time and she was already thinking in movie terms. When you are undercover there is a danger point when you become more the person you are disguised as than your own self.

She thought of how he made her laugh and how he challenged her. She also thought how kind he was and was uncomfortable remembering the sex and how much she thought of it.

She was supposed to turn him, not vice-versa.

CHAPTER 33

Meeting at Starbucks, Roza and Hersh sat at a back table sipping tea.

Then Roza said, "I'm trusting your love life won't interfere with anything you need to do."

He looked over the brim of his cup and shrugged.

"Women weaken legs, Rock."

"So you've told me, Mickey."

They went back to drinking. Hersh turned to the arts section of the paper and Roza perused *The Racing Form.* They met like this for years to iron out problems and point out potential flaws in future plans.

Now they thought so much alike that meeting was just habit. Neither would ever suggest stopping because of how much joy they got and for the goal of having a joke the other never heard.

"A man buys a parrot and teaches him to daven," says Hersh. "Every morning they say the prayers and he even makes a small tallith for the parrot. When the High Holidays roll around he takes the bird to Rosh Hashanah services. The rabbi and the congregation argue the shul is no place for a parrot. When the man tells them the bird can daven they don't believe him, and soon all kinds of bets are made. So the man tells the bird to start the prayers. He gets nothing. He starts the prayers and urges the parrot to join him. Nothing. He yells at the bird in English, Hebrew, and Yiddish. Still nothing. The man leaves in shame and owing thousands of dollars in bets. On the way home the bird begins the prayers. The man screams at the bird, 'Now you start. You made me look like an idiot back there and now I'm going to be paying off markers for years.' The parrot looks at his owner and says, 'Hey, schmuck, think of the odds we're going to get on Yom Kippur.' "

He looks at his grandmother, who allows one side of her mouth to curl. Then she sipped her tea and looked back down at the past performances in the *Form*.

"I think we're going to hit it big today. I've got a Pick 3 that looks promising. You in?"

He slid a pack of money her way.

She didn't count it. She already knew it was $1,000. She swept the money into her purse and enjoyed the moment of the two of them sitting.

"We need to talk about anything else?" she asked.

"Well, you've already put your nose into my dating life," he answered.

She smirked. "Four dates and a sleepover is not a dating life," she responded.

"My God, are you tailing me?" he asked. Then said, "Please tell me Frankie isn't on your payroll now?"

"Frankie would die for you and there isn't anyone who could get him to give up anything on you. Please don't forget that. If there is anything in your life that is unbreakable it is the man's loyalty."

"Betty?"

"Maybe. But if it was you can't blame her. She is a worrier and I'm the person she can talk to."

"Because you are so warm and cuddly?"

"I have my soft side."

"Maybe I'll see it one day."

"Back to the original question. Anything we need to discuss?"

Hersh looked out the window at the black Ford Taurus without really registering it. He saw a few people walk in the PNC Bank but didn't really see them and the folks outside at the tables finishing their coffee were not of interest to him. He did have a question of his grandmother but it touched on her past and she was sometimes reticent about sharing.

"Actually, there is one thing," he said. "When you were young were you ever part of The Nakam?"

Roza raised her eyebrows and simply said, "Book Four?"

He nodded in affirmation.

After a tout from Frankie he had started Philip Kerr's Bernie Gunther novels about the detective in Nazi Germany. Book Four, *The One from the Other*, talked about Jews banding together after World War II to form The Nakam, which was dedicated to killing as many ex-Nazis as they could. The organization took responsibility for thousands of deaths and boasted about their efficiency and their brutality.

"I was too young. And I was a girl. I didn't really like those guys," she said. "They were random and they were vicious. I was all for erasing the Germans but I like a little more order. Otherwise we're just a different version of them. Besides, I'm a loner."

Hersh nodded his head and smiled. "You are more of the 'sun at your back, riding into town and cleaning up Dodge' type of gal."

"Exactly," she said.

"There had to be some kind of reckoning," he continued.

"I wanted the bastards to know who evened up the score. Despite what happened the other day, I wanted them to explain to me how it could all happen. The Nakam didn't give anyone a chance. You didn't get much of a chance with me but you got to say your piece."

"Anyone ever able to walk out?"

"There was one. She was a guard at the women's prison. When I confronted her she didn't make excuses. She said the Nazis explained she worked or her family would disappear. She didn't use it as an excuse and she knew somebody would exact payment one day. She never asked to spare her life. I liked her and so I let her walk."

"Ballsy move."

"About a year after, I get a package in the mail. No name or return address. It was postmarked Phoenix but it looked like it had traveled the world. When I opened it, there was a bundle of papers detailing the actions of seven men. All had performed cruel and unusual acts."

"Were they legit?"

"They were spot-on. I did the follow-ups but it was a waste of time. I don't know how she got such detailed information and briefly worried about her knowing how to find me. Then I realized she was sending me a thank-you note and I never lost a moment of sleep."

"Did you meet again?"

"Yes and no. I tracked her down to a town in Australia. She was leading a pedestrian life as a cleaning woman in a small hotel. She was married with two children. Her husband was an accountant. She seemed happy."

"Did you talk to her?"

"I did not. But I went to her home when the kids were in school and she and her husband were at work. They had a mailbox and I slipped an envelope with her name into the slot."

"Money?"

"Twenty-two thousand," she answered. "In dominations from three separate countries. I wanted to give them a boost but I knew she would be offended if it were too garish. Later I came back and watched through binoculars as she found the envelope."

"What did she do?"

"She opened it. Looked at the money and smiled. Then I saw her cry a little bit. Before she turned to go into the house she gave me a little wave. I don't know if she truly knew I was there or was just making the gesture. About a year later, I sent another $10,000. I included a note: 'Our debts are paid.'"

Hersh made a toasting gesture with his cup. He figured the story was true but he wasn't betting the farm. It was a little sappy for her but then again, who knows, maybe she did have a soft side.

You couldn't tell by looking at her. He never saw total joy and he felt sorry for a woman who lived on her own terms since boarding a train heading for hell.

Somehow, she seemed to read his mind and put her hand over his. He again noticed the slight shake and so he put his free hand on top. Then he grabbed her elbow and led her to her car. He kissed her cheek and handed her the *Form.* As he closed her car door he wished her luck.

He would have a few words with Betty, but really he was thrilled she had spoken to Roza. The amount Betty had progressed made him want to weep for joy. If you were going to unburden yourself no one was safer or wiser than his grandmother. But Betty couldn't make a habit of talking about him.

"Don't ever take sides against the family," he said out loud and then started to laugh.

CHAPTER 34

Not all of Hersh's children made it out.

Sitting in the church pew he looked at the sparse crowd who came to say goodbye to a 9-year-old who got not a single break.

Bobby Jackson was a sweet kid and the streets didn't take the sweetness out of him.

An artsy kid who loved to draw, he was brought to Hersh by Bobby's grandmother, who didn't want him to be eaten alive.

They kept each other alive. She was hanging on for him and when she almost died last year it was hard for him to keep up. He came to the clinic needing a meal or medical attention.

He took two buses to get to the clinic and refused Frankie's offer of a lift. However, he loved riding on Frankie's motorcycle home.

When Bobby didn't show Friday, Hersh got worried. Bobby was automatic on Pizza and Movie Day.

Bobby's death didn't surprise him. This was about a gang initiation and the young man who shot Bobby at the bus stop was starting down a road that wasn't going to get better.

Hersh began to weep and bowed his head. He felt a hand on his shoulder. Expecting Frankie or Betty he was surprised to see Marian.

She didn't say a word but threw her arms around him. When the short service ended, they walked to the parking lot.

A young man approached Hersh on his bicycle. He wore a shirt collar 1½ sizes too big along with a tie, canvas pants, and tennis shoes.

"Are you Mr. Hersh?" the youngster asked.

"I am."

"I'm Bobby's brother Peter."

The boy couldn't be more than 13 or 14 but had the face of someone who had seen too much. There was a scar above his right eyebrow and the way he held himself told Hersh his arm or wrist had recently been broken.

"I'm sorry for your loss, Peter."

"Bobby was a good younger brother, mister," Peter said. "He always listened to me and he always got on that bus. Do you think I got him killed?"

Hersh had never seen such pain but not wanting to shine him on said, "Why do you think that?"

"Because he wanted to stay with me and I told him to go to the bus. It was Friday and he never missed a Friday."

They both smiled.

"Bad things happen even when we have the best intentions," said Hersh. "He knew you were looking out for him. You putting him at the bus stop every day probably extended his life. You can't carry the weight for the evils other people do."

"I guess not," said Peter.

Hersh was horrified that Peter probably knew who pulled the trigger and might try to even the score. He couldn't save Bobby. But he could reach out to his brother.

"Peter," said Hersh. "I know you ride with your own crew here. I know the neighborhood is your home turf but do you think you could come visit me?"

Peter looked down at his handlebars and shook his head. "I don't want to take the bus just now."

Hersh put his hand on Peter's shoulders and turned him 180 degrees.

"Do you see the man sitting on the motorcycle?"

Peter's eyes widened at the biggest and baddest man he had ever seen. He shook his head yes.

"That is Bobby's friend Frankie. He would be happy to pick you up and bring you to the clinic."

"On his bike?"

"On his bike," Hersh concurred.

"That would be super cool."

"Super cool indeed."

Peter again dropped his head.

"You know, mister, I was the older brother but it seems Bobby is taking care of me."

"He was taking care of both of us," said Hersh.

The boy was confused but nodded. Hersh reached into his pocket and brought out a $5 bill.

"Bobby would love for you to have lunch on him. And it would do me good to see someone enjoy Pizza Day."

Peter smiled and rode away but not before looking to Frankie again. He waved at the big man, who saluted as he sailed past.

Marian looked over Hersh's shoulder and saw the black Taurus. Uncomfortable her bosses decided to intrude on a moment of grief she also knew it was part of the job.

You prepared for it all and if it meant being a little less human, then that was a requirement.

Yet part of her loathed it all. Watching Hersh cry while saying goodbye to a child he failed to save was an eye-opener. You couldn't be next to a man like that and not think it was wrong to label him the bad guy.

She looped her arm through his and escorted him to his car. She kissed his cheek and said she would see him later.

CHAPTER 35

On Monday, Frankie picked up Peter and the boy looked like it was Christmas morning.

"What are you doing?" Frankie said to the young man.

"Aren't you going to give me a ride?"

"Wait, I'm supposed to ride you? I thought you would drive and I would rest in back."

That made the boy laugh and Frankie felt he had done his deed for the day.

"You do have a motorcycle license, don't you?"

"I just got a new bicycle," said Peter.

"My mistake," said Frankie. "I thought we would head to the playground and then to the office."

Frankie wanted as many kids as possible to see him with Peter. He wanted to make a statement to the neighborhood.

Peter was afraid of Clemenza but the two came to an understanding. Peter needed no such understanding with Betty. Frankie could tell a young man in love.

Betty recognized a fellow traveler and knew better than to make fun of the crush when the two took Clemenza for his walk.

"Did you and Betty have words?" Frankie asked Hersh.

"Yeah, she told me 'kiss my ass' when I admonished her about talking out of school."

"So, she understood?"

"Perfectly."

"She's a good one."

"That she is. Did you see how she swooped in on Peter and made him feel at home almost before he walked in the door?"

"What do you think they are talking about?" Frankie asked.

"Whatever it is we could never understand," said Hersh. "They are speaking from an experience we can only guess at. How did the ride go?"

"Excellent," said Frankie. "He loved the bike, of course. But I think he also appreciated the short tour of the neighborhood. He won't show it but he's scared. He's got a tough home life and now he's got no brother."

"He does have us," said Hersh.

"God help him," said Frankie.

CHAPTER 36

After lunch, they found Mary and Kathy Doss in the office. Hersh didn't see any bruises. But he had told the mother if she feared anything from Eddie to not hesitate.

They were now under his umbrella and he hoped to keep them safe for as long as possible.

"I didn't know where else to go," said Mary. "But I found your card and so here I am."

"So, tell me how we can help."

The woman looked at her daughter. He understood and gave a low whistle. He tapped his knuckles on the desk and looked at the girl.

"Kathy," he said, "could you do me a favor? I have a friend who needs looking after. Could you do that for me?"

"Where is he?" asked the little girl.

"Well, if I know Clemenza he is just on the other side of the door. He has been waiting for you."

The little girl looked at her mother, who nodded. When she opened the door, she squealed with delight.

Clemenza looked at Hersh, who signaled for him to take the little girl into the playroom.

"All the other kids are out on the playground now so she'll have Clemenza to herself."

"She's always wanted a dog but her dad told her she was not responsible enough," said Mary.

"She can play with Clemenza whenever she wants. But what brings you in?"

"Eddie is working himself up into something bad. He's coming home from work sullen and he's drinking more. He's drinking before he comes home and after he comes home. When he gets like this it is a matter of time."

"But he hasn't done anything yet?" asked Hersh.

The woman paused before shaking her head no.

"So, are you ready to leave?"

"I don't know if I want to take that step right now. I just wanted to have somewhere to send Kathy if it gets bad."

"What will happen until then?"

"I can take care of myself. When he rages, he calms down right after."

Hersh visited many women in the hospital who had that plan and attended the burial of one. But people don't change until ready. Planning for Kathy meant she had a foot out of the door herself.

"Okay," said Hersh. "I'm not totally pleased but I'll back your play. You need money?"

"No, I think we're okay there. If I end up leaving I may hit you up but if I took it now and Eddie found it, I don't know what would happen."

Hersh agreed and spent 10 minutes talking precautions, including setting up a safety zone where she could make a 911 call.

Mary Doss looked about to cry and Hersh thought she would change her mind and leave today. But she kept it together and looked better walking out than walking in.

Hersh would remember Kathy looking back as her mom led her to the car. Mary Doss did not.

CHAPTER 37

If you read mysteries, the Kathy and Mary Doss incident is where you wonder how the hero (my words not yours) could be so stupid.

How could an experienced professional have been led so far afield by a woman and her daughter? It should be documented Kathy was an innocent here. She was too young and damaged to know what was going on.

I don't blame Mary either. She couldn't trust Eddie and took the first lifeboat. I was the one she threw overboard but she needed to be saved.

I'm honest enough to say I was blindsided. It should never have happened and if she weren't dying, Roza would have made me pay for this. All that training and preparation shot to hell over a sad story.

When the feds get involved you can't be too hard on yourself.

Does that make me feel better?

No.

Does it give me a better chance to escape with my life?

Nope.

A true hero would say it was worth it just knowing Kathy was safe. But it would have been nice for her to be safe and me to be able to fight another day.

Hey, stop me if you heard this one. A guy gets into the ring and he looks over to see his opponent making the sign of the cross. The fighter says to his manager, "Will it help?" And the manager answers, "Only if he can fight."

Not really funny but illustrative. I want to call on God to help me out of this but I figured it would only help if I can indeed fight.

Right now, that is negative, good buddy.

I'm sure if I thought about it, I'd get pissed that it was you guys who put me here who are seeing this. This really should be a cautionary tale for a lot of people but I know this confession is going to get boxed up somewhere in a government warehouse.

You'll brag about catching a serial killer but be careful how you tell the story. If you reveal too much people might distrust you and see me as the good.

I'm sure you guys are too much of pros to let me win but I throw out the possibility.

In my version, I'm an underground hero, as people turn my tale into legend in bars and coffeehouses and places you don't talk about. At parties, you'll admire the blanket of freedom I allowed you to sleep under.

You are damn right I'm ordering a code red.

When I start seeing the great Aaron Sorkin you know I'm oxygen-deprived. This should be the moment I begin to conserve energy but getting this off my chest is currently driving me.

Everyone thinks this will never happen to them because they are too smart to make an error this big.

We watch the same movies and yell that people can't be this stupid.

Use me as proof, it can happen. I do want to tip my hat to the other team. As they say, they also got shoes and shorts and were allowed to score the ball. They flouted a few rules. But look who is talking. If you ain't cheatin' you ain't competin,' I guess.

I'm sorry that I'll never again be in a room with the world's bravest children. Of course, I'll miss the dog.

Dogs want to help you out of your worst days. Their tail is always wagging and they wait at the door at the end of the day.

Roza used to say no man ever committed suicide with a good 2-year-old in the barn. I say no man who owned a dog thought about leaving him by doing something stupid.

If you think Clemenza is in peril, forget it. I guaranteed his safety and I meant it. He'll live a life of luxury with plenty of steak on the menu. He won't be paying for my sins.

Now I'm going to relax and try to think healing thoughts. Mind and body. Mind and body. Mind and body.

CHAPTER 38

Riding on a motorcycle raised Peter's street cred but Frankie wasn't so naïve to think Peter wouldn't get challenged or bullied.

Somebody always needed to prove something. But those who looked at Frankie figured there were easier ways to make their bones.

So, that was why on the return trip on the first day, Frankie escorted Peter inside his home. He figured to announce his presence with authority.

When he stepped inside, the mixture of alcohol and cooked food and the smallness of the domicile told him bad things were portending.

But for now, he just wanted to leave his calling card. He just wanted to say, "Hey, I'm here and I'm looking after this guy. You may get him but then you get to deal with me."

The first person he saw was an older woman who needed surgery on her arthritic hips.

There was a kindness and Frankie guessed this was who bought the bicycle for Peter. She didn't react to Frankie's size and that took some doing.

"I'm Maise Williams, Peter's grandmother," she said.

Frankie returned the hand gesture and said, "Frankie. I'm Peter's teacher at the clinic."

"That your bike out there?"

"Yes ma'am."

"Best man I ever knew rode a Harley."

"Harleys are nice," he said.

"You the one who was looking after Bobby?"

Frankie lowered his head and nodded.

"Don't you hang your head, young man," she said. "You gave him more of a life than he ever expected. He thought you were a superhero.

"He was in the wrong place at the wrong time. This is always the wrong place. I know what you all tried to do and I'm obliged to you. The good Lord sent you our way. He needed Bobby for some reason but he told me Peter is going to make it."

He was amazed at the faith people possessed.

"He's a good young man," Frankie said of Peter. "He's already helping us out with the younger kids. He says he wants to be a doctor."

"He's smart as a whip," said his grandmother. "And he minds me. He thinks he has the burden to live his life and Bobby's but I tell him God doesn't want that."

Peter came back in with an ice bag and led his grandmother to the couch.

"The Lord never gives me too much," she said to her grandson when he asked how she was doing. "Although some days I question that. But he also gives me you and I know that I'm going to get through it all."

Peter held his grandmother's hand and Frankie thought of Roza feeding him and making him come back day after day. He silently said thanks these two were together.

"I'm so glad to have met you, young man," she said. "But I need you to leave now. If Peter's uncle comes through that door there is going to be trouble. Nobody is going to start something with you. But Peter will pay. But don't you be a stranger. Please come back during the day or on the weekends. We have things to talk about."

Frankie started to turn to leave but said, "First thing we will talk about, Ms. Williams, is music."

He gestured over to where there was a turntable and albums in a neat vertical row. "Anybody who listens to that much Coltrane has an interesting story to tell."

She roared with laughter and then got up and hugged him.

"Yes sir, the Lord does work in mysterious ways. We'll talk Coltrane and a whole lot more."

Frankie started up his bike. He waved without looking back and left the neighborhood. He wanted to stop when he saw some of the street bystanders staring but he had made enough of a point already.

CHAPTER 39

When the stakeout guys told her about Mary and Kathy, Marian had the idea of approaching them. She knew there was a risk Mary would be too afraid to do anything.

A small risk, in Marian's mind.

It was a matter of time until her husband blew a fuse. There are wives who won't get out of their own way but make sure their children are never in the line of fire.

Of course, she may have seen Hersh as her way out. Posing as a policeman had been a ballsy move.

It was ironic his altruistic nature would doom him and not the murderous acts he committed.

Hersh would offer protection and money but the government could offer her re-location plus money. Mary would see how much better their offer was than his.

It didn't really take much arm-twisting. Mary's lack of faith in all men certainly greased the wheels and getting her to approach Hersh with the deal he offered was a bit easier than Marian figured.

When Hersh talked to her about Mary, Marian was slightly uncomfortable but reminded herself this was the job. When you cash the paycheck, you take everything that goes with that.

With each passing day Marian had more concerns but never considered pulling the pin. Doubt was a killer and she was in this to her eyeballs.

When she met up with Hersh again she wasn't thinking about Mary. She needed Hersh to continue to believe in this relationship. If she lost that she could lose him and that was not an option.

She was taken aback, though, when he brought up the subject and couldn't escape the feeling he read her mind.

"I had a young woman and her daughter come to the clinic today," said Hersh.

"Don't you get that every day?"

"This was a woman I reached out to and didn't think I'd hear from. It is an abusive home and I'm trying to separate them from the abuse."

"Both?" asked Marian. "I thought you only dealt with children."

He smiled and looked around the restaurant. He took a sip of his tea. "Yeah, I'm branching out here."

"How did the woman know you'd be the one to help?"

"She got a referral."

Marian nodded, recognizing the lie.

She knew how Mary and Kathy came to his office because she was proactive in making it happen. She wondered what would have happened if they hadn't come in. Would Eddie Doss be on a slab in a morgue?

She wanted to laugh at the absurdity of being more concerned with a man who created violence in his own home than the man trying to stave off that violence. The better man was the one she was going to bring down.

However, that wasn't true. Certainly, Eddie Doss was a bad human being. But Hersh shouldn't get a pass. You don't make life and death decisions on your own. Even if the system had flaws.

The human degradation he dealt with might be an explanation but it couldn't be an excuse. Marian had worked with too many social workers and family members to give him a pass.

Perhaps they would sit down one day and discuss what pushed him over the edge.

She was kidding herself. When this ended, they would never talk again. He might laugh if she told him, "It's just business, not personal, Sonny," but he wouldn't talk to her. She looked to see him waving a hand in her face.

"Ground Control to Major Tom, take your protein pills and put your helmet on."

She looked embarrassed. "Did I space out there?"

"I thought we lost you."

"Sorry. I was thinking about work," she said in a rare honest moment.

Hersh nodded but he wasn't stupid. He knew Marian was not exactly as presented.

At some point he would have to probe but he knew it was going to be delicate. He didn't want to ruin this relationship because he mistrusted everyone.

Roza and Frankie thought he stopped dating because he had no interest but it was because he had no trust. He had finally met someone he wanted to trust.

He was thinking maybe when he got Mary and Kathy situated he would ask Marian to go away with him. Perhaps a beach or a long train trip would be the answer.

CHAPTER 40

On Tuesdays, the major tracks were dark so Roza had lunch with Betty.

She told the young girl to pack a picnic and she would choose the place.

Betty was surprised when Roza drove into an apartment complex. Neither spoke as they rode the elevator to the 15th floor and entered an empty apartment.

There was the smell of fresh paint and redone hardwood floors. The women stared out a nice view of the city.

"Who owns this place?" Betty asked.

"Me," said Roza. "I own property outside of town but wanted something close by if I decided to live my final years in the city."

"The view is magnificent."

"It is a great location, isn't it?" asked Roza. "Close to mass transportation, easy to get to by car, and the neighborhood has restaurants, shops, and every service a person could want."

Betty marveled at the loft and was surprised to see the room had a computer.

"You moving in?" she asked.

Roza smiled. "Do I look like a person who could climb into that loft? There was a time, though."

"You renting it out?"

"No."

"Whose computer is that?"

"Yours."

Betty looked where her bag sat. She knew inside was her laptop.

Roza laughed. "Not that computer, honey. The one you can use here."

"When would I be here?" she asked.

"Once you and I furnish this place I'm hoping every day."

"What?"

Roza handed Betty a sandwich.

"Betty, I know you hang around the office because you never want to go home. Now you don't have to. You're back to school in the fall and you'll need a place to study and to be a young woman without interference from an old lady and her two gentleman callers."

"But I can't live here."

Roza looked at her quizzically. "*Por que*?

"I just can't live here."

Roza didn't argue.

"A man is caught in a flood and he's trapped in the water. A guy comes by in a canoe and offers the man a place. The man says, 'No thanks, God will provide for me.' About 10 minutes later another guy comes by in a raft and holds his hand out to the man. Again, the man says, 'God will provide.' Five minutes later a cabin cruiser glides into the water and makes the man an offer. Again, he says, 'God will save me.' The cruiser leaves and the man drowns. He goes to heaven and he meets God and he's irate. He tells God what a good person he was and how much faith he had. 'How could you let me drown?' he rails at God. When he calms down God looks at him and says, 'Idiot, I sent you three boats.' "

Roza looks at Betty and says, "Idiot, take the boat."

Betty begins to walk around the apartment. When she comes back she looks at her benefactor and says, "We're going to need a bigger boat."

The two women don't speak through lunch but hold hands and stare out at the city.

"I'm going to have to keep this address secret from my family," Betty says.

"Won't be a problem. The apartment is in my name," answers Roza."

"This is overwhelming."

"Betty," says Roza, "you deserve only good things but I always have a second motive. It does my heart good to see you distance yourself from harm but you may be the only one of us who gets out alive."

Betty's brow furrowed as she looked at the old woman.

"My time is short," said Roza. "A person knows when the party is over and I'm looking at saying goodbye. But that isn't what worries me."

Betty waited while Roza gathered herself.

"Some bad juju is going to happen to Hersh. I think it has to do with the woman Marian. I can't put my finger on it but the bottom is going to fall out. When that happens, Frankie is going to get on his bike and disappear. He'll need to be by himself for a long time. He might send for Clemenza but that also might fall to you."

Betty started to clean up the picnic while she let what Roza said sink in.

"There isn't anything you can do to make this not happen?"

"There isn't. Sometimes events unfold and you deal with the fallout."

"Does Hersh know you feel this way?"

"He wouldn't believe me if I laid it out for him," said Roza. "I don't have anything tangible to show him and Hersh likes tangible."

Roza reached to hug Betty.

"You need a landing if all this happens," said Roza. "You'll need the boat."

CHAPTER 41

Roza would have given odds she would never live in the past.

Of course, then the past was different.

Burt Lancaster in *Atlantic City* talking to Susan Sarandon. "You should have seen the Atlantic Ocean back then."

Then, her past was the camps. Now, she had grandchildren, incredible wealth, and unusual health. The nightmares didn't stop with the first gun but stopped the first time she used it.

The distant past was a horror show; her recent past, a greatest hits collection.

With a past came a revolving relationship with God she still wrestled with.

Always a believer, there were times she was so pissed at Him she could spit. God was a man because no woman would let children die like that.

It boggled the mind to see those continuing to pray while being beaten, starved, put behind walls, in cattle cars and showers, and then thrown into mass graves.

How stupid do you have to be not to know the Almighty had turned His back on you? The old saw, "He has a plan, we just don't know it" was crap.

Nothing says poor planning like six million dead. When you see smoke and people starving it screams out, "Get another plan."

When rescued she didn't thank God but thanked the soldiers who liberated the camp. You could argue that the soldiers were God sending a boat but He waited too damn long to get credit.

Before bed she didn't invoke His name but the memories of family and people who became family behind the wire.

In subsequent years, though, she turned a little. There were too many divine interventions and close calls to not realize she owed somebody.

God and Roza could be in the same room again. Watching her children and their children she had to give Him props.

They would never be square and Roza thought He was a bit of a show-off. The Red Sea thing was a bit much. Moses bringing the tablets down was a little arduous.

The story of Abraham and Isaac was so punitive to Roza she stopped going to High Holiday services. What deity allows a man to entertain thoughts of sacrificing his child?

The Holocaust was such a horror show, it would take her years to entertain the thought of a "good" God.

No question God proved he could kick her ass. Maybe it was a sign of aging or going soft that led her to give Him some due.

However, she never repented what many called a sin and she considered a gift. Never was there a regret over a pulled trigger.

They could talk on Judgment Day but there would be no take backs, even if an eternity of suffering were in the balance.

Troy Maxson said in August Wilson's *Fences*, "Death ain't nothing but a fastball on the outside corner."

Anger was no longer blue hot. What she had was reserved for the thought she'd get out untouched for her sins but her grandson would not.

The only thing keeping her from erasing Marian was a belief you needed to be 100 percent in this business.

You don't settle a score because you have a belief. Equally, she wasn't able to walk away.

If Roza were convinced her hunch was right she would come out of retirement.

CHAPTER 42

Marian and Hersh were walking hand-in-hand out of the movie theatre when approached by a man.

"You guys have the time?" he asked.

Marian said she didn't wear a watch when the man pulled a gun.

This was embarrassing for Marian, who had a team a block away.

They would blow their cover, so Marian signaled them not to get involved.

There are robberies over before anyone can get nervous. She could tell this was not one of them.

She didn't like the guy's eyes.

Hersh stared at the man and then the gun.

"I'll need your wallets," the thief said.

"I guess Al Capone was right. You do get more with a gun and a kind word than just a kind word."

The robber just stared at them and waved his pistol in answer.

"Got nothing in my wallet," said Hersh. "Money is in my pocket."

"Want your wallet anyway."

"Don't make me have to replace the credit cards and driver's license," pleaded Hersh. "Take the money in my pocket."

"I look like I give a damn about your personal problems?" said the man.

Hersh shrugged and reached into his back pocket.

Marian had no idea anyone could move so fast but Hersh had flicked out his arm and swatted the man upside the head. He then broke his kneecap.

While the man screamed in pain, Hersh started whaling on him. At first, Marian was amused at the turn of events but like Betty realized, an enraged Hersh was not something you wanted to see.

Shouting the man was powerless only got Hersh windmilling his punches. The man was unconscious and she didn't think that would stop him, but it did.

When he looked up he seemed unsure where he was and who she was. Looking like a child caught doing something wrong he sat down with head in hands.

When he heard sirens, he jumped up and his face changed.

There was no remorse or guilt but anger as someone whose night was interrupted and didn't care for it. When the first policeman began questioning, Hersh was unrepentant.

"I thought he was going to use the gun so I did what I thought was best,' said Hersh.

The policeman looked at Marian, who was torn on how she should play this. She could show her badge or play the defenseless date. She went with the latter.

While the cop wasn't convinced Hersh was a total victim, he let them go after getting an address.

"That was scary," said Marian.

"Very much so," said Hersh. "He could have killed us."

She shook her head. "Somebody could have gotten killed but it wasn't us."

Looking into her eyes he blinked first. "I'm guessing we need to talk about this."

"Tomorrow," she said. "Tonight, I just want you to take me home and stay with me. In the morning, we'll go through it."

He nodded.

"And Lucy," she said. "You got some 'splaining to do."

Hersh actually laughed as they walked to the car.

CHAPTER 43

Marian was surprised she could sleep but dropped off immediately.

Waking before him she made coffee for her and tea for him. It would be a long morning.

Fifty minutes later he appeared. You wouldn't know he stared down a possible killer eight hours before.

"I woke up and smelled the coffee," he said with a large grin. "See what I did there with the foreshadowing?"

"I saw," she said, equaling his smile. "Now sit down and talk about a few things."

He stared over his cup and raised his eyebrows to signal his readiness. Her prepared speeches seemed inadequate so she led with, "What happened out there?"

He actually chuckled, scaring her more than the altercation. Watching a file coming alive in living color was unnerving. Any doubts about him incapable of violence were shattered in the second he moved his hand.

"I'm sorry you had to be involved," he told her. "But I can't be sorry over a man who didn't get to commit a crime he had planned."

He laid his hand on hers and got a short squeeze.

"Marian, I deal with the victims of this crap every day. But I'm not a defenseless child."

She didn't want to interrupt so she nodded.

"It is funny, you know. I was a little guy in grade school and a candidate to be picked on. Then I met Frankie."

He stopped when he thought about that and chuckled to himself again.

"But my grandmother didn't want me to feel safe because of him. Frankie couldn't be expected to be my bodyguard. Who knows what happens to second-grade friendships."

She smiled because that friendship turned into a love affair. Reading her mind, he smiled also.

"Yeah, turned out Frankie was a stayer but my grandmother had deeper plans for him. As for me, I learned to wrestle and box and you know about the martial arts. I don't get into too many scraps. But I can't apologize for last night except to say I went three punches too far."

"Just three?" she asked.

"He was only in danger on the last three," said Hersh. "The other blows were dealt to deliver pain but the last three were punishment."

"You could have killed him," she said.

"Oh, no doubt," he answered. "But not with the punches I was throwing. I could have killed him with the first punch if that was the intent."

"What would have happened if you had?" she probed.

He smiled. "Then I would have been William Munny."

She looked confused and he said, "The movie *Unforgiven*. A young gunfighter kills his first man and doesn't know how to feel so he asks Clint Eastwood's character what he does now and Eastwood's William Munny says, "Now you live with it."

She cocked her head and looked at him.

"Pretty cold."

"Ice cold. But what else can you do?"

"Have you ever lived with it?"

"Now, as Sean Connery once said, that is a soup question."

"You know," said Marian, "all of life is not a movie."

"Of course it is," said Hersh. "It is available in Technicolor and wide-screen. All 3-D all the time."

"You didn't answer."

"Have I lived with death?"

"Not exactly the question."

"Well, the answer is yes. I have been responsible for the death of another human being."

Marian remained motionless. She had a confession. It was not recorded and probably would be retracted when the time came. But she heard him.

"I don't know how to process that," she said.

"Me neither."

"You think this is amusing, don't you?"

Hersh studied his fingernails and rubbed his thumb to his index finger.

"Amusing? Not really. But I do like to tease you."

"Tease me? Are you saying you haven't murdered anyone?"

"Murder is such an ugly word," he said and then flashed a smile.

"Hersh. This is a serious subject. I'm asking for a straight answer."

Hersh blew out his breath and gave a small cough.

"You may be looking for a lot of things; a straight answer is not one of them," he said.

"What does that mean?"

"You know the answer."

"Why would I know?"

"You don't put together a 112-page file on somebody and not come to some conclusions."

The temperature around her dropped 20 degrees and it was so quiet she heard her eyes blink. Whatever was going to happen depended on what she did next.

"I'm not following you," she weakly said.

"You're not selling this, Marian," he rejoined. "You are a better agent than this. I've read your file."

She tried to stall. "I told you I worked for the Bureau."

"You did but not that you were in violent crimes. You made yourself sound like a bureaucrat."

"How long have you known?"

"The moment you sat down in the restaurant."

"But how?"

"I'm not Sherlock Holmes," he said. "I'm not going to astound with my knowledge of all things."

She actually smiled. When she was a cadet she took a class on Sir Arthur Conan Doyle and had become quite a fan. Her favorite thing was his powers of deduction. Did he know that?

"Then how?" she asked again.

"I saw you in their offices."

Marian had not been an office worker in years and realized he was shining her on. But he surprised her with what he said next.

"Do you remember the Chuckie O'Brien case?"

She froze and had a bad feeling there had been a major screw-up and she was responsible.

"He was a young boy abused by several members of his family. He committed suicide as a teenager. We wanted to tie his family into the death but we could never make the case."

"Did you guys hire an expert?"

"My partner had a guy," she said and then trailed off as she looked at him. She knew she looked shocked but couldn't help it. A screw-up like this was monumental and almost laughable.

"You knew Charlie?"

"I did."

"You were his expert?"

"I was."

"But how would we have met?" she asked.

"I was sitting in Charlie's office when you delivered a document."

"You remembered me six years later?"

He raised his eyebrows and she couldn't help but laugh at the absurdity.

"When we met for a blind date, you knew me?"

"I recognized you."

"You couldn't of."

"You mean because you used to be a blond, 7 to 8 pounds heavier, and no longer wore the sky-blue nail polish?"

Her mouth hung open.

"You are Sherlock Holmes."

"Six years ago, you stopped conversation when you entered a room," he said. "That hasn't changed. But that was only part of it. You walk like an agent and when you sat down in the restaurant you made a move to avoid having your gun hit the table even though you weren't packing."

"Why didn't you say something?"

"It didn't seem relevant."

She thought and said, "You thought I was working you when we first met?"

"Were you?"

"I wasn't," she lied. "You can't think I was working you after the time we spent. Or do you think agents sleep with suspects on a regular basis?"

For the first time, she saw he was disappointed. He looked forward to a game of wits and she failed. She couldn't see the flaw in her lie.

"You think I faked what happened in bed?"

She enjoyed seeing him flush. Despite the high stakes, she couldn't help but like him for that.

"Please do not confuse me with your feminine wiles," he said.

"I was not working you," she answered and immediately regretted the lie.

He was supposed to be on the defensive.

"Do you want to retract anything?" he asked.

"I don't."

"That is a disappointment," he said.

Neither knew how to proceed. She didn't want to dig a deeper hole. He was deciding how far to go.

"Why don't you believe me when I say I didn't know you?"

"Well, there is the 112-page report."

"You were serious about that?" she asked, knowing there was no way he could have known about her research.

She knew she guessed right when he saw a small smile on her face. She breathed a bit.

"Okay, that was a joke," he said.

"So, you don't really believe you're an assignment then?"

"Oh, no, I'm sure I'm part of your case." he countered.

"What did I ever do to give you that impression?" she asked.

"You actually never did anything," he said.

Again, she smiled but not for long.

"It was the two guys in the black Taurus," he said, grabbing his keys and walking out.

CHAPTER 44

Marian sat for an hour after he left. She was too well trained to make a quick decision. Disaster had struck and she had no idea how to fix it.

Yet.

She was too good not to tunnel back. But she needed help.

Two hours later she finished explaining to her boss where they stood. He was grim but she felt a little lighter for sharing.

Given truth serum she'd admit how much she disliked this assignment. Stripped of all the crap of the job and forced to confront her feelings she would admit she liked the guy.

She was playing him but worried he was smarter than her.

"So, what is the alternate plan?" asked Robert Gregory.

"That is why I called you, my friend," she said.

She liked Gregory because he was not always a desk guy with one eye on the next promotion. Gregory had been shot at and shot at people. He lied and cheated to put bad people away.

He was an agent's agent and you couldn't say that about everyone in the new bureau. You couldn't say that about everyone on her team.

"How did he know about the Taurus?" asked Gregory. "Smithson and Jacoby are the best."

"He's good," she said. "Much better than our reports show. We fell down or he played us."

"I don't see how he could have played us," said Gregory. "How would he know we were interested in him?"

"I think I tripped something on that blind date," Marian said. "I can't figure out how. We set it up so well and modesty aside, when I walked in I don't think his first thought was, 'Here comes a woman who is setting me up.' "

Gregory laughed a true laugh and shook his head in agreement.

"I will admit you make a dog strain the leash."

She laughed back at him. "God, that is so insulting to women."

"Isn't it, though?" he said and laughed again.

"You know, Robert, there is only one solution. I have to take another shot at it."

Nodding his head in agreement he asked the $64,000 question. "But how?"

"First, an apology."

"Then?"

Marian smiled and for the second time watched a man blush.

CHAPTER 45

Hersh was at the dentist giving Frankie and Betty time to talk. He told them everything. Betty was surprised. Frankie was not.

"I knew there was something off about her," he said.

"I'm guessing Hersh thought the same," she said.

"My boy is good."

"Why didn't he tell us?" Betty asked.

"Well, darling, I'll tell you why. It might not have made a difference to him."

"How so?"

"Well, you're a woman so you might not understand how dumb man can be around beauty."

Betty processed the statement.

"You guys are stupider than a box of rocks sometimes."

"Giving you the 411 in my opinion."

"No, I can see it. Even I thought she was drop-dead beautiful."

"Sex on a stick beautiful," he agreed.

"How far would he have allowed it to be taken if that robber hadn't forced the issue the other night?" Betty asked.

Frankie drummed his fingers on the table before answering.

"I wanted to pound the shit out of Hersh when we were second graders because even then he was smarter than everyone," Frankie began. "He was two steps ahead of us. I wanted to be like that."

"But you are like that."

"I didn't know it until I met him and spent time with Roza," explained Frankie. "But he knew it."

"Maybe he was looking for a friend," said Betty.

"He wasn't looking, I was," said Frankie. "He knew and put himself in harm's way for me. I could have beaten him up and not thought about him again." Frankie paused before going on.

"Roza changed my life," he continued. "She was the first person I couldn't fool and even as a 7-year-old I knew there was a violence in her I would never rival. I wasn't scared of anything and I was frightened of her. Later I would be afraid of disappointing her but right off I was wary of crossing her."

Betty certainly met a different Roza but had seen a small part of the woman. Her antennae for these things said Frankie was surely correct.

"Roza is so huge in my life," Frankie began again. "But she was an adult and there was only so much she could understand. Hersh was the brave one. He was a second grader putting himself out there for a kid everyone gave up on. Can you imagine being seven years old and seeing the end of the road?"

Betty didn't say anything but Frankie colored a bit.

"Of course you can," he said. "That was incredibly ignorant of me. So, you can imagine the feeling if another second grader reached out. Of course, my first thought was to punch him in the face."

"Of course," said Betty.

"But you know, I fell in love that day. I was a second grader who found his soul mate. Even before Roza I knew my life was going to change. I knew intuitively I was saved."

They let that sink in and then Betty got up to make them lunch.

"So, what could Hersh's plan be with Marian?" asked Betty from the kitchen.

"I wish I knew," he said. "I'm not going to believe there isn't one. I'd ask but he'd give me one of those enigmatic smiles and I'd want to punch him again."

"He might surprise us," Betty countered.

"He might but he also could tempt me to unleash Trotsky and Lenin," Frankie said.

"How come you've never given them feminine names?" asked Betty. "Why couldn't you unfurl Taylor and Swift?"

When Hersh walked through the door he had a new toothbrush and found his colleagues deep in laughter on the couch.

"I'm guessing you've been talking about me," he said.

Frankie looked up. "Yeah, Betty was saying what a complete tool you are."

"I was not," she said. "I would never consider you complete."

That got the two of them howling again.

"You know I could fire you for insubordination," he told Betty.

"I don't think Roza would allow it," she answered.

Hersh agreed and went to make his lunch. Frankie, never one to waste a moment, said, "So, what's next?"

CHAPTER 46

When the horses broke in the fifth race, Roza had her binoculars on the field and was satisfied with the positioning of Rubber Baron. At 17-1, he was the day's best bet.

She had a strong win bet and wheeled him on top with a couple favorites.

"How deep you in here?" Hersh asked.

"GNP deep," she answered.

"This is my inheritance," he said.

"So you say each time you come out here."

She put the binoculars back up and watched the field in the backstretch and returned the glasses to the table.

"Aren't you going to watch the race?" Hersh asked.

"No need," she said. "He'll win. We'll watch when he turns for home but we could go to the window now."

He wasn't surprised when Rubber Baron won by three lengths.

Roza's carpetbag purse was just big enough to hold the cash and the two walked to the backstretch to pass out thank-you notes.

Roza was more generous than usual, bringing huge smiles. The appreciation was delivered in English, Spanish, and Spanglish.

Walking to the parking lot, Roza clutched her bag like somebody was going to challenge her. A half-century later she hadn't rid herself of the fear of being taken.

Intellectually, she knew it wasn't going to happen and with Hersh she was safe 100 percent, but some quirks never die.

"I'm sure you heard about my experience with the police," he said.

"Tales of stupidity travel fast," she said, although it was not delivered with her usual withering sarcasm.

"You know I hate to have my wallet taken."

"It would have been just a wallet," she said. "If you wanted to show off for your date you could have won her a stuffed animal."

Hersh was never surprised by his grandmother's disdain and usually let it pass but he had been angry for two days.

"You know, sometimes I forget how perfect you are," he said.

She stopped and looked at her grandson. She could tell she had crossed a line even though she had been kidding. Things were changing for her and she realized she wasn't the only one.

Roza stunned her grandson when she said, "I apologize. I shouldn't have said that."

"Are you fucking with me?" Hersh said. "Are you fucking with me?"

Roza snorted. "I've warned you about your language. If you don't watch yourself, you're going to say a bad word in front of the wrong crowd."

He kissed his grandmother on the forehead and said, "You are one strange bird."

She grabbed his hand and when they made it to the car said, "I'm going to buy you ice cream."

When he was younger and they needed to talk that was their code phrase. But she actually took him for ice cream. He knew that was where they were headed now.

It was always pistachio for him and fudge ripple for her. Hersh related everything that happened in the last 48 hours.

"So, what is your next move?" she asked.

He chuckled. "How come you all keep asking me that? Do you all think I plot out every moment of my life?"

"Only if you are smart," she rejoined. "All current evidence to the contrary."

"Sometimes I like to let life's events just wash over me and live on my wits."

"There is a recipe for a short life," Roza said.

"I am open to suggestions."

"We could make her disappear," said Roza.

"We could make her disappear? Are you yanking my crank? What are we, *Goodfellas*? That is just too funny."

Roza broke into a grin as she finished her ice cream.

"Funny how? I mean, funny like I'm a clown, I amuse you? I make you laugh, I'm here to fuckin' amuse you? What do you mean funny, funny how? How am I funny?"

The tension was broken although they came up with no solutions. Roza was confident her grandson was faking everyone. She wasn't convinced everything that happened wasn't part of his plan.

She couldn't figure out his game but like Frankie had confidence in whatever it was. But maybe she was wrong. She turned to him and saw his mouth curl and she relaxed.

"What?" he asked.

"Gazing into the face of a genius."

"Don't all grandmothers think that?" he said.

"Probably. But I'm one of the few who believes it for a reason."

"You might want to keep it to yourself for a while. It might make for a good statement at my trial."

"You aren't going to court," she said.

"How can you be so sure?"

Roza stared at him.

"Ahh," he said.

CHAPTER 47

When Hersh returned, Frankie had left to pick up Peter. He found Betty pacing the floor.

"Waiting on test results?" he asked.

"Fuck you," she said.

"Whoa, whoa, whoa!" he answered.

"How do I get myself into these things?" Betty asked.

"What type of thing are we talking about?" Hersh asked back.

Betty made a fist and Hersh thought his protégé was going to strike him. She was near tears and in panic.

"You are behind this, I know you are," she said.

He laughed realizing what the problem was and she was not in danger. At least not the danger she had known.

"Betty, it is just a date," he said.

"Just a date? I've never been on a date, you stupid moron."

"You do know that's redundant."

"You want redundant? How about I let Hillary and Barack go redundant on your smug face?"

Even she couldn't keep a straight face and the two were laughing.

"You don't quite have the menace Frankie does."

"I figured I would try it out."

"Probably not a good fit," he chuckled.

"I'm going to have to come up with a different slogan," she admitted.

"Something will come to you."

"Yeah, I got bigger worries," Betty said.

"I repeat, just a date."

"Says the man who the last time he went on one almost beat a guy to death and then unmasked a federal agent as a sexual fraud."

"That isn't fair," said Hersh. "Marian may be a fraud but there is nothing fraudulent about her sexually."

"Ewww!" squealed Betty. "Double ewww! I've now got a little vomit in my mouth."

Hersh held up his hands in surrender. Betty was petrified and while he wanted to lighten the mood he didn't want to invalidate this big step.

"Betty, you can call this off," he said.

"Can I?" she said with a huge smile.

"Absolutely not."

"Don't give me an out because I will take it."

"Seth seems like a nice young man," he said.

"What do I talk to him about?" she asked. "What do I say when he asks about my face?"

"Well, No. 1, he'll wait for you to broach the subject. And No. 2, you can talk about his brother. I mean, I think he knows things. This is a stand-in parent for a younger sibling. We're talking some maturity here."

"Why did he ask me out?"

"Just a guess, but because he likes you."

"Why?"

Hersh opened his arms and she came into them. He hugged her, then kissed the top of her head.

"As Roza reminded me today, we have options. We can make him disappear."

"Can you do that or me?" she asked.

"You want to take a roller coaster ride?

"Please."

Seth picked her up at 6:30 p.m. and Frankie and Hersh made sure they were two rooms away. Betty could have kissed them for that but was more appreciative of the wide grin Seth gave her when she opened the door.

He looked like a prince in a borrowed and slightly too small sports coat. Taking his offered hand, they walked to dinner.

The night was beautiful and to her surprise she found conversation with Seth easy.

As they shared calamari, Seth looked at her and blurted, "Can I ask a question?"

Her hand went to her face. Hersh knew nothing about men. She launched into a story about the violence done to her and felt better. She was eating the frog first thing.

He looked slightly embarrassed when he talked again.

"Betty, I cannot tell you how much it means you told me that. But what I was going to ask was, 'How come you agreed to go out with me?' "

Her hand flew to her mouth.

"Wow! Talk about jumping the gun," she said when finally getting her laughter under control. "I was so worried about you looking at me I just wanted to get it out of the way."

"It was a fascinating story."

Taking a breadstick, she tapped her wrist before chewing.

"Why were you wondering why I said yes to this date?"

"Well, you are pretty and smart and I'm this guy who only knows you because of his brother. I made the little guy listen to my speech to get you to go out with me."

"Seth, do you think I'm at the clinic because I'm an heiress getting charity points?"

"I had no idea why you were there."

"But you did wonder about the scars?"

"Oh sure," he said honestly. "It was the first thing I noticed."

"Most people do."

"But you know I haven't seen them since."

"How could that be?" she asked.

"Can I take back my comment about how smart you are?"

Betty flushed but before she could answer he had her hand in his and they finished the meal each eating with one hand.

When they returned, she saw Frankie and Hersh watching from the upstairs window, but when they entered the clinic they were absent from sight.

Neither saw the sedan down the street. Had they had eyes for anyone else they might have also noticed the car parked near the restaurant.

Seth stepped in to say goodbye and for the first time looked nervous. She loved him for it and put him out of his misery by leaning in. When they pulled apart each was smiling.

As Seth turned to go, Frankie magically appeared but announced his presence clomping down the stairs. He held two helmets.

"Brother," he said to Seth. "Have you ever felt the power of a Harley on the open road?"

"I have not, sir," he said.

"Well, no time like the present. I'm going to swing the bike around and I'll meet you out front. No bus for you tonight."

"Well, I appreciate it, sir."

Frankie shook his head and exited.

"I think he would like for you to not call him 'sir.' "

"What else can you call a guy who looks like him?"

"Fair point. Why don't you work on it for the second date?"

This time he kissed her. He was about to leave when they heard a commotion coming from the kitchen. They looked to see Clemenza loping at them.

Seth took an involuntary step back but Clemenza was on him and licking his face.

"Clemenza," said Betty, "allow the man the dignity to leave unharmed."

The dog dropped and stared at them.

Seth bent to pet him and Betty looked up the stairs.

"Hersh," she yelled. "Real subtle. Seth was leaving. I don't think you needed to send your henchman."

"Have no idea what you are talking about," a voice came from the top of the house. "I didn't even know you guys were back."

Betty snorted and opened the door for her date. Seth skipped down the stairs and over to Frankie, who was sitting on his bike.

Seconds later, Hersh bopped down the stairs and found Betty sitting on the couch.

"Good time?"

"The best. I feel like Eliza Doolittle."

"But?"

"But what?"

"Betty, Betty, Betty. Do you not know how attuned I am to disturbances in the universe? I can hear a drop of urine falling into the well."

"Well," said Betty. "Thank you for the lovely vision."

"Do not change the subject. I've got a steel trap up here."

She sighed. "My father was at the restaurant."

"Can't be a coincidence," he said.

"It cannot be."

"I'll check into it."

"Be careful."

He nodded. She thought he would lecture her not to worry but he waved good night and returned to his study.

As she was leaving she saw him in the window. She couldn't see his face clearly and couldn't tell he was frowning. He saw the car that she had missed.

CHAPTER 48

"You fucking bitch!" he screamed when she sat down in the diner.

Marian was confused. He couldn't be referring to the other night. When she set up this meeting he was rational and a little remorseful.

"What is this about?" she said.

He was seething and his knuckles red-gripping the saltshaker.

But then his words came out in a level tone.

"If you put a tail on Betty again I will blow up your shit so hard they'll be scraping feces off the wall for a week."

She was dumbfounded and her expression told him so.

"Don't lie and tell me you didn't follow her last night. Don't try. I won't stand for it. When you called, I thought you honestly wanted to get things straight."

"I did and I do."

"Following a teenager on a first date isn't going to feed the bulldog. You people can't be that stupid. Can you? If you are thinking that will push me to do something violent, let me save you worry and manpower. It will. You dumb motherfuckers think you hold all the cards. I know people too."

Too shocked to speak, she hoped he would not stalk out when done.

"Please listen," she pleaded. "I'll make a call and find out whether it was us. If it wasn't, you really need to know."

Calmed, he nodded and she called and then waited.

Seconds later her face went slack and then white. He put his head on the table. When he raised it, she was staring at the phone and her face now red.

"Son of a bitch," she said.

That made him smile.

"We are that stupid."

"Throw a blanket over me, I'm in shock." Hersh said.

"It was us but I swear to you it wasn't me."

"I believe you."

"Just like that?" she countered.

"Just like that."

"Why would you believe me now?"

"You think I've committed a crime. You were clumsy attempting to prove it but you weren't dumb. Following Betty was silly and cruel. Even if you faked being dumb I don't get the cruel part. You know Betty and you don't have it in you."

"Can we start this meeting over again?" she asked.

"It certainly couldn't go any worse."

"Bad rehearsal, good show," she said.

"Since I had the first word last time," he said with a grin, "why don't you take a stab at it."

She was surprised by her opening gambit.

"Why don't I start with some truth since it has been in short supply," she started. "We've had you under surveillance for some time. My bosses think, and I agree, you are a serial killer."

She waited for a denial that didn't come. It threw her off but she stumbled forward.

"We think you are running a Star Chamber. You've been smart about not laying down a pattern. We looked at the families of the children and got nothing. The few deaths among them is within the statistical range for that lifestyle."

Hersh made a pyramid with his fists and rested his chin.

"We can't pinpoint your MO. That hasn't stopped us from believing you're guilty. We'll be there when you make a mistake."

Marian stirred her coffee and waited for a response.

"Interesting," he said. "Would it be rude to ask the names of those I've helped cross to the other side?"

Sliding a sheet of paper over, Marian wanted to look at his reaction as he perused the list.

After a minute, he pushed the list back.

"Just fascinating," he said. "I like where you detail how each person was killed. That's anal even for you guys."

"Denials?"

"Are you asking if I killed all those people?"

She nodded.

"I did not kill all those people."

"Don't play word games. If you think you can pass a lie detector test, I assure you the box is more sophisticated."

Bemused, he looked up from the table. "It takes stones to preach to me about a machine that detects lies since you guys couldn't pass if you copied off the person next to you."

Marian quickly agreed but added, "That really isn't the conversation. We'll pay for our sins, but don't do the 'you're a sinner so don't look at my sins.' "

He raised his eyebrows.

"It is intellectually weak and you're better than that," she said. "If you want to argue justification, I'm all ears. If you want to explain this sickness, I'm your girl. But don't yank me around with dodges and feints. It diminishes you."

The waiter asked if they wanted to order and Hersh took the opportunity to grill the man on the specials. Then he ordered a hamburger. Marian was going to pass on food then went for a turkey club.

As the waiter disappeared, Hersh drummed his fingers on the tabletop and then spoke.

"A man is dying and a priest comes in to give last rites. The priest asks, 'Do you renounce the devil?' The man says, 'I do not.' The priest says, 'You don't renounce the devil?' and the man says, 'I don't.' The priest says, 'Son, why won't you renounce the devil?' and the man says, 'Because, father, a man in my position needs all the friends he can get.' "

She stares at him and he says, "I got that from a Louis L'Amour movie."

"As I said, dodges and feints won't keep me here."

He waved his hand toward the door and shrugged his shoulders.

"Quick tip. When the guy shows aces, don't bluff with eight as your high card."

"Meaning?" she asked.

"You are here to deliver a message and not leaving until the message is sent. I could read the phone book and you'll be here. So, stay seated and try to outsmart me."

Before she could respond he picked up the pepper mill and moved it to a table across the room.

"Now that it is just you and me talking this might go a little bit faster," he said.

Marian's face turned the color of the ketchup bottle but she really had to laugh.

"Why didn't you do that when we started this conversation?"

"Thus far you haven't asked me anything I felt needed to stay between us."

"So now I'm going to get a confession?"

"What would you like for me to admit?"

"Any name on the list would be a start," she told him.

"Why don't we start with Elmore Givens and Gabby Revson."

"I'm listening," she said leaning in.

"Givens died in New York. Revson died in Florida."

She nodded in affirmation.

"Did you enjoy your visits?"

He scowled like she asked the wrong question in class.

"Well, unless I can teleport, I could have only enjoyed one or the other. Check the time of death."

Givens and Revson were killed on the same day, hours apart.

"Please tell me you guys aren't running a pathetic con game to clear your case load?" he said. "How can you be two places at once when you're not anywhere at all?"

"Just because you couldn't have done both doesn't mean you didn't do one of them."

He clucked his tongue.

"You came into this meeting with that 'high and mighty' bureau confidence you were going to clear 20 some cases. You told me at the outset I was guilty of all of them. We're two names in and you're down to 50-50 at best. Have you no shame, senator?"

"Hersh, you are a brilliant man and I'm not just pumping sunshine up your skirt," she said. "You might skate on this. But we both know you're not innocent. Can we start with that?"

Saved from answering by the food being served, Hersh chose to eat in silence. When he finished, he pushed his plate to the side and cleared his throat.

"Marian, have you killed anyone?"

"I have," she responded with no hesitation.

"Self-defense?"

"Yes," she said with a pause and then thought about it before nodding her head again. "Yes."

"Was it hard?"

"The hardest thing I've ever done," she said and then got a sad and resigned smile. "And now I'm living with it."

"Was there a second time?"

"There was not."

"If there is a second time do you think it will get easier?"

"I don't," she said.

"So, you are a person who is trained to protect not only yourself but others. And with all your training you don't think killing another person will get easier. Yet you come to a diner, give me a list of 20 people and think I'm some kind of avenging angel."

"I never said you were an avenging angel," she countered. "I think you are a stone-cold killer."

"How come you were never afraid to be alone with me?" he asked.

It was her turn to pause. An honest answer would be right but it wouldn't be the only right one. Yet, she went with the truth.

"Because we had a chemistry and I liked you. I liked you so much. I don't know when that happened. I think the first time we shook hands. It scared me then and it scares me now. But let me tell you, I'm not letting you go."

He raised his eyebrows and she realized how that could be taken.

"I'm not letting you escape."

"Yeah, I wasn't confused by your verbiage."

She frowned and said almost inaudibly, "Maybe I was."

Reaching into his pocket, she thought he'd come up with money to pay the bill but instead had two tickets.

"Loudon Wainwright III is playing Tuesday. You still want to go?"

Flabbergasted, she stared at him and then at her fork. Maybe if she punctured him he would wake up to this being serious.

"You asking me on another date?"

"I am."

"Are you joking?"

"Not at this time."

"Are you delusional?"

"How long does this go on? I just need a yes or no."

Dropping her hands into her lap and counting to five she finally gazed back and said, "Yes."

"Excellent," he said. "This doesn't mean you have to stop investigating. This gives you a chance to get closer. I caution you, if you put two guys in the audience, don't have them wear the black suit, black tie combination. I'll spot them."

CHAPTER 49

Peter and Maise Williams were on the stoop trying to catch a breeze. Maise was content to sip on her ice tea but Peter kept looking and listening for a motorcycle.

His eyes dropped when he saw his uncle. He was carrying a brown bag. That was never good news.

Peter moved closer to his grandmother but knew his uncle was going to do what he was going to do.

"Mama, Peter, what are you guys doing outside?" he asked.

"Just getting some fresh air," she said.

He pointed a finger and the brown bag at Peter and said, "And I guess you needed someone to protect you while you came outside?"

"Son, there is no need," Maise Williams said. "We're not bothering anybody and neither should you."

"Mama, I was talking to the little man and he knows he'll never be a big man if he doesn't get from under your skirt."

"You mean like Bobby?" Peter said.

His uncle looked at him, as did his grandmother. Peter had no idea why he said it but he was tired of being afraid and no matter what his uncle did, Peter would not regret it.

"What did you say, boy?"

"You already got my brother killed with the mess you talk. You want both of us dead?"

"Don't make me come other there," said his uncle. "I had nothing to do with Bobby's death."

Peter took one more step toward his grandmother but his uncle was too fast and grabbed him by the arm.

"Please don't start nothing, son," said Maise. "Let's enjoy the day with family."

"Little man has to respect his elders and he needs to know what happens when he doesn't."

Peter braced for the first blow and it made him unaware the three weren't alone anymore.

He heard his name called and he smiled.

"Hey Peter, how is it going tonight?" Frankie said. "You ready to ride?"

Totally ignoring the uncle, Frankie extended his arm to give Peter his helmet.

"Evening, Ms. Williams," he said.

"Evening, Frankie," she said.

"Nice night for sitting out."

"Sure is."

Frankie didn't see the uncle step up to him as much as feel him.

"Who the fuck might you be?" said Peter's uncle.

Sticking out his hand, Frankie introduced himself, but the uncle didn't reciprocate.

"Peter and I were in a discussion," said the uncle.

"I apologize, sir. But Peter and I are late. I had trouble with my bike. He has an appointment and I need to get him there. I'll wait by the bike until you guys finish."

Walking over to his Harley, Frankie stood with his helmet tucked under his arm. He winked at Peter and looked up and down the street.

"I think Peter and I can finish this when he gets back," the uncle said. "You make sure we do, okay, Peter?"

"Sure," the young man said, walking toward Frankie.

Before the two pushed off, Frankie handed a package to Maise Williams. Her eyes got wide at the complete set of Coleman Hawkins recordings.

"Oh, my," she said.

"I have a friend, who has a friend," said Frankie as he touched her hand.

Walking back, he heard the uncle say, "We'll talk too later."

Frankie answered in his softest voice.

"Maybe we'll have coffee."

"Coffee?" said the uncle. "We don't need to have any damn coffee."

"Yeah, I don't drink coffee myself. But I figured our third friend does."

"What are talking about, a third friend?"

"Well, while I was waiting for Peter the other day I got chummy with your neighbors. You know Radio Joe, don't you?"

A fist to the face would not have stunned the uncle any more. He gazed at Frankie, who hadn't moved from his spot.

"When did you want to have that talk?" Frankie asked.

"Whenever," said the uncle.

"See you whenever," said Frankie, who jumped on the bike, fired it up and roared down the street.

Maise Williams looked amusedly at her son.

"Now, how do you suppose that young man knows Joe?" asked Maise.

"He don't know shit," said her son.

"You know, I don't like that type of language. Why don't we listen to some Coleman Hawkins?"

Her son never answered. He stormed out on the street toward a group of men. She couldn't help but recognize Radio Joe among them.

CHAPTER 50

Marian looked at her watch, snatched up some papers and rushed into her boss's office.

"Hey, Robert, you know James Marshall over at the 111?"

"Didn't he help us with the banking case two years ago?"

"That's him. I've got an appointment. Thought he could give us local information about our boy Hersh."

"What kind of information?"

"There is no way this kind of activity could go on and Marshall not know."

"I would agree in normal situations but this is anything but a normal case."

She didn't have trouble locating Marshall since he was the only detective in the bullpen. He was tapping away at his keyboard.

Marian was used to getting the double-take from men but Marshall merely gave a "one moment" sign.

He hit two more buttons and closed his laptop.

"Because I am an outstanding detective I'm guessing you are the federal agent who called a few hours ago," he said, extending a hand.

She sat down in the seat closest to his desk. He raised his coffee cup in the universal gesture. She shook her head and reached into her briefcase for a file.

"As I said on the phone," Marian began, "I've got a case that involves someone local and was hoping you guys had a file on him."

"Yeah, you didn't say who that was so I can't tell you yet whether we can help," Marshall said, topping off his cup.

He took a sip and made a face.

"Good choice not to go with the 111 brew," he said.

"I've had enough cop coffee to last me two lifetimes and rarely do I regret turning down that offer."

"So," said Marshall, "exactly what bad man is running through town here?"

Throwing a thick folder on the desk she opened it up and took a rubber band off the thickest stack.

She nudged the file over to Marshall and he picked it up, weighed it with his hand and laughed.

"I pity the poor SOB who you're trailing. You guys must know when he goes to the bathroom."

"Not his morning routine but in the evening . . ." she trailed off to let him know she wasn't some humorless bureaucrat.

However, he hadn't been listening. He was staring at the file and reading page by page.

"I can sum up for you," she said.

He continued to read. He turned his desk light on and fumbled in the desk drawer for reading glasses. He held up one page while he read another. Finally, he put it all down, took off his glasses and rubbed his eyes.

"Hersh?" he said.

She took the file and gathered it into one stack and put the rubber bands back on. She swept the pile into her briefcase and shut it.

"You know of him?"

"Indeed, I do."

"What can you tell me?"

"Well," he said scratching his head. "You know how there is a civilian who is always getting into police business? And the police will do anything to get rid of the guy?"

"Yes, I do," she said.

"Well, Hersh is the opposite of that guy. He is the civilian who police go to for information. He knows more about deviants and criminals in this city than most people on the force."

"You've never suspected him of stepping outside the lines?"

"Suspected him? Yes. Convinced? No. I will say too many problems disappeared for me not to think he was involved. Throw in Frankie and you'd be a bad cop not to think something was cooking."

"Have you guys done anything?" she asked.

"Well, the mayor has given him two commendations and we show up in our dress blues when it happens."

"You're kidding me?"

He scooted to a metal cabinet and thumbed through folders. When he scooted back he had eight folders under his arm.

He slapped them on the desk.

"I know federal officers are trained to look at the black and white. We're more gray here," he said.

She gazed at the folders. "Meaning?"

He ran his fingers along the edge of one folder.

"Well, here are eight cases listed in your report. Six of these fine citizens are dead and two are serving time."

"Yes, I know," Marian said a bit wearily.

"Do you know what would happen if the higher-ups found out Hersh had a hand in any of them?"

She gestured for him to tell her.

"I'd have to get my dress blues out and watch him get another commendation."

"Catching those guys should be your work, not some renegade citizen's."

"I don't disagree and maybe if I was sitting at a desk talking with other feds I might be able to enjoy the smugness you guys have."

"What does that mean?"

He debated what to say next and then just came out with it.

"When two fine federal officials talk, they think everybody is on one side or the other and there is a big fat line between them. That isn't what happens on this level."

She didn't interrupt him because she knew he wanted to make a point.

He nodded his thanks and continued.

"Ma'am, I have no doubt you are a fine law officer. I'm not one who gets his back up when the feds come in. We're all working the job. So, I'll ask you for help. What do you suggest when a victim's mother comes in and pleads for justice for her injured or deceased child? Later, when she thanks me for something we didn't do but the problem is cleaned up anyway, what should I say?"

"The job isn't supposed to be easy," she said.

The detective grew grim and held up a file.

"Let me be specific," he said. "This is the file of Jackson Cabot. I'd been a law officer for 20 years when I caught the case. When I saw the body of his victim I puked. I didn't feel bad because the coroner was a little green too."

"I am not denying there are tough cases," she interrupted.

"I haven't gotten to the point of the story," said Marshall. "I knew it was Cabot. I couldn't prove it was Cabot. I lost 22 pounds. Do you know why?"

"Why?" she asked.

"Because while I tried to make a case we got another body," he said. "I stopped sleeping and eating."

He got a whimsical smile. "I didn't stop drinking."

Opening the file, he showed her a photo.

"That is Cabot after we found him on a meat hook," he said. "I slept like a baby that night. When I thought about finding no more mutilated children, do you think I gave a good goddamn whether Hersh Grundstein decided to level the playing field?"

Marian waited for calm.

"There has to be a right way and a wrong way to get justice," she said.

"In theory. But look at the cases in front of you and tell me as a human being, not as a law officer, that the world is not a better place with them off the grid."

"But I am a federal officer," she countered.

"And if you weren't?"

"I can't separate that out."

"Our type of justice and the justice people want don't always match up," he said.

"That is why we make the decision."

The police detective looked at Marian and held his hands out wide to the length of about five feet.

"Do you know what that is the size of?" he asked.

"I'm afraid to know."

"It is the size of a child's coffin," he said. "I've seen too many to debate you."

"So you won't help us to catch him?"

"No, we'll give you everything you need."

"Then what are you saying?" Marian asked.

"I'm saying, don't expect anyone to thank us for doing our jobs."

"That is not why we do our jobs."

James Marshall gave Marian the saddest smile she had ever seen.

"So, are we better than him?"

CHAPTER 51

In your file is the information I'm claustrophobic. It didn't change when and why I did things but sometimes changed the where.

I also had a bout of anxiety, another reason I screwed up. I could have fought a one-front attack but when the police got interested I found myself overwhelmed.

No matter how fast you were someone was faster.

Maybe I was outgunned, not outdrawn, but does it matter now? When you are face down in the dust in Dodge, and the crippled boy who sweeps the saloon gets two bits to run and get the marshal, does it make a difference how it happened?

I'm a romantic and figured I would escape this mess.

I'm getting wordy for a guy who should have shuffled off. This is my version of Martin Luther's 95 Theses on the church door. It is the missive you find next to an empty pill bottle.

The great philosopher Donna Summer said it best:

Last dance
Last dance for love
Yes, it's my last chance
For romance tonight
I need you by me
Beside me, to guide me
To hold me, to scold me
'Cause when I'm bad
I'm so, so bad
So let's dance the last dance
Let's dance the last dance
Let's dance this last dance tonight

If only Plato and Aristotle had been introduced to disco the world might have been a better place.

I'm fading and I've got a fever and the only prescription is more cowbell. Perhaps I am delirious and will wake in my bed, or more likely a bed paid for by the taxpayers.

Truly, I don't expect to make it to a bed but you might call me a dreamer. But I'm not the only one.

CHAPTER 52

Roza picked up a random file and smiled. This was a favorite. She was coming into her own when she had a chance meeting with Rudolf Strider. What else can you say when you see a war criminal in the neighborhood butcher shop?

He had been sentenced in the Nuremberg trials and served five years. It was supposed to be life but like many defendants he was released prematurely.

The USA needed Germany to deal with the Russians. It was more important to win the Cold War than punish those who ran the last one.

So, Nazis were walking the streets. Roza was a devotee of the Nuremberg trials and knew Strider right away. She wasn't surprised he was free.

She was past being shocked by life's cruelty. She didn't get mad and didn't want to get even. She wanted to be one ahead.

Strider was too arrogant even to believe he was being followed. He wouldn't have cared. Working for the USA helping to find Soviet agents, he was handsomely paid, protected, and compensated.

He was doing a job now and a job then. He didn't even mind working with Jews. He had not agreed with the plan to eradicate them but only because he thought it a waste of energy and manpower.

He wasn't surprised many didn't hold him responsible. When you fight many wars, you can't be surprised by who your allies are.

But Roza did hold him responsible. When he signaled for a cab on that October morning, he had no idea it would be his last day.

He had wanted to go to 18th Street and when he figured the car was headed elsewhere, it was too late. She pulled into a neighborhood of warehouses.

He was amused when she pulled a gun and ordered him out of the car.

"Is this a robbery?" he asked.

"No," she said.

He waited for more but nothing came. He had been a soldier and knew who could pull the trigger and who couldn't. This wasn't the first time he'd been accosted.

True, she carried a gun but there was a difference in holding one and using one. He stared at her tattoo so he knew what camp and what year she arrived.

A quick calculation told him she entered as a child and probably was the only family member to walk out.

She led him to an empty building, where he saw two chairs. There would be a lot of talk. Holocaust victims couldn't stop talking. It seemed to be a badge of honor to compare horror stories.

Why couldn't these people live with it? Things happen and then you face another day. What good did it do to talk about it?

Still, the talking worked to his advantage. Most talked and talked. Then they explained they were better than him by letting him go. They weren't monsters like he was.

He wondered how Germany lost the war to these people.

The Russians were ruthless and gave the British credit for steeliness but the Americans and Jews just seem to want to prove a moral superiority. Like that was going to stop somebody in power.

He wanted to tell this woman to skip the preamble so they could get on with their day.

When she shot him, he was more shocked than hurt. She put a round in his shoulder and it blew him back off the chair. She ordered him to put the chair upright and sit down again.

Tossing a towel to press on the injury, she asked him a question.

"Do you know why you are here?" she asked.

He blinked a couple of times and realized he had a flesh wound. So he focused on her.

"I'm here so you can get some kind of satisfaction."

She swiveled her head to indicate he was mistaken.

"You are here to die," she said. "I won't be satisfied but happy for a while. Killing you will be like a drug. Immediate relief but it won't last forever."

"You won't kill me," he said.

She tilted her head and regarded him through one eye.

"I'll admit I was surprised you shot me. But you and I know you don't have it in you to commit murder."

This time she shot him in the foot.

He didn't spill out of his chair but it hurt like a mother.

"What are you trying to prove?" he said.

"I'm not trying to prove anything," she said. "I'm trying to heal myself and I'm trying to get some payback for people who can no longer do it for themselves."

"So you are going to kill me."

"Probably," she said.

"Probably?"

"I figure I'll give you a chance to explain yourself and then decide."

"What would you like for me to say?" he asked in a mocking tone.

She shot him again. This time in the other foot.

"It would serve not to have an attitude," she said. "We can be civil or you can continue with Teutonic arrogance. The choice is yours."

The pain was excruciating and so he decided subservience was in order.

"Okay, please tell me what you want me to say."

"Explain to me the thinking that went into what you guys tried to accomplish."

"Well, that would take days and I don't think you are patient."

"Try," she said.

"It was war, not a tea party. We tried to win and our opponents tried to win. How much more explanation could there be? We were brutal, the Japanese were brutal, and the Russians are still brutal. I mean, you guys dropped the bomb."

"So it didn't take days, after all," she said.

"There are nuances those who weren't there wouldn't understand."

She turned her wrist to him. "I was there."

"You know what I mean. You had to be on the inside. You don't stop mid-war and say, 'Are we doing this right? Is the master plan really masterful?' It wouldn't have done any good. There was only one man who could make that decision anyway."

Roza thought maybe he was right. Maybe you did your job and when you figured you did it wrong you were onto a different job.

She considered him again and asked a question he couldn't see the relevance of.

"Do you watch movies?" she asked.

"What?"

"A simple question, Colonel."

That shocked him. Not many knew his work with the SS. Most thought he was a bureaucrat when he was a ranking party member.

"I watch movies. Spencer Tracy is my favorite actor."

That brought a snort of laughter from her.

"So you think you know how this will end, don't you?"

"Look, I don't know what you want but I'm in a lot of pain."

"This won't take a lot more time," she said.

"Tell me what you want me to say and we can both return to our lives. You get me medical help and I won't tell anyone what happened here."

"How old do you think I am, Colonel," she asked him.

"I have no idea."

"Of course you do. Young women were a specialty of yours," she said.

For the first time, Strider was truly frightened. This woman had way too much information for his comfort."

"I'm going to say 19 or 20."

"Close enough."

"Why should that make a difference?" he asked.

"I should have a sister who is my age," she answered him without addressing his question. "So, for a moment pretend you are facing two of us."

"You think your sister would want you to exact some sort of revenge?" he said, mocking her.

She put her finger on the trigger but didn't pull it.

"I admire your ability to remain arrogant through this. You are not a disappointment in that regard. But I thought you would have been more perceptive. That is disappointing."

He leaned back to regard her. She thought she was in control and wanted an apology. She would have to wait a long time for that.

"If you kill me, you'll have to get rid of my body and that is going to raise questions. So, dispense with this charade and get on with it."

"I thought we could have had a dialogue. I want to get a better understanding of Nazi thinking. I was too young to form many opinions while it was happening but I've done research since."

"I don't care for your tone," he said. "We are in a warehouse and soon the owners will arrive and you'll have to explain why we're here."

"The owners won't be showing up," she said.

"How do you know?

"The owner is here," she said.

For the fourth and final time, she shot him. She walked over to a curtain and pulled it aside. There was a large hole and she dragged the body over and rolled it in. She emptied a bag of lime and filled the hole with dirt. At some point, someone might enter the warehouse but she wasn't worried. Her name wasn't on the lease and any attempt to track down the owners would be a chase.

She picked up the two chairs and put them in the trunk. She locked the doors and drove away. Strider was disappointing but she would learn and next time be patient.

After parking on the street, she walked to the bus station and headed out of town. By early evening she'd write this up and figure out what was next.

Roza marveled at her younger self. She shook her head at the woman who hadn't become quite the huntress she would be. It did get easier and less brutal.

Even early on, Roza didn't have the hubris to think what she was doing was right. Or righteous. She never believed she was doing good work. If found out she would have never given excuses.

Anger fueled her in the years following the war but cooled quickly. There was never a time when she tried to justify her journey. If you claimed she was like the Nazis, she agreed you could make the argument.

Arguing about justification was silly. Sitting in the bank, she wanted to feel remorse. It was the time of her life for reflection.

Years ago, she asked Hersh to take measures if she weakened. She wanted to protect everything if she got a dose of remorse.

Whether Hersh would execute the plan was the question. Not for the first time she considered getting rid of all of this. But she couldn't bear watching her life's work disappear. If it disappeared, she would disappear.

Looking at her watch, she began to put things away. She liked batting practice and made sure she arrived in time.

Hersh would be there, as would Frankie and Betty. In recent days, Hersh had been distracted. She preached staying on task but he had gotten a faraway look. Maybe she'd lightly mention it.

Looking at the files she chuckled. A light touch was not in her arsenal.

CHAPTER 53

The beer was cold and the sun was warm. Roza and Betty had gone for food and each man was enveloped in his thought.

Frankie broke the silence.

"I'm thinking of bringing Peter to a game," he said.

Hersh said, "I love the idea. How he's doing?"

"For a kid who lost his brother I'd say he's improving."

"He's lucky to have his grandmother. He's lucky to have you."

"His grandmother has trouble with her son and I can't be around 24 hours a day."'

"We do what we can do," said Hersh.

"So we tell ourselves."

"You have another solution?"

"I'd like to get them out of there."

"How would you do it, Frankie?"

"They could live with me," he said.

"They could, and then what?"

"Then they would be safe."

"Maybe," said Hersh. "But they would also have been extracted from their home. Peter might benefit but I'm not sure about Mrs. Williams. No matter your jazz collection."

Frankie put his face toward the sun and didn't speak for a moment.

"You know how much I hate it when you are right," he said.

They didn't talk about Peter again but Hersh knew if they lost Peter he'd have trouble reining in his friend. Bobby's death had almost destroyed him.

Losing himself in the game, Hersh put all of that to the side. The others picked up the vibe because other than talk about the game the four didn't engage in any conversation.

When it was over, they made dinner plans. Betty colored when she begged off. They knew she had a date with Seth.

"I hope you are practicing safe sex," Frankie said, then threw his hands up when they looked at him.

"Frankie!" exclaimed Betty.

"What?" he said, looking at them again. "We all were thinking it and you can't close the barn door once the animals are loose."

"That is a strange metaphor," said Hersh.

"Look, I don't want there to be a shotgun wedding," Frankie said.

"I think we are all in agreement there," said Hersh.

"Betty needs to be careful," said Frankie.

"Hey, you guys do know I'm standing here, right?"

The men looked and pretended she just appeared.

"I can handle my own dating life if you don't mind," she said, giving them a playful punch on the shoulder. "As for my sex life, please let us not talk about it. You'll embarrass Roza."

The older woman gave a pained look. "Why does each generation think they have a handle on the morals of their time?"

Frankie shocked them all by starting to sing Cole Porter.

"In olden days, a glimpse of stocking was looked on as something shocking. But now, God knows, anything goes."

Hersh laughed but then picked up the song.

"If driving fast cars you like, if low bars you like, if old hymns you like, if bare limbs you like, if Mae West you like, or me undressed you like, why, nobody would oppose."

Roza walked away as the two men began to harmonize the end of the song.

"You all are children," she said.

CHAPTER 54

Roza and Hersh were sitting in the reading room. He was speeding through Stephen King and she had the new Tim O'Mara. When each finished, they would switch.

A book club for two was all they could manage after finding their eclectic tastes were only similar to each other's.

Normally they read until being served but Hersh unexpectedly asked a question.

"What about the Judenrat?" he asked.

"What about them?"

"They have been on my mind," he said. "I know you don't read books about those times but I was just reading Jim Shepard's *The Book of Aron* and it got me to thinking."

"About the Judenrat?" she asked.

"Well, I've always been interested in self-preservation and I've always wondered what I would do in the direst of circumstances. Would I become a policeman in the ghetto and the camps and would I lord it over my fellow Jews?"

"Would you sink to the lowest depth to save yourself?" she asked.

"Exactly. I could be hungry or scared enough. I would like to think I'd be the type who looked the other way and did favors. But there are millions of people in Germany who believe they would have been the same kind of Nazis."

"Can I surprise you?" she said.

"You always do."

"All of us are capable of turning. In the worst of days, we become the worst people. I can't hold anger for anyone who tried to survive. Do I think less of the women who surrendered themselves to the soldiers? I don't. Survival was the finish line and most of us put what we did and what happened to us in a pocket we never reach into."

He looked at his grandmother with skepticism and she threw up her hands.

"I did say most of us," he laughed. "I'm working on being a better person."

He took her hand and rubbed it. "You're the best person I know. Don't go changing on me."

She squeezed his hand back and patted the top of it.

"We should get back to your original question," she said. "I'm a hunter but I never hunted that species. If you go in too many directions, you dissipate your anger and it becomes less meaningful."

Hersh put his hand over his heart and feigned injury.

"I've lived a life not many would be proud of. But even I had standards, places I didn't go. We all had missions to retrieve what we lost. Most people figure what we did we did for revenge."

"And it wasn't?" he broke in.

"It was but it wasn't the totality of what we were hunting for. For some it was dignity expelling the anger for not doing more when it started. There was a tipping point and to a person we believe we should have done more."

"That is a nice chunk of guilt to carry," he said.

"No matter what we did we were going to lug that around. I think I'm right when I say none of us thought we would come out a winner. We just didn't want the score to be so lopsided."

He knew she was also speaking for him. The damage done by his chosen path was broken irrevocably the first time he took action.

"You are a better person than I," he said. "I don't think I would have been able to separate the Judenrat from all of it. I might have blamed them more. You could make an intellectual argument for the horrors of war and the expectations of things happening. I don't know where the discussion of turning on your own people would have a satisfactory conclusion for me on any level."

Roza wiped her lip with a napkin and played with her fork before she looked back up at her grandson.

"Do you remember Philip Larker?"

"Sure, the nice man who umpired and refereed. When we struck out or fumbled he'd say, 'You'll get them the next time, big guy,' or, 'Even the greats have tough times.' "

Roza stared at him after he was finished. She opened her eyes wide and his mouth hung open.

"No?" he gasped

"Yes."

"Get the heck out of here."

She wagged an index finger.

"Everyone had a plan and most never look back. We don't want to see what we were. Life is a struggle and it is a blessing when we forget."

"Mr. Larker?" he brayed again.

"Mr. Larker," she repeated.

He frowned and cocked his head toward his grandmother.

"I could never understand why you didn't like him," he said.

"The answer was always in front of you," she answered.

"But you said you understood."

"I did but that doesn't mean I ever wanted to be in the same room."

"Did he know?"

"I'm sure he did. You can't look at anyone with a wrist tattoo and not feel guilt and shame."

"So, you knew him during the war?"

"I didn't but you only have to listen to people talk about their times back then and you know what everyone did."

"You could be mistaken."

"I am not," she said.

Hersh realized she didn't make a mistake.

"There was never a time when you were tempted to fix things?" he said, air quotes around the word "fix."

"I have limits, you know."

Hersh considered it and his mouth curled.

"Fair criticism," he said. "More than anyone I should know how unfair that belief would be."

She touched his face and then closed her eyes.

"However, in full disclosure ..."

He laughed and leaned in.

"There was one."

"Ah ha," he said.

Shaking her hand mirthlessly she let out a sigh.

"The man who picked my sister and myself for the experiments was a nasty twist. He wasn't burdened with guilt or remorse. He enjoyed his job and loved the power. I was a child and even I knew this was an evil man."

"So, you found him after the war?" Hersh questioned.

"He never made it out of the camps," she said. "My childhood ended the day the Nazis marched into my hometown. But even in the ghetto and then the camps we tried to hang onto at least a speck of something. We learned to enjoy tiny things. Maybe an extra roll for your birthday or a magic trick. We have a tremendous capacity to hang on as long as we can."

She paused and a single tear rolled down her face.

"But when my sister died I was no longer a child but a survivor. And little hands are quick hands. Watching grown-ups do magic tricks led me to try. I gained a capacity for making things disappear and reappear. Like a cigarette lighter on an officer's desk."

While she talked, she made her fork evaporate and come back on the other side of her plate. She fiddled with it and then the saltshaker was off the table.

"I could get things because no one suspected a child. We should have been the first ones you suspected, though, but who knows what goes into the thinking of monsters? I couldn't get big things like guns but I could nab a bullet or a small knife. But small items were my specialty. I could pick your pocket and be gone before you knew I was there."

"I can see that," he interjected.

"But a better trick than making something disappear is have it reappear somewhere else.

Hersh pointed his finger at his grandmother.

"Even someone high in the Judenrat had trouble explaining how a colonel's lighter ended up under the mattress of someone in his employ.

The Nazis aren't big on explanations and especially not big on sorting out the problems of the campers."

"So, what happened?" Hersh questioned.

"Well, he didn't get a jury of his peers," she said. "They shot him, of course."

"Of course," said Hersh.

"You want to hear the funny part?"

"I knew there had to be a punch line," he said.

"I was part of the cleanup crew. We stripped the room and cleaned up the blood and then re-made the room. While three men carried him out into the yard I stole the lighter again."

"You did not."

"I did."

"You little bitch," he said.

"This time we hid it until the colonel was transferred out and we bartered for extra food."

"Ballsy," he said.

"You want to know what ballsy is?" she asked.

He nodded and she reached into her purse and pulled out a gold lighter.

"No!" he screamed in delight.

She flicked it and got a flame before snapping the cover shut. She slid it over to him and he turned it over and over.

"How?"

"I always kept track of it. I probably stole it a dozen times. The Nazis were so careful in many respects and so sloppy in others. Keeping track of all the stuff taken was a little overwhelming, even for those anal bastards."

Hersh shook his head.

"You are a caution," he said.

"A scamp," she agreed.

He handed the lighter back to her but she shook her head and gestured for him to keep it.

"Time I passed it on," she said. "It can be a talisman for you and perhaps a cautionary object. A reminder you have to be both cautious and a gambler and know when to be one and the other."

Hersh slipped the object into his pocket.

"Every meeting is an education, isn't it?" he said.

"Only if we are lucky," she said. "Since I supplied the lesson you can supply the money for this meal."

CHAPTER 55

When someone had the idea of putting someone inside the clinic, Marian was apoplectic.

"Robert, that is bad karma," she said. "We're going to hell if we interfere with those kids."

Her boss reminded her they were using an abused wife to snare their prey.

"I'm not comfortable with that plan either," she said. "But if we disturb the sanctity of the clinic we might as well turn in our badges," she said. "I didn't agree with Detective Marshall about Hersh being a saint but his point is taken. If we mess this up we're going to be crossing guards in cities we never knew existed."

Robert Gregory chuckled but in the end agreed for the time being they would leave the clinic alone.

He gave no thought to telling her at this moment they were wiring the place. It was lonely at the top time.

He'd feel terrible if this blew up but he had been a cop and an executive too long for it to splash back on him. He would protect her as best he could but he wasn't putting his badge on the line.

"They are looking for results, Marian," he said. "So why don't we report progress next time they ask."

"So the slow and steady has gone out the window," she answered.

"It went out the window the first time he caught us spying."

"I guess," she sighed. "I only have myself to blame for being sloppy."

Gregory swiveled his head.

"You didn't get sloppy," he said, closing his door. "You said it before. This guy is good and it doesn't benefit me to deny that. There aren't many who could smoke us out and he's now done it repeatedly."

"So, what is next?" she asked.

"Next is your date at the concert."

"Can't wait," she said.

"We do what we have to do," he said.

"You know I like him, right?"

'I know you think you like him," he said.

"We will agree to disagree."

"But it won't affect your performance, right? You are still a pro?" he interrupted.

"A pro's pro," she said.

"Enjoy the concert then."

CHAPTER 56

The music was good and she found Hersh in great spirits. Neither talked business and Marian hadn't been this happy for a long time. They were holding hands when Loudon Wainwright played his first encore.

Exiting the venue, he suggested Thai food. She put her arm through his and they window-shopped while walking.

At the restaurant, she excused herself to use the restroom. Washing her hands, she looked in the mirror and didn't appear as stressed. She touched up her lipstick and returned in time for the hostess to seat them.

Both ordered a beer before picking up the menus.

"Thank you for inviting me tonight," she said.

"Well, thank you for coming."

"Wow, that sounded so stiff," she commented. "How about we pretend we didn't have a disagreement and we're not trying to get our balance?"

"No shop talk then?" he asked.

"God no," she shrieked. "That is the last thing I want to bring up."

He reached out a hand and she shook it.

"Good deal," he said. "We'll pretend you don't think I'm a criminal and I'll pretend you're not devising plots to have me arrested."

"Hey, way too harsh, my mellow," she said.

"Marian, I truly like you," he said. "But we're not going to have a relationship if we put our differences on the back burner. It is who we are."

She took a pull on her beer.

"I can't be Faye Dunaway to your Steve McQueen," she said.

"Understood. But Dunaway was trying to stop a thief. You think you're trying to stop a murderer."

"But the plot is the same," she said. "I can't and I won't let my feelings get in the way. If I get the goods on you then I'm going to pull the trigger."

"If I prove to you that you couldn't be more wrong, what then?" he asked. "How will we get past that? How will I be able to trust you again?"

"Somehow, I don't think I'll be assuming that guilt," she answered.

"So there is no real chance for us?"

"Only in the movies," she said. "But we can enjoy ourselves. I look at it as two people playing chess. Only there won't be a draw here. One of us is going to lose a queen and then concede. I can't see any scenario in which it is me."

"You may win," he said. "But you won't win with honor."

"What does that mean?"

"Let us say, for argument's sake, I'm guilty of everything you claim. Would bringing me down justify any means?"

"Are you asking me what is acceptable collateral damage?"

"Collateral damage is a Fed word. I'm asking how many innocent people have to be hurt for you to bring me in."

"The goal is zero but I'm not naïve. I know the toll these things take. But when you ask about innocent people you have to be clearer and more honest."

"I'm listening," he said.

"If bystanders get hurt physically, that is one case. But if taking you off the streets hurts the clinic, well, that is an abstract argument open to debate."

"So any means necessary is the mantra," he said.

Flashing an angry look, she made herself calm down before answering. "You know I'm not saying that," she said.

"So, the tail on Betty was justified?"

"No, that was a mistake and it happened without my knowledge."

"When people get hurt they don't care who had knowledge," he objected. "They just hurt."

"No argument," she agreed. "But the past is prologue and we need to learn from it."

"I won't let the clinic be compromised by anything you federals do to put me in a noose."

"Hersh, we've got 10 men and a dog on your case and we're going to prove you are out there disposing of people. I won't get into a debate as to who is a worthy candidate for your version of cleansing. Some people on the list would be on our list to shut down but your definition of shutting down is different than ours. And please don't tell me you're more effective."

"Wasn't going to raise an objection on any level," he said. "And I won't deny anything because you wouldn't believe me. But please don't piss down my back and tell me it is raining. I won't stand by and let my kids be hurt."

Looking around she noted happy couples and wished the two could be included. She wanted to have them jump into bed and let the world spin without them for a dozen hours. But they couldn't do anything if they didn't clear the decks.

"We're not investigating the clinic," she said.

"So you have no interest in what happens there?"

"Why would we? Unless we believe you are conducting other business in there we have no angle."

Marian reached over and brushed his face and let her hand linger for a moment.

"I hope you are not wearing a wire," she said with a sad smile. "I'll deny I ever said this but I couldn't be prouder of somebody for what you are doing with those kids. You are a G-D hero in my book. If you had only stopped there we could be a normal couple who read the paper and discussed our day over dinner."

"I do read the paper," he said. "I do eat dinner."

They laughed and enjoyed the respite from sparring. She did want to enjoy this evening and wait until tomorrow to resume her chase. She was nervous he had a different timetable.

"Hersh, I am trying to be as honest as I can. We are chasing you. I've been upfront about it. I'm not going to detail our game plan but you have my word I'll play it according to Hoyle."

Knowing that wasn't 100 percent true she colored. She just wanted this conversation to end.

The waiter cleared the dishes and she was happy to see Hersh order dessert. When the strawberry shortcake was served he asked for two forks and handed her one.

The first bite was always the best but before she could speak he pulled a tiny box from his pocket.

She prayed this would not be a bad surprise. Her prayers were not answered.

He opened it, looked, and then spun it so she could see.

"Our federal dollars at work," he said.

Marian knew what she was looking at, but picked it up as if confused. She rolled it around her palm and put her eye closer to what was a listening device.

"You guys went minimalist," he said.

"Where did you find it?" Marian asked, hoping against hope.

"This one was in the kitchen," he said. "Can you guess where the brothers and sisters were located?"

"Save me the misery," she said.

"Do you mind if I ask you a question?"

She nodded and dropped her hands back toward her lap.

"We found one in the nap room. We call it that for obvious reasons but it is also where kids can go to talk without us around," he said.

She kept her eyes closed taking in every word.

"Do you know what they call the nap room? They call it the Safe House. Because they reveal their secrets to someone whose secrets are as scary. As good as we are, you can't understand certain things unless you've lived them."

"Like soldiers," she said just to hear herself.

"Exactly," he said.

Hersh was not angry and she began to feel clammy and tight.

He continued to eat his dessert and talk. Anyone looking over would not have grasped the gravity of the situation.

"So now in this safe room comes Big Brother, possibly the largest bogeyman these kids could imagine," he continued. "They want to listen in. I'm going on too long but my question is a simple one," he said. "Why?"

Marian wanted to vomit but instead she shocked her herself by weeping. Not just shedding tears but actually sobbing.

Other than offering a handkerchief he allowed her to cry it out. She looked at him with red-rimmed eyes and then blew her nose so violently she could feel it in the back of her head.

"There are no words," she said.

"You might want to try," he said, but not in a snide way.

"It is cowardly of me to say I didn't know but I'm saying it anyway," she confessed. "I don't have an explanation to satisfy either of us. But I will get you one."

He made a steeple of his hands and bisected his face with them. He pushed out his lower lip with his tongue and then dropped his hands.

"What do we do now?" she asked.

"Well," he said picking up his fork. "I'm going to finish this cake and then I thought we could take a ride."

She raised her eyebrows and he laughed.

"Not take a ride like in the movies," he assured her. "Take a ride and see the city and maybe talk about something less depressing."

For some reason, she giggled as she agreed to the plan.

"I got a little dramatic there, didn't I?" she said.

"You mean the crying? Or were you referring to your fear I would dump your body somewhere it couldn't be found?"

"All of it, I guess," she confessed.

"Well, since your phone has a tracking device I won't be dumping your body," he opened with. "As for the crying, that was understood."

"Thank you for your understanding," she said.

"I'm nothing if not a gentleman."

As they walked to the car she spotted a man across the street with his girlfriend or wife. They only had eyes for each other but Marian knew better. She flipped them the bird. Hersh took the same sightline and could only laugh.

CHAPTER 57

None of them was surprised about the listening devices although they agreed the nap room device was particularly vicious.

Hersh was surprised none seemed angry. Betty was nervous about the talks she had in there but Frankie explained the bugs were swept before anyone could have been caught on tape.

His paranoia had him investing in a sweeper that daily ran through the place. It was a good enough program to catch the feds because a former government employee designed the system.

After Betty went to pick up lunch they talked of putting all projects on hold. The law was going to stick like a barnacle for a long time but there was no harm in waiting until they became less vigilant.

"I guess Peter's uncle got a reprieve," said Frankie.

"He doesn't know how lucky he is," said Hersh.

Roza spoke next saying, "I know this will sound crazy coming from me but we have to let the police handle anything over there for the time being."

Hersh and Frankie looked at her and knew how serious the situation had become.

"I am going to have to expedite my exit plan," he said.

There was nothing any of them could say. Hersh's exit plan meant one of two things. Either his plan would fail and he'd be dead or arrested or his plan would be a success and he'd be so far away from the action you'd need a map and a compass to find him.

Either way they would probably not see him again. If he failed, they needed to distance themselves. He was too clever to put them in a vice but they needed to avoid getting caught in his wake.

If he made it to the other side, he might send them a message but it would be so coded and so cryptic it might as well be from a stranger.

"How close do you think they are getting?" asked Roza.

Hersh had his fingers just an inch apart.

"They circled for so long I thought we could get by. But bringing in Marian was a master touch. She'll hang onto this case until it is gristle and bone."

"I repeat my offer of erasing her from the board," said Roza.

"That isn't who we are," said Hersh.

"I'm not entertaining Roza's offer but I do want to add we can't be who we are if we're not here to be who we are," said Frankie.

Before they could explore deeper, Betty came back with lunch. She was worried because they looked worried. That was something she never saw.

It was a quiet and quick lunch. Hersh got up to check the children in the nap room. He cracked open the door and stuck his head in. Clemenza led him to where he found Peter curled up but not sleeping.

"Not sleepy, big man?" Hersh asked.

"Not sleepy," he said.

"I figured you'd be tired after spending all those late nights with the ladies."

The boy giggled and Hersh smiled. He knew this 13-year-old had grown-up worries. He suffered the death of a brother he couldn't probably grieve. He tiptoed around his uncle and imagined all sorts of dangers for his grandmother.

At any other time Hersh and Frankie would have been more help. Hersh kissed the boy on the forehead and whispered to him, "You are not alone."

The boy smiled and Hersh watched his eyes get heavy and close. Clemenza and Hersh didn't move but when it was clear Peter was truly asleep they moved around the room checking on the other mats.

Finally, Clemenza was satisfied and circled before throwing his body down and closing his eyes. Hersh took a final glance and shut the door.

When he returned to the kitchen he found himself as the topic of conversation, and Betty gave him a hug.

"I don't want you to leave," she said. "But I'll be prepared for it if you do. And I'll be okay."

He put his forehead on hers. He picked at his food but never really ate and then wrapped it in the wax paper and placed it on the bottom shelf of the refrigerator.

When he closed the door, they were looking at him and he said, "Scorched earth."

"No," said Roza.

"No," said Frankie.

"Why not?" he asked.

"You said it before," answered Frankie, "it is not who we are."

"It is never too late to be who we might have been."

They shook their heads.

"Nobody thinks in terms of human beings. Governments don't. Why should we? They talk about the people and the proletariat; I talk about the suckers and the mugs. It's the same thing. They have their five-year plans; so have I."

They looked at him now like he was delirious.

"You know where that speech came from? Anyone?"

He waited a beat or two.

"Harry Lime in *The Third Man*," he said.

"So now you are Orson Welles?" said Frankie.

Hersh put his finger on his nose.

"But Welles wasn't the hero," said Frankie.

"I've stopped believing I'm going to be a hero," said Hersh.

"You can never stop thinking that," said Roza. "That is death."

Betty stared around the room and knew the mood needed to change.

"A fish walks into a bar," she shouts.

The room is still and all heads swivel toward her.

"The bartender says, 'What do you want?' The fish croaks, 'Water!'"

There is a second delay before the room explodes in laughter. Before they can stop, Frankie says, "A penguin walks into a bar and says to the bartender, 'Have you seen my brother?' The bartender says, 'I don't know, what's he look like?' "

As everyone continues to howl, Clemenza trots in to announce the kids are starting to wake.

This time Roza takes the dog and goes to settle the kids.

"She never does that," says Hersh.

"Roza knows if she stayed you'd continue with that crap about death and scorched earth," said Frankie.

"I'm not saying we do it, I'm saying we hold it out as an option."

"You are a scary person these days," Frankie said.

Hersh got a big grin and punched his friend on the arm. They wrestled briefly but as soon as Frankie got Hersh on the ground it was over. He reached and pulled Hersh up. He wanted to say something but didn't.

Instead he put on his jacket and grabbed his helmet.

"I'm going to take a ride and when I come back I expect sanity to have returned."

"No promises, brother," said Hersh.

CHAPTER 58

There was a time I suggested a scorched earth policy and got shouted down.

I was probably not serious but sitting here in this mess I'm thinking I could have done worse.

When you cast the film, look for a middle-age Al Pacino who roams the clinic out of his mind on power and fueled by alcohol.

"I'll show you 'out of order.' You don't know what 'out of order' is, Mr. Trask. I'd show you, but I'm too old, I'm too tired, I'm too fucking blind. If I were the man I was five years ago, I'd take a flamethrower to this place!"

I know what Pacino meant when he says he's too old, tired, and blind. I'm two of those now and will be the third when my organs shut down.

Before this I was in great physical shape. The upside is I'm going to finish this. The downside is the end will be sloooooow and painful. I want to believe I'll cowboy up but I'll probably be squealing like a newborn.

Trust me when I say if that happens I won't be putting it in this report. I want to keep some pride. Since they won't lower the flags at half-mast for me I at least want to hold onto the dignity of death.

Straight up, I was never fooled by the feds' use of Mary Doss. I'm not an idiot.

Mary was a perfect choice in their minds. But it showed laziness to me. It was transparent.

But you are thinking of how it ended and figured they must be geniuses. They weren't. I got too cute and heroic. I thought I could save her, the child and myself. I wasn't totally wrong but this isn't a business you win with percentages.

It is hard to comprehend the things I did. If I didn't know myself, I might agree I needed to be punished for my sins.

A jury of my peers would say "guilty, your honor," but they would feel bad and I don't think any would talk about it with pride. In fact, some would lead lesser lives because of what they had done.

Is this a touch of poor sportsmanship on my part? Probably. But why should only the winners get to write history. The losers' side is sometimes more interesting.

But back to Mary Doss.

She's free but I hope she doesn't think the feds were responsible. There will be bad nights for her when she's sitting with her beautiful daughter and she'll realize the man who made it possible didn't make it out.

She'll carry that weight. She'll curse me for what I did to her husband, then she'll thank me. She'll know this was never going to end without bloodshed.

As I said before, I am not the Lone Ranger or Roy Rogers. I'm not shooting the gun from your hand.

What is it Robert De Niro says in the *Untouchables*?

"I want you to get this fuck where he breathes! I want you to find that nancy-boy Eliot Ness. I want him dead! I want his family dead! I want his house burned to the ground! I wanna go there in the middle of the night and I wanna piss on his ashes!"

So first I'm Al Pacino and then Robert De Niro. Talk about a complex. And the strange truth is, I'm more of a Spencer Tracy, Henry Fonda in *The Grapes of Wrath* kind of guy.

"I'll be all around in the dark - I'll be everywhere. Wherever you can look - wherever there's a fight, so hungry people can eat, I'll be there. Wherever there's a cop beatin' up a guy, I'll be there. I'll be in the way guys yell when they're mad. I'll be in the way kids laugh when they're hungry and they know supper's ready, and when the people are eatin' the stuff they raise and livin' in the houses they build - I'll be there, too."

I feel better getting that off my chest. If I can believe this is a movie, then I can believe someone will call "Cut!" and I can walk out of here and wait for the next two-reeler.

But it isn't going to happen, is it? No, it isn't.

I coulda been a contender.

CHAPTER 59

Peter showed up with a bruise on his cheek and a cut lip.

It was all any of them could do to keep Frankie from jumping on his bike.

None could physically restrain him but they calmed him down. It was Peter begging him not to leave that did it. That and the teenager claiming it was his fault, something they had heard so many times.

So Frankie didn't do anything about Peter. He figured to play the long game. In the end, when it hit the fan, Frankie was not involved.

Two days after Peter was "disciplined," his uncle was shot coming out of a bar. He would live but somebody shot him from behind, blowing out both his knees. The cops chalked it up to a bar room disagreement. When it happened, Frankie and Hersh were on a long-distance drive picking up a client.

Betty was alone but no one thought of her.

Hersh heard about the shooting before Frankie and if he hadn't been with the man 90 miles away he would have marked his friend suspect No. 1.

The TV and newspaper gave little detail and no one was talking. Frankie had taken a ride to talk to Maise Williams. He made sure she was okay and assure her he was not involved.

"I can't say I'm surprised," she said. "I know what kind of life he's led. I don't want to be one of those parents who thinks her child is never responsible. The way he treated Bobby was a sin and the same with Peter. I want to say, 'He's not bad, he's just drawn that way,' but I know it wouldn't be true."

Not being able to help himself, Frankie laughed.

"What?" she said with a smile. "You think I'm too old to watch *Who Framed Roger Rabbit*?"

"I would never think that, Mrs. Williams."

"Not hip enough?"

"Definitely a 'no.' "

"Not white enough?"

"Well, maybe there is that," he said.

Now she laughed.

"It is good to laugh," she said. "Otherwise, I don't know if I could get through the day."

She got up and fiddled in the cabinet behind her. A minute later music was playing and Frankie was smiling.

"I love Art Tatum," he said.

She closed her eyes and soon she had drifted off to sleep. A mother and a grandmother spent a day worrying about her family and the only thing she got was another day older.

When he got on his bike Frankie noticed he was still getting stares, but some were smiling and a few older women waved hands in appreciation for what he had done for Maise Williams.

He roared off with mixed feelings about Peter's uncle. The man lived a life that promised violence but he wouldn't revel in bad fortune.

When Frankie returned, he sensed something off. It was quieter than usual and the easiness usually surrounding the place was missing.

Clemenza was refusing to leave Betty's side.

When it was nap-time, and the bills had been paid, Hersh looked at the dog and asked, "Which well did Timmy fall down this time?"

Hersh called Frankie in and both studied the dog and Betty. Clemenza figured his work was done and trotted into the nap room to be with the kids.

"Soooooo, Betty," Hersh said in a light tone. "Anything you want to tell us?"

The young girl was cleaning but Hersh calmly got up, took her by the arm and sat her down in the chair opposite them.

"Please don't make me unleash Frankie. He'll be so cloying and sanctimonious you'll admit to the Lindbergh kidnapping before the day is over."

Frankie gave his friend a withering look and took Betty's hand in his. "Does this have something to do with Seth?"

"No," was all she said.

Then she cried. They didn't press her but after a minute she walked to the closet. She bent down to the floor safe, opened it, and pulled out a handgun.

"How do I clean this?" she asked.

Frankie got up and took the gun. He didn't speak but smelled it and checked for missing bullets.

He mouthed "two" and put the revolver on the desk.

Betty broke the silence and she didn't waste a lot of time getting to the crux.

"I've known it was there," she said. "It scared me at first but I figured it couldn't harm anyone being where it was. I convinced myself it was for protection but I'm not naïve. I've known violence all my life and I know violent people. I love you for it all the more."

As they talked, Frankie brought out oil and a rag and started to clean the gun. He broke it down on the table and wiped it piece by piece.

"Did you fire this?" asked Hersh.

"Yes," said Betty.

"When?"

"That is not a soup question," she said with a sad grin.

"Did you go down to the bar and put two into Peter's uncle?" he asked.

"Well, I knew Frankie couldn't do it. And I knew you wouldn't do it."

They nodded.

"The two of you have performed miracles with Peter and there are days when I forget why he's here. But I'm the one he confides in and I wasn't going to let him go undefended."

Wrapping up each piece in a different cloth, Frankie put them in a bag. When he returned an hour later he nodded at Hersh.

To Betty he asked if she had been seen.

She shook her head and her friends breathed a sigh of relief.

"Now what?" asked Betty.

"Now you live with it," the two men said in harmony.

"That's it?" said Betty.

Getting up from his chair, Frankie kissed her on the forehead. Hersh cupped her chin and looked her in the eye.

"No, that isn't all," he said. "Not by a mile. You killed Miles and you're going over for it."

She looked at him blankly and he smiled.

"Just a little Sam Spade for you," he said. "What we need you to do is live your life as normally as possible for the next few weeks. Do you think you can do that?"

"I can try," she said. "Then what?"

"By then you'll know whether you can live with it," said Frankie. "If you can't we'll figure out how to get you over it. If you can, and God help you if you can, then you live your life and hope something like this never happens again."

Handing Betty the leash he indicated she needed to take Clemenza on a walk while he talked to his partner.

"How long of a walk?" she asked.

"He'll know," said Hersh.

When Betty closed the door, they slumped into their chairs and joined their hands, making it look like a prayer meeting was going on.

"This is not good," said Frankie.

"You think?" answered Hersh.

"Really not good," repeated Frankie.

"Well, our little girl has grown up," followed Hersh.

"How did this happen?" asked Frankie.

"We're contagious," was the answer he got. "We got sloppy and let Betty too far into our business. I knew it at the time and didn't do anything about it. I'm still not sure I was wrong."

"With the feds on your tail this probably wasn't the time for her to make her bones," said Frankie.

"You have to kill somebody to make your bones," said Hersh. "So we need to lower the temperature in here."

"Are you afraid she won't be able to live with this?" his friend asked.

Hersh shook his head and Frankie nodded. He had the same fear.

CHAPTER 60

Sleep was not going to come for Marian. As she looked at Hersh she wondered whether he had demons.

It was beyond her how he could sleep the sleep of the innocent. He told her about the shooting and she couldn't shake the feeling he was involved.

She spent a lifetime looking at perfect alibis and he had the stink of the shooting all over him.

She wanted him off the streets but not erased. If it came to him being harmed, she would allow him to go free. It was the way it was now and she'd live with it.

But she did want him caught. Like Bogart she would lose a few nights' sleep. She'd visit him and explain she wanted the violence to stop.

Yet, here she was in bed and nothing entered her mind but enjoying their time together.

Now he was sleeping and she wasn't, and it pissed her off. The competitive part of her wanted to send him over the edge of the bed with a kick.

Looking around she wondered if there were any clues. If she could get something on him now, they might not have to have a final showdown where violence was guaranteed.

Slipping out of bed, she threw on clothes. She wanted there to be a big sign flashing "clue, clue, clue." Short of that she just wanted anything allowing her to kick this can down the road. Something she could get a fingernail under and pry loose.

Even the most careful of men, and she had left one of the best sleeping, let something hang out. They either don't expect someone to catch it or they don't expect someone to be in a position to notice.

Certainly he knew she would be in this place. And maybe that was the clue she was looking for. What would you do if you knew ahead of time your nemesis was going to enter your sanctum sanctorum?

"I would try the floor safe underneath the kitchen table," came a voice from behind her.

"How do you do that?" she demanded. "How do you sneak up on me so easily"?

"Well," he yawned. "First of all, I wouldn't call rolling over and waking up exactly sneaking. But you say tomato …"

"I'm guessing there is no way for me to plausibly deny I was looking for proof of your guilt."

"You can try," he said.

"No. I'm going to be upfront about my deception. I was prying and praying there would be a confession typed out."

"I do my confessions longhand," he said, scooting out of bed. "It plays better on film."

"So, I should be looking for a special pen somewhere."

"In the desk are my writing utensils. And there is a Mont Blanc there."

She looked at the roll-top desk and considered opening it. But she knew she would find a Mont Blanc. She sighed and walked into the kitchen to make breakfast.

"Oh, come on," he said to her back. "You can't be giving up this easy. It can't be the getting there, it has to be the going that is good."

She extended her middle finger over her head as she walked. By the time she made eggs and toast, he had showered. She threw the plate down and took off for the bathroom to start her day.

When she came back 30 minutes later she was smiling and looked like the agent she was.

"You figure something out?" he asked.

"I did," she said. "I'm wasting my time trying to catch you the easy way. This is going to be damn hard and I should have not wasted time looking for the giant clue. I also realize I won't catch you but you'll get yourself caught."

"Please enlighten me,'" he said.

Waiting a beat, she smiled and then began to explain. "You're good, you're really good," she said and waited for him to make some kind of snide comment. When he didn't, she continued.

"You might be the smartest person I've dealt with. But you can't help yourself. You have to show off and show me how clever you are."

He didn't say anything but chuckled.

"Laugh all you want, funny boy, but it is going to happen," she said.

"Let me see if I have this straight. I'm going to be hoisted on my own petard because of my hubris."

"Pretty much so," she agreed.

"Your proof is your belief you are so stunning and so important I'll have to prove my brilliance to you. The case will hang on your belief of my inability to resist your charms. Well, one of us is hung up on themselves."

He caught her off balance for a second but only for a second.

"The proof will be in the pudding," she said.

"And will the frost be on the pumpkin?" he countered. "And will I be advised not to count my chickens before they hatch or will those chickens come back to roost?"

"You should put yourself on the stage," she said. "And the next one leaves at 5:15 out of town."

He laughed again.

"I could banter like this all morning but I've got children to see and you've got a trap to set."

She actually smiled, and then he dropped her off at her car. Even though she knew they were under watch she kissed him as she exited the car and gave him a little wave over her shoulder as she strolled to her car.

He knew she was putting on a show but it wasn't as showy as she thought. Their time together was ending. Neither would admit how sad that was but it did spice up the day.

When he got to work, he found Mary Doss but didn't see Kathy. He panicked but realized the girl was probably with the other kids.

"I didn't think she needed to hear any of this," the mother said.

"Understood."

"We are ready to get out," said Mary. "I don't want Kathy to live like this anymore."

"Do you want to leave right now? We've got places to put you until the real move but if you want to disappear we can make it happen."

She considered what he was saying and shook her head.

"I think we're going to be okay at home," Mary said. "I don't think we're in any danger from Eddie. He isn't home a lot of the time anyway. But when we leave I want it to be forever and I don't want to mess this up by leaving too soon."

Hersh didn't like the plan but said, "Any indication, and I mean any way the plan isn't going your way, you need to call and we'll be there for the two of you. You take no chances."

"I won't," she said, then paused. "And thank you."

"Don't thank me until you are miles out of this and your daughter is in a new school. And maybe not until she's walking down the aisle."

Mary laughed but when Hersh went to his desk to write down a number she got a sad look. And before Hersh turned back she had to refrain from crying. When he handed her the slip of paper she was smiling again.

Before she left she put her hands on his face and stared into his eyes.

"I also want you to be careful," Mary said. "Do not take any unneeded chances for us. We will be okay. It will be fine if you can't give us everything you promised."

He took her hands and held them. He also had a look of sadness but quickly switched to a cheerier demeanor.

"We're a full-service institution," he said. "We will deliver the best we can. But I appreciate what you are saying, so don't leave thinking I didn't hear your offer."

He watched as she and Kathy walked hand-in-hand up the street. They appeared happy. He ran his tongue around his teeth and remembered he had another dentist appointment.

The game was afoot.

CHAPTER 61

Hersh found Roza watching a workout and taking notes. He noticed the tremor but more worrisome was seeing her pull her sweater tighter on a day when most people were in short sleeves.

"Working or playing?" he asked.

"Mostly working but I'm enjoying myself so much I can't really say I'm breaking rock."

"As long as you break the bank," he joked.

She looked at him. "Remember the chat we had where I told you to think about what you say, and if it isn't clever then just don't say it?"

"I remember."

"But you chose to ignore it?"

"Well, who took the cookie out of your lunch this morning?" he demanded.

"Okay, now that is better. Give me a kiss."

As he did he realized she felt a little cool. He watched her work the numbers and didn't interrupt. When she finished, he began to speak.

"A guy is at the track and standing in the front row as the horses cross the finish line. All of the sudden he grabs his chest and falls over. A crowd surrounds him and someone shouts, 'Is he alive?' A friend looks at him and shouts back, 'Only in the double.' "

He feels he's back in her good graces.

"So, I'm talking to Marian and she thinks no criminal can get away with their crimes because at some point they have to brag about it to someone," he said.

"And what was your witty riposte?"

"She was taunting me and I almost told her I knew somebody."

"Then you realized I wouldn't appreciate that."

"I realized you'd have me silenced."

"So you can learn a lesson, then?"

"I didn't tell her because it wasn't her business and I'm better trained than that. Do you really think I'd let a pretty face unravel the past 30 years?"

She paused.

"Well?"

She smiled.

"I'm thinking. I'm thinking."

This time he smiled.

"That woman is right, you are going to get yourself in trouble."

"That woman?"

"I'm not going to say her name."

"Very mature," he said.

"I was in the bathtub the other night and my wife called me immature. I disagreed and then she sunk all my boats."

"I love Jacob Cohen," he said.

"That's Rodney ..." she said before stopping herself.

'You are just too easy," he said with a laugh.

"Well, laugh at this, Junior," she said with triumph in her voice. "We've got dinner at your parents tonight."

He stopped laughing.

"Nice touch," he said. "I'm going to assume this was your doing."

"You don't see them enough."

"I see them three times a week," he said.

"They want you to bring that woman."

That stopped him.

"Please don't say, 'Are you shitting me?' First, I am not and second it has become your go-to phrase."

"Any other surprises?"

He felt sick when she grinned at him.

"Well, Betty will be there and so will Frankie."

"Are you shitting me?" he said.

"I am not, in fact, shitting you," she said.

He put his face in his hands and began to laugh and when he looked up he saw his grandmother was also laughing.

"I guess this is proof hell exists," he said.

"It could be fun," she said.

"No, it couldn't," he answered.

"I meant for the rest of us," she said with another grin.

"Payback is a bitch," he said.

"Is that her name?" said Roza.

"Wow, you are really six years old, aren't you?"

What he saw flash in her face made him kick himself for his insensitivity. But the look passed. He loved her for changing the subject.

"Who will be making money for us today?"

"You won't believe it when I tell you," she said with glee.

"Try me."

"There is a horse running in the feature called General Sternwood."

"Oh, come on!" he shouted.

"They might as well just give us the money."

"Who could be that big of a Raymond Chandler fan?" he asked.

"Not our concern. When God puts a gift on your doorstep you don't ask why."

Hersh put his hand to his grandmother's forehead.

"You mentioning God? Do I need to call a doctor?"

"I've a got a fever and there is only one cure," she said.

"More cowbell?" he asked.

"More cowbell," she agreed.

When General Sternwood pissed on the field, Roza and Hersh went to separate windows to collect. This time they needed more than her satchel bag to take home the winnings. While Roza was sweeping the bills into her purse, Hersh was stuffing $100 bills into every pocket.

They met back on the bench near the finish line and watched the final two races without betting.

"What should we do now?" he asked.

"Why don't you walk me to the backside," Roza said.

"Can do."

"I feel like John Rockefeller," she said.

"But you won't be handing out just dimes, will you?" he asked.

During the short walk to the barn area, Roza began to shiver and Hersh took off his jacket.

As they got closer to the shedrows he sensed her getting stronger. He was amazed at what the mind could convince the body to do and thankful to see the vintage Roza.

Sidling up to her favorite grooms and exercise riders she slipped them some bills. He could tell by their faces she was adding some spice to her normal tips.

"How much did we give away back there?" he asked.

"About $7,000," she said.

He whistled.

"We're not done," was her only comment.

"Figured we weren't."

By the time they left the track, her bag was much lighter and so was her step. But as they approached the car she began to lag. She needed help getting into the front seat and before he reached her apartment she was sleeping.

He scooped her up and carried her into the elevator. She woke, said a word or two, and then slumped onto his shoulder.

She slept for two hours and when she came into her kitchen for tea she found him reading a book.

"What are you doing here?" she said.

She never asked how she got home and he let it go.

"Did you think I was going to go to dinner without a game plan?" he asked.

"Did you get ahold of the woman?"

"I did."

"And?"

"I'm picking her up in an hour."

"So why are you still here?"

"I need to give you a ride to your car."

She surprised him when she said, "Don't bother. Betty is picking me up."

He asked for her to be gentle at the dinner and was thrilled when she laughed.

Roza had not told the whole truth about the evening. When Hersh arrived, he found not just his parents, grandmother, Betty, and Frankie but also his three sisters.

"Et tu, Brute?" he said to his oldest sister.

"I wanted to tell you," said Sophie, "but Zora and Harper said I couldn't."

"Oh, you lying bitch," said Harper.

Hersh held up his hand and looked at his grandmother. "You guys don't need to protect her, I know who the lying bitch really is."

"Hersh!" said his mother. "Don't talk like that."

"Don't worry," said Roza. "He already knows I'm leaving everything to the girls."

That brought laughter and Hersh introduced Marian to his family. She sensed the coolness from Roza but the others were glad to finally put a face to a name.

"So how did you two meet?" asked Zora.

"Blind date," said Marian.

"You did not?" squealed Sophie.

"Do you use that voice with your patients?" asked Hersh. "Because you wouldn't be my doctor if you sounded like Betty Boop."

"I am your doctor," his sister said.

"Well, I'm shopping for someone else."

"Please let me know where I can send your files to," Sophie said. "You were always a lousy patient."

"That would be too much of a coincidence," he said and dodged the napkin she threw.

"So," said Harper to Marian. "Word on the street is you are a fed."

"Guilty," said Marian.

"Do you carry a gun?" asked Harper.

"Does she carry a gun?" countered Hersh with a shake of his head. "That is a question a child asks. She works for the government. Does she need to put her weapon on the table?"

"Is that what you say to her when you are alone?" giggled his sister. " 'I'm putting my weapon on the table.' "

"I won't have that kind of talk during dinner," said her father, but he couldn't keep a straight face.

"So, what kind of child was Hersh?" asked Marian.

"I can answer that," said Zora.

"Please don't," her brother said.

Zora pointed her finger at him and said, "Payback is hell, my brother."

"That should be 'my brotha,' " said Harper.

"Don't get me sidetracked," said Zora. "He was the sweetest boy ever. He used to play dolls with me when my friends couldn't come over."

"He still makes me play dolls with him," said Frankie. "I have to be Ken to his entire collection of Barbies."

"Ken is gay, you know," said Sophie.

"Why does everyone think that?" asked Frankie. "Can't a guy dress well and be a gentleman and people not think he's gay? Well, we've got an expert here. What say you, Hersh?"

The sisters laughed at their brother's discomfort.

"He had a mean side, though," said Sophie.

That stopped them as they stared at her.

"Hersh had a mean side?" asked Harper. "Please tell."

"Like you don't know," said Zora.

Harper looked confused and saw her brother shaking his head at her older sister.

"Is there something I don't know?" she asked.

Zora looked around the table and said, "William Mackerson?"

"What about that bastard?" Sophie asked.

"You know we really don't have to go into this now," said Hersh.

Zora looked at him and picked up her fork and stopped talking.

"Whoa, whoa, whoa," said Sophie. "You need to spill. We have no secrets in this family."

"I'm sorry, Hersh," said Zora. "I thought she knew."

"Tell the story. Harper should know," repeated Sophie. "We *don't* have secrets."

Hersh put his face into his hands and signaled to his sister to continue.

"You remember your junior prom?" Zora asked.

"Of course I do," said Harper. "Son of a bitch tried to get me drunk."

Her parents looked at her and the group realized secrets did exist.

"Then he tried to force me to have sex with him," Harper said. "Then he spread it around the school that I did have sex with him and my reputation was ruined. Even my friends didn't believe me. He was a football star."

"Well, your reputation wasn't ruined for long, was it?" asked Sophie.

Harper thought about it and smiled.

"Yeah, it turned out he wasn't that bad of a guy," Harper said. "He told some friends later he made it up because he was embarrassed I got out of the car and walked home."

"Oh, he was that bad of a guy," said Zora.

Harper looked confused and saw his sisters were looking at their brother.

"What could Hersh have done?" she said. "He was still in middle school."

Everyone was surprised when it was Roza who said, "You had a talk with him, didn't you?"

Hersh smiled weakly and lifted his head to agree.

"What could you have said?' said Harper. "You were just a kid."

They all looked his way.

"I asked him to reconsider his position," Hersh said.

That brought a huge laugh from Frankie. "Reconsider his position. That is so rich."

"Well, what did he say then?" asked Harper.

Frankie slapped his friend on the back and massaged his neck as he began to speak.

"Hersh caught your prom date walking home and asked if they could talk," he began. "The peckerwood had no idea who he was. When Hersh said he was your brother, the guy laughed and said something I won't repeat here."

"So, what happened?" asked Harper.

"Hersh went medieval on him," said Zora.

"It happened so fast," said Hersh, as if apologizing. "One minute I was asking him to stop talking about you and then I stopped talking."

"It was good I happened to be trailing my boy," said Frankie. "He would have killed him and I don't mean metaphorically."

Marian looked over but Hersh refused to meet her eyes. She knew what Frankie was talking about. She had been up close and personal just recently.

"Hersh?" said Harper.

"Our brother has a temper," said Sophie as she ruffled his hair. "I got the story from Frankie and the funny thing was, I never doubted it. It never entered my mind he would embellish a single fact."

"How could I not have known this?" asked Harper. "How come I never saw this side of you?"

"You guys talk like this was a weekly thing," said Hersh. "The guy insulted my sister and I asked him politely to desist."

"Then you introduced him to Rodgers and Hammerstein," said Betty, who looked over to see Frankie giggling and then holding up his hand for a high-five.

"You've been keeping one in reserve," laughed Frankie. "I'm stealing it for my own."

"But he never looked like anyone had hit him," said Harper.

"He missed gym for a few days," said Frankie. "Then he shrugged off the bruises as football-related. But the guy was passing a little blood for a while."

"You will remember, Hersh had to go to the doctor himself," said Zora.

"Dr. Himmelfarb," said her brother under his breath.

"Yes!" Zora. "I had forgotten his name. He straightened you out, didn't he?"

"Completely healed me of all aggressive thoughts," said Hersh. "Now, can we go onto another story?"

"What ever happened to William Mackerson?" asked Marian.

She was confused when they all started laughing, including Hersh.

"Well," said Sophie. "First he was a Division II All-American football player. He got into some NFL camps but nothing came of it. And now ..."

"And now?" asked Marian.

Sophie let the question linger for a bit, savoring the punch line.

"And now he's in the Justice Department. He uses his middle name."

Marian stared at her and then her eyes flew wide open. "W. Michael Mackerson?"

"Small world," said Zora.

"Unless you have to paint it," said Hersh in his best Stephen Wright deadpan.

Marian slumped in her seat like she had been sucker punched. It explained so much and it was humiliating Hersh knew why he was being investigated before she did.

She hated being played.

"Motherfu ..." she said before realizing she was in someone's home, and halted.

Hersh looked at his family. "Hey, she's just talking about Mack."

That got a laugh but not as big as when Zora started to sing and then dance.

Mack
Who's the black private dick
That's a sex machine to all the chicks?
(Mack!)
You're damn right
Who is the man that
would risk his neck for his brother man?
(Mack!)
Can ya dig it?
Who's the cat that won't cop out
When there's danger all about
(Mack!)
Right on

Even Marian smiled being entertained while in the belly of the beast.

Robert certainly had to know Mackerson was involved and it would be hard to believe he didn't know why.

She felt a bit ill, like she was on the side of the cheaters.

"I should probably go home," she said to Hersh.

"Or you could just have a big stiff drink," he said.

"How come I'm always humiliated whenever I'm with you?" she asked.

"Don't feel bad," said Frankie. "We are all humiliated to be with him."

Even Marian laughed.

"Does anyone mind if I change the subject to something more pleasant?" asked Hersh.

He waited a beat and said, "Grandmother and I bet on a horse called General Sternwood today."

That brought a grin from his family and a look of confusion from Marian.

"General Sternwood is the father of Lauren Bacall's character in *The Big Sleep* and for some reason my grandmother thought reading Raymond Chandler to that miscreant over there was a good idea," said Harper. "It might explain a few things."

Marian nodded and made a mental note.

"These two," Sophie said, pointing at her brother and grandmother, "sometimes talk like they were from the 1940s."

"He used to be so happy when I read to him," said Roza. "It relaxed him more than the children's books you girls used to love."

"I like *Blueberries for Sal*," Hersh protested. "I'd like to think I was just appreciating literature. I mean, I still remember the opening from *The Red Wind*."

Hersh closed his eyes and started reciting.

"There was a desert wind blowing that night. It was one of those hot dry Santa Ana's that come down through the mountain passes and curl your hair and make your nerves jump and your skin itch. On nights like that every booze party ends in a fight. Meek little wives feel the edge of the carving knife and study their husbands' necks. Anything can happen. You can even get a full glass of beer at a cocktail lounge."

When he finished, they all clapped and he took a mock bow.

"I still don't see how that was appropriate reading for a baby," said Hersh's mother.

"It gave me a taste of the good stuff early," he said. "It also kept me from getting beat up as a second grader."

Frankie smiled.

"I'm about to pound this little guy and he says to me, 'Dead men are heavier than broken hearts.' I look at him and before I can do anything there is Roza, and Hersh quickly became the second most frightened second-grader."

Before anyone knew it, they had changed the subject to Zora's students and Sophie's patients. Harper told about a passenger who thought he could fly better than her so she got up and left him in the cockpit.

Hersh and Marian left with a shopping bag of leftovers. Before he took her hand, he whispered in his grandmother's ear. She smiled but it wasn't the happiest expression Marian had seen.

"She okay?" Marian asked when they were walking to the car.

"She's slowing down and I never thought that could ever happen," he answered. "I thought she would run forever."

"She seems pretty hale and hearty to me," she said.

"You should have seen her then?" he said and couldn't help chuckling to himself. 'My she was yar."

"That is from a movie, right?" she asked. "I have a lot to learn."

"And a short time to get there," he added.

She looped his arm and they walked without further conversation. She knew at the house there was plenty of talk going on about her.

Marian's hunch was spot-on.

"I like her," said Zora.

"You like everyone," said Harper.

"You don't like her?" asked Sophie.

"No, I like her but I was just saying Zora is not the litmus test for likability. She's too easy."

"Funny, that is what they used to say about you in high school," Zora zinged her younger sister.

Sophie and Harper looked at her with astonishment and then all three were howling with laughter.

"Idaho?" said Harper. "You da 'ho.' "

That started them in another round of laughter.

While they were snapping dish towels at each other, Roza walked into the kitchen to say good night.

"What do you think about Hersh's date, grandmother?" asked Zora.

Roza knew she couldn't tell the truth. But she wasn't going to fake affection either.

"If you have nothing good to say about someone you shouldn't say anything," Roza said. "I've got nothing to say about her."

"Grandmother off the top rope," said Harper.

"The bitch is back and drops the mic," said Zora.

CHAPTER 62

One positive about having your life flash before you is you're a short time from asking questions of those passed to the other side.

In fact, I think I see Raymond Chandler coming me for now. What is it you're saying, Ray?

"What did it matter where you lay once you are dead? In a dirty sump or in a marble tower on top of a high hill? You were dead, you were sleeping the big sleep, you were not bothered by things like that. Oil and water were the same as wind and air to you. You just slept the big sleep, not caring about the nastiness of how you died or where you fell. Me, I was part of the nastiness now."

Fooled you, didn't I? You didn't really think I saw Raymond Chandler. Let's get real. I'm about to take the dirt nap but it doesn't mean I have to be morose.

More than ever I need to keep my sense of humor. But it would have been cool to have these people helping me to pass over. That would have been worth reincarnation.

It is my belief Kathy is too young to know what happened. She just knows she's living a life without the dangers her father brought home. But Mary has to know the cost. When you see her, tell her I know she never expected someone to die in her place.

There can be no guilt. She never expected the price would be this high. And if it is any consolation, tell her I had a plan and it blew up in my face.

Both of us were supposed to get out, but as the great philosopher Mike Tyson used to say, "Everyone has a plan until they get punched in the face."

If saving a mother and child is my final act, then I can live with that. A little gallows humor.

CHAPTER 63

Marian spent the week prepping Mary Doss. She wanted her ready. When it was Thundercats Go, there would be no time to improvise.

Mary picked New Mexico to disappear and Marian thought vanishing into the Badlands had a karmic ring. It didn't hurt to put thousands of miles between you and your troubles.

If Mary had second thoughts she didn't voice them, and if she was nervous she didn't show it.

For obvious reasons, they kept Kathy in the dark but the little girl had to play her part. No one wanted to trust a child with a secret this big but neither did they want the plan to crater because she wasn't prepared.

It was a tightrope walk Marian and Mary were walking. Three women hatching a plan that would damage a man they all owed was a fact too cruel to dwell on.

When they were done for the day, the adults hugged and Marian gave the girl a piece of candy and told her it was for being so patient while grown-ups discussed boring stuff.

She knew if everything went as drawn up only Mary and Kathy would get a happy ending.

They would be free and clear. Eddie Doss would lose his family, Hersh would lose his freedom and maybe more. Marian would lose Hersh.

Alone in her office she wanted to cry but stared at the wall instead.

At some point she heard her name but only when she shifted her gaze did she see her boss in the doorway. He was waving his arms and smirking.

"Just finished up with the Dosses," she said.

"Everything go okay?"

"Perfect. Mary is locked and loaded."

"So why the faraway look."

Laughing to herself she gazed at her boss, who was expecting a long explanation.

"A horse walks into a bar and orders a beer," starts Marian. "Bartender says, 'Hey buddy, why the long face?' "

Gregory looked puzzled.

"I'm not following," he said.

"I just thought a little levity was in order," she said. "I think I've been on this case too long. The opposition is starting to affect my moods."

"As long as they're still the opposition," Gregory said.

Marian gave a sharp look but her voice was calm.

"Questioning my commitment?" she asked.

"Are you questioning it?" Gregory fired back.

She didn't answer that question but asked another.

"How come you didn't tell me about Mackerson?"

Stung by the quick jab, Gregory's head snapped back. Then he smiled.

"There really are no secrets, are there?" he asked.

"So you knew about Mackerson's past with Hersh and his family?"

"Not at first."

"When?"

"I'm not sure that is important," he said.

Marian took measure of a man she trusted with her life and career.

Now she doubted herself. She wished she woke every day with a friend like Frankie.

"May I speak freely, sir?" she said.

Not since her first year had she called him "sir."

"You've never had to ask," he said.

Marian gathered herself by closing her eyes and taking a few breaths.

"How did I miss the fact you've turned into an asshole?" she said.

"Wow," he said with a chuckle.

"I'm sorry," she quickly said. "What I meant to say was, when did you become an asshole and untrustworthy?"

"I think you made your point the first time," he said.

"One of the reasons I liked working with you, sir, was you weren't a desk man. You knew how dangerous things are out there. But you kept me in the dark on this one and put me in danger."

"You were never without backup," he said.

She continued like he had not interrupted her.

"The Robert Gregory I knew would have never done that to an agent. It would be a point of pride. I will finish this assignment, sir, in the exact way you tell me. We will put these people away. When it is over, one of two things will happen. I'll either be fired or we will never work together again. I realize the former is more likely but I live in hope."

"What is this all about?" he said sharply. "Be careful what you say next. Our friendship, your job and your future all depend on it. Most bosses would have sent you packing already."

He looked over and realized she wasn't affected by what he said. So, he changed tactics.

"Can we talk this through?" he said. "Maybe I made some mistakes here but I made them thinking it was best for this investigation. You are right, I've been on the street, but don't forget you've never been in my job."

Gregory was uncomfortable by the look in his agent's eyes. But he was surprised when she said, "Fair enough," and went back to looking out her window.

"So, we're good?" he asked.

"Yes, sir, we are."

"I need a better answer," he said.

"Yes, sir, we are clear. You want to run this investigation your way and you are the boss. So we run it your way."

He nodded and should have let it go. But he couldn't.

"You know, I've overlooked a lot of things you've done," he said and immediately regretted it.

She looked at him with such pity he grew angry.

"What does that look mean?" he demanded.

Again, she ignored his question.

"Let me know when you want the Dosses to make the move," she answered instead. "Everything is in place and we should wrap this up within 24 hours of them being in the clear."

This was not the time for a showdown but she was right, the two would not work together again. He had seen this in agents before. He owed her a soft landing but she was a danger to herself and the bureau.

She had crossed a line.

"So I can tell Chief Mackerson everything is ready?" he asked.

One side of her mouth curled.

"I assumed he had been listening to our conversation already."

She picked up her purse and walked past her supervisor, who let her go before he adjusted his tiepin.

CHAPTER 64

W. Michael Mackerson wasn't a man who dispensed pleasantries so Gregory wasn't surprised when the chief was all business.

"Will she conduct this investigation like we asked?" Mackerson said. "Because I have to tell you, Robert, I have great doubts."

"Sir," he said and smiled when he realized he was paying his boss the same mocking respect, "she's a pro."

"Not that you could tell by her actions," Mackerson growled.

"In fairness to her she thought we were having a private conversation," Gregory said. "Which reminds me, how did she know you were wired?"

Gregory shrugged.

"I'm not sure she wasn't fishing," he said. "She was angry being kept in the dark."

"We'll we make those decisions," said Mackerson.

"She felt blindsided because the suspect knew about you before she did," said Gregory, treading a line.

"My past relationship with the subject was none of her business," Mackerson said. "We are tracking a cold-blooded killer and that is what she needs to keep in mind."

"She has never forgotten, sir. This was her plan and it was clever. It plays on the weakness of this guy. If you can call loyalty and sympathy a weakness."

"Robert, don't make a mistake thinking he's the good guy. He was a violent prick when we were kids and he's only ratcheted it up since."

"Understood, sir. For what it is worth, I think Marian agrees with you. She might admire some of the things he's done, but in the end, she'll have him in cuffs."

"If the rumors are true it won't be the first time she's slapped cuffs on him," said Mackerson, who followed with a bawdy laugh.

Gregory gave his boss an appreciative chortle but only because he didn't want to show his disapproval for such an immature reaction.

"I heard she's gone quite the distance for us," added Mackerson. "In fact, you might say she's gone all the way for us."

This time Gregory didn't bother to humor him. It was frustrating to play footsies with a guy he didn't like.

But he would sacrifice Marian's career to get up another rung. He wished he were like Mackerson, who truly believed he was ascending on merit.

Gregory stepped over bodies and hoped he would still be able to sleep.

Marian was wrong about him being an asshole. He was just a nasty bastard.

"You get it?" roared Mackerson. "All the way?"

"Good one, sir," said Gregory.

"She is gone as soon as this is over," said Mackerson.

"I think she knows, sir."

"Don't put your career in jeopardy by helping her," said Mackerson.

Gregory snorted.

"You need to keep her on a tight leash, Robert, until we get the SOB behind bars."

"Understood."

"If this goes sideways you can't be standing on the path," said Mackerson.

Gregory wanted to tell his boss he'd be standing next to him, far enough away to avoid splashed mud but close enough to accept the kudos and promotions.

"I look forward to the day when I'm going to be toe-to-toe in an interview room with him," said Mackerson.

Gregory thought, "No you don't," but merely nodded.

"Good things come to those who wait," said Mackerson. "We'll see how smug he is when he's answering questions from the bureau. We'll eat him and his lawyer alive. Then we'll deal with his girlfriend."

Gregory got himself out of the office and left the building. He needed fresh air. He had many great days as an agent. This would not be one of them.

Marian was looking out the window and saw her boss crossing the street. Her anger was gone but sadness had invaded.

CHAPTER 65

A few weeks before it hit the fan, Roza was rushed to the hospital.

When Hersh made it to the fourth floor, Frankie was there.

"Glad to see you, big man," Hersh said before noticing the man was crying.

"She scared us," said Frankie. "Heart attack but the doctor says she should recover."

They looked at the sleeping woman, who appeared to be another senior citizen rushed to the hospital.

"But those aren't tears of joy," Hersh said.

"They did other tests," said Frankie. "She's got a mass in her chest."

"How bad?"

"They don't know," said Frankie. "More tests."

"Well, we're not going to get a lot of information from the doctors. They're cowboys," said Hersh. "Maybe a nurse will be forthcoming."

Frankie actually smiled.

"I don't think we'll have too much trouble. I'm guessing the doctor will be more forthcoming than you think."

Frankie was a good patient advocate without saying a word and Hersh didn't doubt a few words went a long way.

"So, we prepare ourselves," said Hersh.

"She's too scary for cancer," said Frankie.

"I pity the fool," said Hersh.

When Roza opened her eyes, Hersh was holding her hand and Frankie was napping in a chair.

"Well, I know I'm not in heaven because you two are here," she said.

"I guess the experts were wrong," said Hersh. "Don't they say a medical emergency can change a person's personality? She's as unlikable as before."

Frankie chuckled and reached and squeezed Roza's other hand.

"Tell me at least your subconscious gave you some winners at the track while you were out," said Hersh. "I'd hate to think all of this was for nothing."

Roza gave a weak smile.

"You better hope I don't live long enough to actually change my will," she said.

"Old lady, don't threaten me or I'll pull the plug right now," Hersh said.

Roza started to laugh but choked a little instead. That brought in a nurse, who didn't say a word after clearing the tubes running in and out of her patient.

When she left, Roza had Frankie close the door.

"We are going to get a flood of family and friends soon," said Roza. "So I want to ask you guys a favor quickly."

They looked at her.

"Don't let me linger," she said. "If it comes to that I need to go."

Frankie looked stricken.

"Well, answers one question," she said. "Turns out the big man is too much of a pussy. So Hersh, you need to be the guy."

Hersh nodded and asked, "You want me to do it now?"

Roza pointed her chin at Frankie and said, "You know, he's a Nancy-boy but he can still hurt you."

"First," said Frankie, "'Nancy-boy' is a pejorative term and not nice. Second, I'm preaching nonviolence these days."

Even Roza was able to laugh. By the time the hospital room began to fill, the two men were so exhausted they excused themselves.

Frankie kissed the old woman on the forehead, and when Hersh leaned in to do the same he made his grandmother smile when he whispered, "I promise."

CHAPTER 66

When Mackerson and Gregory left for the day they took an elevator together. On the street they were going separate ways, but before Gregory could take off, his boss put his hand on his elbow.

Gregory looked where Mackerson was pointing and saw Frankie and Hersh sitting on a bench. They didn't get up and only a pro like Gregory knew the duo was looking at them.

"What do you think they are doing?" asked Mackerson.

"Right now, they are having a late lunch and if I'm not mistaken they are having it on us."

"Well, I'm going to stop this right now," said Mackerson.

This time Gregory was the one to reach out a hand.

"You don't want to do it, sir," he said.

"Why the hell not?"

Gregory wanted to tell his superior he was overmatched but said, "Because you'll give them the satisfaction of knowing they got to you. Best to ignore them."

Then Marian came out and followed her bosses' gaze. When she saw Hersh and Frankie on the bench she barked out a laugh.

"You didn't tip them off, did you?" asked Gregory.

He was allowing her to tee off with her frustration. She returned the favor by shaking her head. She didn't have to agree with Gregory to show the respect he deserved.

He smiled and wished he were standing next to her and not Mackerson.

It should have ended there but Mackerson was a bureaucrat, not a pro.

"You better not have, agent. If I find out you did, it will cost you your badge."

Gregory rolled his eyes and prayed Marian had cooled down. He didn't want any confrontation out in the open.

Marian again showed her training and smiled.

"I'm the one who is going to catch them," she said. "I'm not likely to bring in more people to confuse the issue. Besides, Hersh doesn't seem to need help, he appears to have our office wired."

Gregory winced. He knew she didn't mean literally wired but Mackerson wasn't a man who had a lot of nuance to him.

But he wasn't listening to Marian. He turned to leave. If he didn't say it, it wasn't worth much.

"Thank you for that," said Gregory.

"Mackerson is an asshole but he's your asshole," Marian said.

He smiled.

Marian was about to say something but saw Frankie was alone. With horror, she saw Mackerson and Hersh headed in the same direction.

Tugging on her boss' sleeve they took off at a trot and after two blocks caught up with Mackerson.

Surprised, he halted in the middle of the block.

"We thought you might be followed," said Gregory.

"By whom?" his boss asked.

"We weren't sure," said Gregory, surprising everyone with the lie. "Marian saw a guy in a hat appear twice and we wanted to make sure."

When the two didn't see Hersh they shrugged like they were embarrassed.

"Sorry, chief," said Marian. "I guess the case is making me jumpy."

Getting dismissed with a wave of a hand, Gregory hopped into a cab and Marian retraced her steps. At her building, she found Hersh and Frankie back on the bench.

"Now what the hell was that all about?" she asked as the two howled.

"She's calling you a snail," said Frankie, unable to contain his mirth.

Marian wasn't about to be shined on.

"Why did you do that?" she asked.

"Because I can," said Hersh.

"You can be such an ass sometimes," she said.

"Sometimes?" asked Frankie.

She sat down on the bench and stared at people passing by.

Then she turned to Hersh and got a huge grin.

"Even on Central Avenue, not the quietest dressed street in the world, you guys looked about as inconspicuous as a tarantula on a slice of angel food cake."

Hersh giggled in appreciation. "You've been reading Chandler."

"Guilty," she said, feeling pleased at scoring a Marlowe point.

"Roza might have to change her opinion about you," he said.

That got them all quiet as they thought of the woman who probably didn't have much time to change her mind about anything.

"How did we find ourselves here?" she asked.

"Is that rhetorical?" asked Frankie.

They stayed quiet and let the time pass. It was Frankie who would look at his watch and break up the meeting. He was meeting Peter.

Frankie nodded and moving quicker than a man his size had the right to. Frankie disappeared, only to reappear moments later gunning his bike.

"He is one scary dude," she said.

"Only if you're on the wrong side," he said.

"How do you make sure you're on his right side?" she asked.

Hersh smiled. "By not trying to arrest me."

CHAPTER 67

With the Racing Form opened on her bed, Roza looked like a new woman when Hersh visited.

Her hair washed, she had thrown away the hospital gown and dressed in her own clothes. She didn't look vintage but passed for healing.

"Please don't forget to walk over to the backside if we win today," she told her grandson.

"I'm not likely to pass it up," he assured her.

"It does put the piss into it," she agreed.

"Everyone is asking about you at the track," he said. "I told them the doctors were at your beck and call but the best medicine would be some winners."

She smiled and passed over her list of horses. He studied them, then folded the paper and put them into his jacket pocket.

"How are they treating you here?" he asked.

"Three hots and a cot," she said.

She looked at the clock and implored him to go so he could bet the early double. He kissed her. "No famous last words?"

"Large bills."

When he disappeared, Roza moved the *Racing Form* to the chair, now too weak to pick up a water glass. Picking horses and talking to her grandson took her strength. She didn't wake until moments before he returned seven hours later.

Out of sorts when he walked into the room, she thought she was seeing her father, but her mind soon cleared. She smiled when she saw her carpetbag at his side.

"How good?" she asked.

"Pretty good," he said, popping the clasps and letting her look.

Pulling out a fistful of money, she held tight.

"You are the anti-gambling lobby's worst nightmare," he said. "They want everyone to be a cautionary tale and you keep piling up wins. If this were a movie you would have come up a cropper and learned your lesson."

"I've had losing days at the track," she said. "I just happen to be on a hot streak."

"People dream of these kinds of streaks," he said.

"It helps to have friends," she reminded him. "I've been called off by a lot of trainers on their horses. Helps to even the odds."

He reached for the money and put it back in her bag. He went to rest it in the corner of her table but she shook her head.

"You need to keep it," she said. "It won't do me any good in here. Share it with your sisters."

This was the first time his grandmother acknowledged how sick she must be. There was no way she would part with her winnings no matter the circumstance.

"What about the nurses?" he said.

"Already taken care of," she said.

"I thought they looked unusually happy for people working 14 hours a day."

"Nurses and teachers are proof of God's existence," she said.

"Wow, you must be taking such strong stuff if you are again admitting there is a God."

"I'm an old lady who has lived a full life. And for almost 50 years I've been a gambler. So, I know there is no upside not placing a little saver bet on the chance I've been wrong all these years."

"Fair and smart enough," he said.

"Now, how are you hedging your bets?" she asked.

"How do you mean?" he answered.

"They are coming at you hammer and tong and I won't be here when it is head-clobbering time. I can't be your consigliore."

"You're not a wartime Consigliere, Tom. Things could get rough with the move we're making. But I never thought you were a bad consigliere. I thought I was a bad Don."

Without the energy to laugh she just smiled.

"I saw where Alex Rocco died," she said. "I loved him as Moe Green."

"He was making his bones while I was dating cheerleaders," said Hersh.

"We had a good run, didn't we?" his grandmother asked him.

"When you look in the dictionary under 'great runs' the picture of us is there," he said.

"You know, I learned English with a dictionary. I'd learn 40 words a day and after I was fluent, I learned 10 definitions. I was a demon for knowledge," she said.

"You still are," he said.

"My I was yar."

"You were, Ms. Hepburn. You were."

She fell asleep and he left. He was tired and he felt bad for the agent sitting in the waiting room. So he walked to him and sat.

"I'm not coming back tonight," he said. "She's resting and I'm tired so why don't we all take the night off," Hersh said.

"Pardon me, sir?" said the man.

"Look, we could do the dance and you could try to convince me you're here for a loved one but you don't have the jewelry for it," said Hersh. "Give yourself a break and take off. I give you my word I'll call your office if I do anything that needs someone to tail me."

The agent looked at his shoes in confusion and then looked at Hersh. He got a slow smile. "You promise?"

Hersh gave the scout's honor salute and the man walked him to the elevator.

"Do you mind me saying you're a strange one, sir?" said the agent.

"I don't mind and you're not the first to say it," Hersh said.

"I'm a good a good agent and I like to be able to tell my children I chase the bad guys and put them places where they can't be bad anymore," the agent said.

"Give them some security," said Hersh.

The agent nodded. "But sir, I just wanted to tell you, when we get you I won't be telling my children anything."

"I think that is the nicest thing anyone has said to me in weeks," said Hersh.

The agent sadly nodded and pushed the button down. The two didn't talk during the ride.

CHAPTER 68

Mary and Kathy Doss were moved to one of Hersh's safe houses on Tuesday, and on Thursday they were gone. By Friday, Eddie Doss needed two planes and a bus to get near them.

Marian knew where they were; she had given Mary a tracker and in case she got cold feet had slipped another into her luggage and a third into her purse.

She should have felt worse about using them but felt so close to ending this that the adrenaline eliminated most of her standards. Hersh had covered his tracks so she didn't think the family was in danger but she had to admit that wasn't at the forefront for her right now.

Hersh had given no indication he had hidden a family. He acted like his day had been normal. Besides worrying about his grandmother, he didn't show any disturbance in his routine.

She had to admire that but she also had to mirror it. It was show time for her also.

When she awoke, he was gone and although she didn't know at the time, she would never see him again. She first thought he had stepped out to get them breakfast but saw he had made coffee and laid out pastries.

Walking around his place always made her feel creepy because she never resisted a chance to see if he had mistakenly left her something to go on. She called him to assure he would not walk in on her snooping.

Not getting an answer she hesitated only a minute. Again, she didn't expect to find anything but this wasn't the time to play percentages.

Getting on her knees she looked under the bed, the sofa and even the refrigerator. She felt stupid but she'd feel worse if somebody else found something après-capture.

Scouring the bathroom, she thought he had employed a cleaning service. She knew how silly it was but the absence of anything in the place was telling her something.

In the bedroom, she glanced at the open door to his closet and saw reflected light. She moved his dress shirts to find the biggest home safe you could have without damaging your floors.

Knowing she couldn't open it frustrated her but it was nice to know it was here. Somebody with different skills could take a crack later.

The safe wasn't going anywhere and the risk of him moving documents or whatever else resided there was a chance she would take.

In a few days, this would be moot. She didn't figure he would be able to manipulate a move from prison. Though she should not count out an attempt.

She took a shower and walking out of the bedroom she almost had a heart attack when she found somebody in the kitchen.

"Betty, what in God's name are you doing here?" she said.

Betty looked at the agent with a mixture of rage and pity but her gentler side broke through.

"I'm here to warn you," she said.

"From what."

"Not what but whom," the young girl said.

"From you?"

That made Betty laugh and it took time to be controlled enough to talk again.

"Oh, I wish," Betty said. "Wouldn't it be great to inspire that kind of fear and respect?"

"It is a little overrated and sometimes sad," said Marian.

Betty shook her head in agreement and smiled again. But there wasn't a lot of humor behind it.

"Right now you're deep in bat guano, but it hasn't reached the level of suffocating you," said Betty. "You need to watch your step."

Marian was not about to interrupt the girl but motioned they sit.

"It is not a state secret that you are after Hersh," Betty said. "You think he's guilty of something and I respect the hunch on your part. It wouldn't do for me to say you're wrong. But he's a god in my eyes and I'd lay down my life for him."

"Of course, he'd never ask you to do that," interjected Marian, who matched Betty's smile.

"That is what makes my declaration safe," she said. "But he'd lay down his life for me. He's made that clear in any number of ways. In a cruel twist, he'd probably lay his life down for you."

That was a piercing arrow but Marian did not give anything away.

"I know you and your brother officers think you have everything figured to the fifth decimal point," continued Betty. "I'd venture to say none of you believe Hersh will be able to shimmy out."

Marian wasn't going to disagree. The plan was top-heavy with agents and it would be tough for Hersh to do anything but surrender when it was over.

"I want to throw one variable into your mathematical plan," said Betty. "I'm not sure you guys gave enough weight to the X-factor."

"X-factor?" asked the agent.

"Frankie is the factor no one can claim to know the true value of," explained Betty. "He may do what Hersh wants. He may do what you expect. And he may surprise us all."

"What do you think he'll do?" asked Marian, who was surprised to get an answer.

"You know, my two guys are *Godfather* fanatics," said Betty. "Men can't get enough of the first two movies because Vito was so smart and in some ways heroic. We know that is romantic bullshit but be that as it may . . ."

"So, Frankie is Vito?" asked Marian.

"Don't convince yourself it is far-fetched," countered Betty. "People look at Frankie and see Sonny or Luca Brasi. That is a mistake. But Frankie is not Vito. We both know Hersh is Vito. Always has been. He's got the brilliance, the balls and the patience. But here is where Frankie becomes your worst nightmare. He is Michael. He might wait for the death of Vito and the baptism but he'll come after you."

Betty went to stroke the damaged side of her face and looked for a moment like she was aping Marlon Brando.

"What if our plan includes neutralizing Frankie?" asked Marian.

That brought on a paroxysm of laughter.

"You don't have enough agents," she said.

"That's a pretty high opinion of someone's power," said Marian.

Betty gave a backhand flick and continued.

"You would have a better chance of turning Frankie," Betty said. "It would be a million to one and it would be a better bet than making him a non-factor."

"Suppose we just arrested Frankie," the agent asked.

"Where is Frankie right now?" countered Betty.

Marian realized Betty wasn't here to warn or threaten her but as a messenger.

"So he's into the wind already," said Marian.

Betty confirmed that.

"So why don't we arrest you and flush him out?"

Betty put out her hands. "A girl always loves to get more bracelets."

"Frankie sent you, didn't he?" asked Marian.

Betty put her finger on her nose.

"Betty, you need to get some distance. This is going to get messy for a lot of people on both sides."

"Is that what you think keeps me up at night?" asked the young girl. "Do you think my nightmares include a federal agent taking me downtown and slapping me around?"

The two women looked at each other and both began to laugh.

"Too dramatic?" asked Betty.

"A little," said Marian. "But I liked it. More importantly I believed it. You won't be the weak link. We thought maybe Roza but I don't think she's going to be a factor for either side."

A tear came to Betty's eyes and she turned away. Marian smiled thinking she had found the weak link.

However, when Betty turned her face back toward the agent, Marian knew she had been mistaken.

"You don't want to put Roza on the board at any time," said Betty. "I said I would never tell anyone how to do their job and now I'm going to break my pledge. You cannot imagine the carnage being unleashed if you try."

"I'm not sure you aren't giving Roza's statue a bit too much weight."

Betty grimaced.

"Lady, imagine the worst shit storm you've ever gone through and then lace up your gummy boots for something to the nth power," said

Betty. "You think you're wading through bat guano now? Please take what I'm saying seriously. I'm not saying don't go after Hersh. That is your job and we can have a discussion about the merits at a later date. We'll agree to disagree on that. I'm telling you the body count is not on your abacus if you bring in Roza. You might as well shoot his dog at the same time."

Like he knew he was being talked about, Clemenza trotted in. He had been gone and Marian figured he was spending the night with Frankie. But here he was and he looked at the agent.

"You remember what Clemenza tells Michael while he's making the pasta?"

At first the two women thought it was the dog speaking to them, but when they turned around they saw the man who followed him in.

"Frankie!" shouted Betty.

He nodded and called the dog.

"He tells Michael to take a long vacation," said Frankie. "And Michael asks him how bad it is going to get."

Frankie had the floor, so he continued.

"Clemenza says, 'Pretty god damn bad. Probably all the other Families will line up against us. That's all right. These things gotta happen every five years or so, ten years. Helps to get rid of the bad blood. Been ten years since the last one. You know, you gotta stop them at the beginning. Like they should have stopped Hitler at Munich, they should never let him get away with that. They was just asking for trouble.'"

Marian wasn't about to ask who was Hitler in this version.

"You warned me early," said Marian to Frankie. "I'm giving you that. I never thought it would come to this but here we are."

The devilment on Betty's face couldn't be contained as she looked at Frankie.

"Herr Janning, it came to that the first time you sentenced a man to death you knew to be innocent."

Frankie hooted and put up his hand for a high five.

"Outstanding usage," he bellowed. "Just outstanding."

Betty beamed but Marian didn't lose her resolve.

"You guys want to believe you're on the high road but you're not," she said. "Your boss is a stone-cold killer. Don't quote chapter and verse of his good deeds. It doesn't cancel out the other. You can quote from all the movies and it still won't make you on the side of the angels."

"Don't expect us to disagree with you," Betty said, surprising the agent. "About Hersh, we have no comment. But even if what you say is true, even if he's the killing machine you paint him to be, don't make the mistake of making you guys the good guys."

"Explain to me how taking a killer off the streets doesn't fit us for the white hats," the agent said.

"Marian, you may be the dumbest genius I've known," said Betty. "You are not the good guys because you'll sacrifice a good man at the altar of public opinion in the belief this is going to get you a corner desk in Washington, D.C."

"Betty, I have more experience so believe me when I say you can never confuse a man who does good deeds with a good man," said Marian.

"Oh, you don't need to have experience to know who the good guys are. This is so easy for me. The guy who throws hot grease in your face is the bad guy. The guy who kills the grease thrower is the good guy."

Marian didn't comment. This had to be a non-starter for her.

"Marian, there are things you will never know," said Betty. "Both of us know what it feels like to walk into a room and have every eye on you. But you'll never know what it feels like to know those eyes are cringing, judging or about to thank God it wasn't them. Hersh didn't kill my tormentor, as you know. He's still running around in an almost constant drunken state. But if I asked Frankie or Hersh to erase him from the planet they would close shop for the day, walk into my neighborhood, and get the job done. Do you have any idea of what kind of loyalty that engenders?"

"Surprisingly," said Marian, "I do. I admire it, I truly do. I'm not shining you on. But we just draw the line at different points."

Frankie and Betty looked at each other and both stuck out their lower lips as they took in what the agent was saying.

"Fair enough," said Frankie. "No argument there."

"Hey, is the coffee still warm?" asked Betty.

CHAPTER 69

"And now, the end is here

"And so I face the final curtain."

Please tell me you didn't see this Sinatra song being on the movie soundtrack?

I wanted to wait until the hour was nigh. And it couldn't be more nigh. It is so nigh I'm busting out of my skin.

"My friend, I'll say it clear,

"I'll state my case, of which I'm certain."

Here is where the band really has to swell. You need to sell it with emotion. There can't be a dry eye in the house when Frank finishes singing. Even the people who thought I got what I deserve have to be moved.

"I've lived a life that's full.

"I've traveled each and every highway;

"And more, much more than this,

"I did it my way."

When I said earlier the plan blew up in my face it didn't mean nothing good came of it.

I got to see Roza one more time. We are both in a race for time and while I wouldn't give a tinker's dam for either of our chances I'll give odds I'm getting to the finish line ahead of her. She'll last me out just for spite, and if there is an afterlife she'll give me grief for it.

But she won't be far behind me. When I went to see her "she was using her strength as carefully as an out-of-work showgirl uses her last good pair of stockings."

Don't look that up. It is from *The Big Sleep*. I just can't help myself. I think the oxygen is starting to get blocked to the brain.

I'm going to sign off because I've got to comb my hair and try to get some of this blood out. I promised myself I'd live fast and leave with a good-looking corpse.

This is a promise I'm going to try to keep.

CHAPTER 70

Letters came for Frankie and Betty and they shared them with no one. Including each other.

Frankie was with Peter when he got his and a mention of the boy made Frankie admire his best friend even more.

Frankie:

If you are reading this then I must have put my plan into motion. I don't know if it is waterproof but I am hoping it doesn't leak too early.

Roza does not believe in God but I knew there was a higher power the day you threatened to beat the crap out of me. I was scared but knew God had rewarded me for something I had done.

We had a great ride and hopefully this isn't the end. But let us not be a couple of little bitches that complain about it. If you are one know I'll come back somehow and slap the living shit out of you. And if you even dream of slapping me you better wake up and apologize.

We've done some dodgy things but I'm not going to regret one. I know you want to take care of business with Peter. I can only say God bless you. If you decide to take it to the limit, let me say I'm there in spirit.

Take care of Betty and take care of Clemenza. They both are going to need you now.

You are now the head of the Five Families. Hopefully you'll rule with an iron hand but with a fair one.

Don't take any wooden nickels and if the phone doesn't ring you'll know it was me.

Betty got hers at the clinic. She kept it in her shirt pocket until the break and then found a quiet spot and opened it.

Betty:

In the words of Neil Young, I am gone but not forgotten. This is the story of Johnny Rotten.

The plan is unfolding and the game is afoot, my friend. Hopefully, this letter will be one in which you can tease me about being a drama queen.

But if turns out not to be the case please know my life was made better knowing you. The courage you showed was inspirational and the happiness you spread was legendary. For all the good Frankie and I try to do it pales to what someone like you can bring.

I'll be writing Mrs. G about other things but I'll also thank her for having the foresight to ship you to us. As you know, the woman is a genius and there is no way any of us can thank her for what she's accomplished and hopefully will continue to accomplish. You are at the top of that list.

If for any reason I don't stick around, please remember there is no situation in which a piece of movie dialogue or a song lyric does not make it better.

If there is time, I'll be thinking of some of my regrets but I won't be thinking long. It wouldn't do me any good anyway. I wouldn't trade what happened nor would I alter the game plan.

We all would like more time but tomorrow is never guaranteed to any of us. I've known and accepted that.

This is not a letter suggesting you live the life I did. That would be selfish and rather stupid of me. But in all honesty, it was a pretty cool ride.

I can tell how you feel about Seth. Don't let life get in the way of that.

Don't take any wooden nickels and if the phone doesn't ring then you'll know it was me.

Betty folded the note. She didn't notice Clemenza sitting by her chair but she wasn't surprised to see the pup there. She scratched his neck and sat there for a few minutes before she rose to check on the kids. The letter made her both sad and elated.

CHAPTER 71

When Mrs. Grimes walked through her door she was sorting the mail and didn't look up until she felt a presence.

She dropped everything when she saw him in her rocker.

"Jesus Christ, Hersh, you gave me a heart attack," she said.

He smiled, then got up and picked up everything she dropped.

"Sorry," he said. "I'm trying to stay below the radar."

Now that she had her breathing under control, she prepared tea. Nervous, she spilled the loose tea on the counter before she was able to make a pot.

"Can I assume this is not a social call?" she hollered from the kitchen.

"Assume away," he said. "I was going to write but I figured I'd go with the personal touch."

"You wanted to say goodbye in person?" she said, bringing in two mugs.

Looking a bit surprised he told her yes.

"Yeah, no surprise with everything going down," she said. "Going to the mattresses or disappearing?"

"I don't want to say," he commented.

"Because then you would have to kill me?"

"No, but I wouldn't be able to say that for everybody."

"Well, here's another nice mess you've gotten me into," she said.

They sat and talked. At times she was amused and at times she was horrified, but when he left she was oddly lifted and she had a little hope.

After leaving Mrs. G, Hersh disappeared for a few days. He prepared for this day. It would have been near impossible for his friends to find him so he wasn't worried about anyone else.

He read and watched his favorite movies. He had enough food for months. He made no calls, turned off all electronic devices and let time pass.

When he emerged, he would be in combat mode and ready for the outcome. Since the feds had camped on his doorstep, he was out of rounds and he was weary.

He punched Slaid Cleaves on his iPod.

I'm not living like I should
I want to be a better man
A sinner's prayer upon my lips
A broken promise in my hands
I know that there will come a day
A heavy price I'll have to pay
I keep pretending to be good
But I'm not living like I should

Thinking all bases were covered he was stunned to receive a package on what he figured would be his final day.

He grinned like an idiot when he saw it addressed to Terry Lennox.

Only Roza would use a character from *The Long Goodbye.*

Hersh:

If you are reading this then the end is near for either you or me or both. I wrote this a while ago, so if anything has changed, excuse the small errors.

If you are wondering how I found your "secret" hideaway, let me say you are not Bruce Wayne living in Wayne Manor. You had to rent this place from someone and that someone was me. I've known for years this day would come.

You are old enough and wise enough to make your own choices but it never hurts to have another voice, so I'm going to show hubris and be the voice.

I might even fill in gaps in your knowledge. I've got so many secrets and there seems to be no need to keep all of them.

The first thing I'm going to say should go without saying but here goes anyway. No matter what happens, no matter the blood splatter, don't let any of it get on Frankie. We both know he'll wade through a river of fecal matter to be at your side. That can't happen.

I always felt he would continue to produce when we were out of the picture. He didn't fit the profile of a long-termer but life can kick you in the rear end. We need proof we existed and Frankie is our proof.

You'll need at least two exit plans and three is always better but only if the third is as brilliant as the first two. The goal is not to drown, so keep your head up. That means some tough choices and some people and things you don't want to sacrifice.

This isn't Abraham and Isaac stuff. You know that story was crap. If Abe was any kind of father he would have given the middle finger to the All Mighty and said, "Not with my family." But I digress. If you need to throw me onto the fire, do it. And this is not an idle suggestion. I'll handle whatever happens.

I'm a survivor and in all modesty, I'm smarter than you and more experienced.

I developed a blood lust you've never had and while you are a better person it makes me more likely to get away with what we've gotten away with.

Before I go medieval on your ass let me clear a few things up. People think I lived a life of vengeance and payback with little thought to anything else. They would be right about the first and wrong about the second.

To my own surprise, I had a wonderful life. I fell in love and that was the biggest shock of all. I had a happy marriage and your father is the light of my life. I love your sisters and you and I've done so many things I didn't think possible. I'm rich and powerful. Most people would sell their soul for that. I came out of the camps with no soul but I found it again and I'm thankful I wasn't just a ball of rage and hate.

You'll find legal papers in this package. If you get out of this and I don't then the legacy continues. I'm giving you this now because no matter how things work out for you, I won't be around long. I know because the doctors told me and I know they are right. I won't give you the medical mumbo jumbo but it spells out to "get you shit in order now."

Consider this getting my shit in order. Don't worry about sharing this. As far as money goes everyone is taken care of. I made money and I stole money from people who shouldn't have had it in the first place.

I have more money than many countries and I've invested it well. People are going to live on my dime for a long time.

But the real message of this letter is to survive and advance. There is no substitute. Last man standing and all that.

You will find loyalty is a valuable commodity but one you cannot count on. Do not expect from everyone what you get from Frankie. No need for me to try to illuminate how rare it is.

Last thing. You are smart but so are other people. Be careful of believing you can think your way out of every box. Sometimes you have to shoot your way out. Violence is an ugly thing and I am thankful for my ability to deal in it.

Hersh's eyes widened when he got to the financial aspects. He would indeed be able to live on this money if he lived at all. He assumed the clinic would also be getting cash but he had already taken care of them.

Time was up for Hersh and his window of greatness was slim, but it was there. His legacy would be in others' hands and he recognized the possibility of his family's disgrace. But you couldn't do this job with an eye on the clock.

It was show time.

CHAPTER 72

Maise Williams was drinking iced tea and talking to neighbors when she heard the motorcycle. She called for Peter, who came outside and had a broad grin when he saw his friend.

Taking off his helmet, Frankie waved at the two people he now considered family. He hoped it was reciprocal because what he wanted to do would take some convincing, and only family would understand.

He pulled a package and gave it to the older woman.

"What on earth did you bring this time?" she asked.

"If I told you there would be no surprise," Frankie said.

"Well, come on in and let us see how surprised I'll be."

While Peter made lemonade, the adults sat down as she made a production out of unwrapping the paper.

"Oh baby!" she said when she saw a rare Dexter Gordon recording. "This is too much."

"It isn't," said Frankie. "A guy I know owed me a favor and I got a great deal. I don't have the turntable to do it right and you are the person I thought of."

"Why are you so good to us?" she asked.

"Someday," said Frankie, "and that day may never come, I will call upon you to do a service for me. But until that day, consider this just a gift on my daughter's wedding day."

The grandmother began to giggle at Frankie's awful impression but stopped when she saw he had something on his mind.

"You sit down and you tell me what you need," she said.

Frankie turned sheepish and realized the two toughest people he knew were women and both now elderly. If Roza and Maize Williams ran the world it would be a lot different place.

"Ms. Williams," he started.

"Anybody gives me Dexter Gordon better be calling me Maise."

"Maise, he said with a smile. "I need to do something and I need you to accept it. It is going to be hard but I want you to not reject me out of hand."

"Is it illegal?" she asked.

He chuckled and said, "No."

"Too bad," the old woman said. "I was up for getting into some trouble."

He laughed again and held up a finger for her to wait, and he walked outside. When he returned, he had a briefcase and he set it down on the coffee table.

"Things are changing in my life, Maise, and I'm in a hurry to cover some bases. There is a chance I won't be around in the future. It's likely I'll be going away. Either by choice or by demand."

"Does this have to do with my son?" she asked.

"It does not," he said. "I've done some bad things in my life but Peter's uncle was not one of them."

She signaled for him to continue.

"I may not be physically available for Peter," he said. "But somebody will always be looking out for you."

"Someone always has," she said.

He colored. "I'm not comparing myself to the Almighty, ma'am. I just meant somebody peeking in from time to time."

The old woman touched his face and began a silent prayer.

"Somebody will now be peeking in on you from time to time," she said. "As for us, we're going to be okay. What you've done is save this family and we won't forget you. We never expected you could stick around forever. That is not the way things work sometimes. We've been blessed and we thank you."

Taking the briefcase, Frankie opened it so only he could see. He seemed satisfied and closed the lid and looked back at his host.

"I love this briefcase," he said as a preamble. "Makes me feel like Matlock or Perry Mason. So I won't be leaving it behind. But there is something I want you to have."

He pulled out a sheet of paper and handed it to her.

"There is a lot of legalese so let me cut to the chase," he said. "This is a document that sets up an education fund for Peter. It will be enough to go to whatever school he chooses. That includes high school if you want to put him in a school in town."

Maise Williams' eyes filled with tears. "I accept," was all she could manage.

"Good," said Frankie. "But that wasn't the thing I needed you to consider."

She dabbed at her eyes.

"Well, well, well," she said. "The Lord is going to test me a second time."

Frankie looked back into the briefcase.

"Yes ma'am. He is. The fund for Peter can only be used for education. A family member can't tap into it for his or her pleasure. You can't pay bills with it and you can't start a business with it."

"Understood," said the grandmother, who knew exactly what he meant.

"But," continued Frankie, "I know you have obligations and so I want to leave you some money."

"Oh, no, that isn't necessary," she protested.

"Ms. Williams, you promised you would listen."

She sat back and pursed her lips.

"My business is about to split apart and we had an executive meeting about the cash that needs to be dispersed. We've got a list of people. If you all don't take it the government or people we don't want will get it."

She knew most of what he was saying wasn't true. But this was a good man trying to do a good thing and she figured if she accepted the few hundred dollars he wanted to give then she could consider it a good deal.

She looked at him and told him yes.

He pulled out a manila envelope and put it on the table next to the education document.

She gasped when she opened it.

"How much is there?" she asked.

"A little over $82,000."

She put the envelope down.

"I know you have expenses."

"Well, I could pay my son's hospital bills," she said.

Frankie looked a bit shaken.

"I can't pay the hospital bills with this?" she asked.

He shook his head no. "That has already been taken care of."

She was dumbfounded.

"I was telling you the truth when I said I had nothing to do with it," said Frankie. "But I know who was responsible and this is to help assuage their guilt. The other money is for you to use as you see fit."

"I might go to the casino with it," said Maise Williams. "Learned how to throw the dice from my father."

"They say craps has the best odds of any," said Frankie.

"I might buy me some of that crack cocaine," she said.

"You might."

"Might buy me some company for the night. Call up one of those services. Get me a fancy man."

"Well, now you have the money," he said.

"I do," she answered and reached out and hugged him. "I've got a special hiding place for this so don't you worry about the safety of it."

"Never crossed my mind," said Frankie.

"Will you be saying goodbye to Peter?" she asked.

"When the time comes, I will. And if the time doesn't come then I'll leave it to you. But the plan is not for me to disappear. Hopefully, the plan is better than that."

"Man plans and God laughs, according to my Jewish friends," she said.

"Nobody is laughing here, Ms. Williams."

"You take care."

"You too."

He paused when it looked like she wanted to say something else.

"Shoot first and shoot straight," she said before going into the kitchen to get her grandson.

Seeing Maise Williams was the easiest part of his day. Spreading joy doesn't take anything out of you even when you might be saying goodbye.

Frankie's next stop was the hospital. That was the toughest part.

Roza was resting but fading. Of course, they had no idea who was taking up a bed on their wing. When people see a tattoo, they see a survivor but miss much more.

But he was here for a key and a name.

He wasn't surprised when Roza opened her eyes when the shift was changing. They would have about four minutes before the new arrivals came to take vitals.

"Your timing is impeccable," she said.

"Bottom drawer, right hand side and under the socks."

He palmed the key and put it in his pocket all in one motion.

"Name?"

"Dr. Frederick Bauschbower."

Frankie arched his eyebrows.

"He owes me," she said.

He didn't embarrass her by asking what Roza had done or more accurately hadn't done to get this favor. By the time the nurse came on shift, they were talking about the mundane things a visitor and patient chat about.

Shortly, he was on the streets and then to a safety deposit box. Moments after he left the bank a black Taurus pulled up and an agent hustled in. Thirty minutes later the agent exited with a small key.

CHAPTER 73

The agents who were watching Eddie Doss were instructed to keep a low profile, and so they sat playing bridge. They didn't know what day someone was going to show up but they knew it would be soon.

When Marian knocked on the van door she found a loose bunch. Sometimes long stakeouts could get nasty, with agents starting to dislike each other and the smell getting ripe.

But this was different. They were parked far enough away to allow for easy come and go. It allowed them to rotate shifts, so no one had to sleep or even eat in the van.

"Nothing?" said Marian.

"Well, Eddie's had company but not the company we are on the lookout for."

Marian tensed. She had no idea what Hersh's first move would be and it would not surprise her if he hired a hooker to make contact. She grilled the men, who assured her it was strictly business.

"How do you know?" she demanded.

"I know her," said an agent, who was looking at a monitor showing the front of the Doss house.

"Know her from where?" asked Marian.

"The neighborhood. She and Eddie go way back."

Mollified but not convinced, Marian asked an agent to track her the next time she showed.

The second worst thing was Hersh getting hurt or killed. That was nothing compared to what would happen if this blew up in their faces.

Marian looked at her phone and thought about trying Hersh. She knew she wouldn't get him but she wanted to let him know the game was starting.

Once Mary Doss reached out, Hersh wouldn't back off. He probably was looking forward to matching wits. It would be fun until handcuffs came out.

She smiled thinking of Hersh taking her to see *The Maltese Falcon* on their last date.

"I thought you were a Raymond Chandler not a Dashiell Hammett guy," she said.

"Have you ever seen the movie?" he asked.

"I'm embarrassed to say I haven't."

As promised, she loved it. Especially when Bogart threw Mary Astor over.

Sam Spade: *I've no earthly reason to think I can trust you, and if I do this and get away with it, you'll have something on me that you can use whenever you want to. Since I've got something on you, I couldn't be sure that you wouldn't put a hole in me some day. All those are on one side. Maybe some of them are unimportant – I won't argue about that – but look at the number of them. And what have we got on the other side? All we've got is maybe you love me and maybe I love you.*

Brigid O'Shaughnessy: *You know whether you love me or not.*

Sam Spade: *Maybe I do. Well, I'll have some rotten nights after I've sent you over, but that will pass. If all I've said doesn't mean anything to you, then forget it and we'll make it just this: I won't because all of me wants to, regardless of consequences, and because you counted on that with me the same as you counted on that with all the others.*

Surprised when the phone chirped she was stunned when she saw his message: "It is the stuff that dreams are made of."

She excused herself from the vehicle and took a walk. She didn't see him but that didn't mean he wasn't there. What was he trying to tell her?

She liked to be deliberate but Marian could also gin it up to warp speed when things began to unfold.

Hersh was trying to change the pace of the game, and so he was pressing her. She knew that and she had to admire his tactics. A little pressure wasn't going to rattle her with the end in sight.

Hersh could see her from the restaurant window. He was comfortable being anonymous for another hour but she wasn't going to arrest him before he did anything.

He saw Marian look down at her hand and then put the phone to her ear. She nodded.

Hersh laughed when she rolled her eyes. The game was clearly unfolding to a conclusion so speedy that just holding on was going to be a major task.

Showtime.

CHAPTER 74

Maise Williams and Peter were playing chess when her son hobbled by. He was on crutches facing a long rehab. He wasn't drinking but the medication made him mean.

"Afternoon, son," she said.

"Lunch ready?" he barked.

"Been too busy to cook but there are leftovers to make a sandwich."

"I look like I can make a sandwich?" he asked testily.

She looked at Peter and sighed. He wanted to giggle but knew his uncle was watching, so he dropped his head and studied the board.

He heard his grandmother throwing plates around and minutes later she plopped a roast beef sandwich on the dining room table. Then she moved her bishop.

"You get me something to drink?" her son asked.

"No. I figure you can twist the top off a bottle."

Her son started to say something, then hopped through the kitchen door. He returned with a 7Up and dropped himself into a chair.

The two paid him no mind and he returned the favor until Peter started cackling when he took his grandmother's knight off the board.

"I never saw that one," said Maise.

"Quit letting him win," her son said. "You'll turn him into a sissy. The boy has to learn how to survive."

Neither acknowledged him and he thought about letting it drop but realized he had to reassert himself as head of this house.

"You listening to me?" he barked.

Maise Williams looked at Peter and said, "You listening?"

"I am, Grandmother," he said.

She looked over at the table. "Seems we are both listening," she said.

"Well, don't let him win."

"Peter doesn't need help winning; he's quite the chess player."

Her son glared at them. “Yeah, well, chess is a game for pillow boys too. He’s going to be beat up if people find out.

“Frankie plays chess,” said Peter.

“Don’t talk to me about that motherfu…”

“Not in my house,” warned his mother.

“Your house?” he said. “Since when did you figure this was your house?”

“Since your grandfather built it,” she retorted.

“That was then, this is now and I’m the man around this house.”

“I looked at the mortgage and there was no name under ‘Man’ there,” she said. “In fact, the only name is Maise Williams. Now, your name Maise?”

This time Peter couldn’t help laughing and regretted it right away. The man was coming at him and his face was twisted in rage.

“You think this is funny, you little faggot?” he screamed.

“Not in my house,” his mother said.

“I’ll deal with you after I teach this boy a lesson.”

He never saw her pick up the chessboard but he felt it when she swatted him across the face. If the couch hadn’t been there he would have fallen. His crutches were separated from his body.

“What the …

“Careful what your next word is,” Maise Williams said, brandishing a forearm. “I’ve coddled you for a long time but that doesn’t mean I can’t serve you up a little of this African soup bone.”

He was stunned for a second, then came for his mother.

It was Peter who stood between them and he got the rubber end of the crutch across his face. He screamed and felt wetness.

Even with screams of pain and anger the sound of a pistol cocked was heard. The two stopped to see Maise Williams with a handgun.

“You out your damn mind?” her son snarled.

“Take another step toward Peter and we’re both about to find out,” she said.

His smile was scary but he stopped. He was judging how serious she was. He brandished his crutch and moved toward her.

"This is going to cost you, old lady," he said. "I'm going to have to show you."

He took a step.

She closed her eyes.

He raised his hand.

She did too. Then she pulled the trigger.

When Frankie rode up, Peter was waiting on the doorstep. They didn't speak. Maise Williams was kneeling and pressing a wet towel to her son's shoulder.

"How bad?" he asked her.

"Not bad but the bullet is still there."

Frankie nodded and kneeled. The man was in shock so he didn't see the syringe. Then he was out cold.

Frankie reached into his bag and brought out a scalpel and tweezers. He made a small incision, reached in and plucked out the bullet.

He dropped it next to him and sewed the wound. Placing the bullet in his pocket, he grabbed the gun and placed it in his bag.

Laying the man on the couch he covered him with a quilt. Then he cleaned up. By then Peter had packed an overnight bag.

"Will you be okay when he wakes up?" Frankie asked.

"I think so," Maise answered and grinned. "I don't think he'll doubt my intentions."

Frankie laughed. "No, I think he'll take you at your word now."

"You think he'll make trouble?" she asked.

"Not likely. His street cred drops if anyone finds out he was shot by his mother."

"Can't believe I did it," she said. "I didn't see anything but Bobby before I squeezed the trigger."

He patted her shoulder and then looked to make sure the room was spotless.

"Peter can stay at the clinic for as long as you need," he said.

"Appreciate it. I'll let you know when it's safe to come back."

There was nothing more to say, so he threw his arm around the boy and they roared off.

Betty didn't say anything until they had put Peter in a room.

"Tough day, big man," said Frankie.

"I've had worse," he said.

The boy looked like he wanted to say more, so Frankie waited.

"I have a terrible secret," said Peter.

"Your secret is safe here," said Frankie.

The boy whispered in case anyone but Frankie was listening.

"I'm not sorry it happened," he said.

Frankie wasn't sure how to answer so he said, "Your grandmother isn't someone to trifle with."

Peter nodded and closed his eyes. Frankie envied the ability of kids to get through things, even though he knew this was not the end.

Betty was not surprised by the story and even found some humor.

"I'm probably not the person to admonish the grandmother," she said.

"Probably not," concurred Frankie.

"That man brings the worse out in everyone," said Betty.

"Might get hot up in here," said Frankie.

"True dat," said Betty. "Will it affect what Hersh wants to do?"

Frankie was thinking about it hours later when Betty and Seth were out and only Clemenza was there to bounce ideas off of.

He read and when the boy woke they ate a late dinner. Peter chose *Ghost Dog: The Way of the Samurai* as the movie. He spent the night pretending to be Forrest Whitaker.

He said to Frankie before dropping off to sleep again that "it is a good viewpoint to see the world as a dream. When you have something like a nightmare, you will wake up and tell yourself that it was only a dream. It is said that the world we live in is not a bit different from this."

Frankie loved that Peter took to the character and wondered if that was Peter's destiny. Being a samurai wasn't a bad life, even if it could be a short one.

Whitaker's character was a lesson for everyone who watched the movie that night.

"When one has made a decision to kill a person, even if it will be very difficult to succeed by advancing straight ahead, it will not do to think about doing it in a long, roundabout way. One's heart may slacken, he may miss his

chance, and by and large there will be no success. The Way of the Samurai is one of immediacy, and it is best to dash in headlong."

Maise Williams was right about her son. When he awoke, he was not only weak but rather contrite.

He didn't fight his mother when she changed his bandage and he didn't threaten her. That, of course, might change, but when she got in touch with Frankie she let him know things were good.

They agreed to let Peter stay with Frankie but it was a relief to know that Maise was safe and Frankie could take that off his worry list.

Still, Hersh needed to know what was developing. Years ago, Frankie and Hersh devised a plan to stay in touch no matter what hit the fan.

So … Hersh got Frankie's message, with both knowing there wasn't a lot he could do.

Other than concerns about Eddie Doss, Hersh cleared his mind and mentally went through the file on the man.

The carelessness was mind-boggling. It was like Eddie Doss thought no one was looking. Being sloppy never worked and Doss stuck his chin out so far, it was a wonder no one took a swing.

Doss didn't seem to get it and that was a puzzler. Hersh had no allusions of settling things with a conversation.

Smart people don't ever think the other guy has no way out.

Hersh had learned the lesson early and never forgot it because it was drummed into him on a daily basis.

It wasn't enough for Roza to learn from her mistakes. It was important that Hersh also benefit. So while she was short on exact details, Roza made sure that failure was not an option a second time.

Hersh thought about that, wondered if he was about to break that rule. You can get shot out of a cannon so many times before breaking your neck. Free fall is exhilarating until the last moment, and then it is all pain.

Knowing he would be in the house for hours before Eddie arrived, he got comfortable. He could have fallen asleep and felt safe but why take a chance.

Hersh looked for a clean place to wait. Whatever Eddie Doss was doing since his wife and daughter left didn't include a broom and mop. If things went sideways for Hersh it would take CSI a long time to sort for clues. This place would be a technician's nightmare.

Wandering about Hersh noticed the absence of reading material save for two children's books forgotten in haste. The family had a CD player but most of the music was heavy metal.

This would be an opportunity to catch up on reading. He had two *New Yorkers* to get through plus a new biography on Richard Nixon.

"I am not a crook," Hersh said.

He wasn't the only one getting in position. Marian reserved the best seat in the house. She was looking into the monitor and sitting by the van door.

When it went down she'd be in the fray. She didn't want to be wading ashore when the bombs started falling.

"Almost Thundercats Go," she said.

The agent next to her wasn't sure whether she was kidding or not. A superior too calm or too amped got you killed.

"Yes, ma'am," was all he said.

Walking up the street like he didn't have a care, Eddie Doss was whistling.

And why not? He had the U.S. government at his back. This was the luckiest break of his life. Not that he'd take advantage. Even with their protection, Eddie could mess up a one-car funeral. They were offering him a new life and odds were he would go back to his old one. Certainly, Eddie Doss would not be applying for a Mensa membership in the near future.

Of course, he still had to walk into his house and find himself facing Hersh. He was covered by the Feds from all angles except for being shot point-blank when he opened his door.

Part of Marian wished she'd hear a gun shot when the door opened but it was the part of her who believed in bad guys getting what they deserved.

She didn't have a chance to think about anything more. Her eyes flew wide open when she heard the explosion and she was running toward the house before anyone moved. Her biggest fear was coming true and she threw out a quick prayer there would be no fatalities on this day.

Bursting through the door she saw Doss was fine. She drew her gun when she saw one in his hand.

"What the hell?" she screamed. "What the hell?"

Doss looked at his hand and seemed confused at the weapon there. He mentally checked out but then smiled.

"I shot the asshole," he said.

"Who did you shoot?" Marian screamed as the house filled with agents.

"I shot him," Doss said again.

Marian followed his gaze to a small pool of blood and drops leading toward the back of the house. She followed the pattern to an open window, where there was a smear on the bottom pane and another on the ledge. She looked out and saw Hersh staggering away. His back was to her but he was holding his side or stomach.

She yelled at him to stop. He didn't but did swivel his head toward the house and appeared to grin. That had to be the adrenaline. Then she heard a shot and he went down. Just as quick he was up and now clutching his back.

Marian's professionalism kicked in and she jumped through the window. As she ran she wondered how things went downhill so fast. For the second time, she prayed.

Agents flanked her as they raced after the injured Hersh, but turning a corner they found no one there.

Marian told three agents to continue the search while she returned to the house.

She found Doss no less pleased with himself.

"I guess he learned his lesson," said Doss.

"You are going to have to tell me exactly what happened," said Marian. "Start from you opening the door."

He couldn't have been happier to tell the tale.

"I open the door and I see him sitting in my chair," he said, gesturing to the La-Z-Boy. "He starts telling me I'll have to pay for my sins. He reached for a gun in his jacket pocket. So I shot him."

"Why did you have a gun?" she asked.

Doss looked confused.

"What do you mean?" he asked. "You guys sent it to me."

"What are you talking about?" she said, sharper than she intended. "Why would we send you in armed? The whole point was to draw him here and arrest him after he threatened you. You should never have been in danger."

The feds didn't include Doss into their total plan but figured he needed to know a minimal amount so he didn't go rogue on them.

That little amount still fried his brain somehow.

"Well, he was reaching for his gun."

"Are you sure he was armed?" asked Marian.

"Well, I don't think he was looking for a comb," Doss said with a smirk. "What's the difference? I was protecting myself and you guys can arrest him for attempted murder."

Marian wasn't about to tell him Hersh had gotten away. They would have to provide protection for this jackass. Another headache in what Marian figured would be a cluster before the day was finished.

By the time the technicians finished, Marian had alerted her superiors and was sitting in Mackerson's office.

"What moron gave him a gun?" asked Mackerson.

Marian stared at him and then Gregory.

"I certainly didn't," she said. "I thought maybe you guys authorized it without telling me."

There was a silence as the three of them let her accusation sink in. Mackerson wanted to say something but Gregory held up a hand.

"Marian," he began. "You know me well enough to know I would never compromise an agent. Screw-ups get people killed. We actually lucked out."

Marian studied her boss and nodded.

"I apologize, Robert. Uncalled for on my part," she said. "I'm letting this all get to me."

Gregory got up and poured himself and Marian a drink. After she gulped the whiskey he started again.

"What are the chances Doss is lying and decided to go cowboy on us?" said Gregory.

Marian pondered the question for only a second. "It was my first thought. But it seems peculiar he would go rogue when we laid out a plan too generous to him by half."

"He wouldn't be the first to think he's smarter than us," Mackerson said, joining the conversation. "He's not the steadiest guy we've joined hands with."

Gregory and Marian agreed and they walked the case backwards to see a pattern.

Thirty minutes into the postmortem, Marian went white.

"You okay?" Gregory asked in alarm.

She gave him a thumbs-up and then said, "We've looked at everyone who could have had a hand in this and come up empty. But there is one person we've left out."

Gregory was the first to see where she was headed.

"Grundstein?" he asked with such incredulity Marian almost laughed.

"He's got the stones for it," she said.

"Well, it backfired on the genius," said Mackerson with glee.

The two looked at him and then at each other.

"What?" said Mackerson.

"Sir, if Grundstein sent Doss the gun we have to entertain the thought it was part of a plan."

"He planned to get shot? Pretty stupid plan."

"He has disappeared," said Marian. "What if Robert is right and this was a setup?"

Mackerson snorted.

"Boy, you guys make this guy out to be a superstar," the supervisor said. "He's probably dying by inches right now."

His words pained Marian but she forged on and explained if the techs found it wasn't Hersh's blood they would have to consider they had been played.

Mackerson tapped out a number. Whoever answered got a code number from the chief and he hung up.

"We'll know in a few," he said.

When the phone rang 30 minutes later it wasn't only Marian who jumped.

Mackerson listened for a few seconds. He smiled and kept the grin after he replaced the receiver.

"The blood belongs to Grundstein," he said with a triumph off-putting even to Gregory. "The son of a bitch is running and running out of blood. How far could he go with two bullets in him?"

"Depends on how bad he was hit,'" said Gregory.

"And how soon he gets medical attention," added Marian.

"We've got the hospitals covered," said Mackerson.

"Good, sir," countered Gregory. "But probably a waste of manpower. He won't go to a conventional place to be patched up. He's got an underground network for this type of thing."

"There can't be a long list of people who can help," said Mackerson defiantly.

"You'd be surprised, sir," said Gregory. "The network of people working for cash is astounding on the surface but not shocking when you think about it. No paperwork, no insurance companies. Medical help for a chunk of money is a doctor's dream, if you ask me."

"Let us put that to the side for a moment," said Marian. "Tell me why he would give Doss a weapon and be so stupid as to get shot?"

Then she gave a laugh with no mirth.

"Something funny, agent?" demanded Mackerson.

"No, sir," she said quickly. "Something cinematic."

Gregory and his boss looked at her quizzically.

"Hersh thinks of his life in terms of movies and books. Half of what he does he gets from one or the other. He gets his code from them."

"What does it have to do with what just happened?" asked Gregory.

Marian thought for a moment and looked at Gregory. "Suppose he's Jason Bourne."

Even the seriousness of the situation couldn't stop Gregory from laughing. "Nicky Parsons."

"Who the hell is Nicky Parsons?" Mackerson demanded. "And how does he figure into this?"

"She, sir," said Marian. "Nicky Parsons was an agent in a movie. Her superiors are discussing a mistake Jason Bourne has made and she informed them it was not a mistake. They don't make mistakes. They don't do random. There's always an objective. Always a target."

Gregory picked up the thread.

"So, the person who would be me in this scene says, 'The objectives and targets always came from us. Who's given them to him now?' "

"And," finished up Marian "the Nicky character says, 'Scary version? He is.' "

"God, I loved that movie," said Gregory.

Mackerson scoffed and not for the first time wondered whether he could trust them.

"Stop treating our suspect like he's a mythical creature. He screwed up on a grand stage," he said. "When you find him you'll just have to pick him up, patch him up, and send him up."

Mackerson thought he was witty. The other two realized you couldn't explain this to someone who never walked the line.

Gregory and Marian agreed they needed to interview Doss again and make sure they had overlooked nothing. There were enough agents looking for Hersh.

Frankie and Betty were reading to the kids when the first agents showed up there. Betty was confused at first but Frankie was not. He knew his friend was up a well-known tributary without a means of conveyance.

"Have you seen Hersh Grundstein?" an agent barked.

"Yes, we have," said Frankie.

"Where?" barked the agent.

"Here, of course, since he runs the clinic. At his home, at dinner, and just recently on the beach."

"How recently?"

Frankie looked at his watch, trying to buy some seconds before answering.

"Last time was about 15 hours ago," he said before looking at the watch again. "More like 13 hours."

The agent knew he was getting jerked around but waded back in.

"Where?"

"Here," said Frankie.

"We had a meal together," said Betty. "I had the chicken. Frankie had a salad but I don't remember what Hersh had."

"He had leftover Chinese food," said Frankie.

"Oh, yes. He nuked the crispy chicken."

"Said it tasted like glue," added Frankie.

"Ate the rice cold," added Betty.

"Said he wished he had not eaten the egg roll the day before."

The agent held his hand up and tried to regain control of the interview.

"Did he say where he would be going?"

"He did not," said Frankie.

"Wait," said Betty. "He was going to do research and turn in early. We got two more clients and he was exhausted."

The agent tired of their verbal games and took satisfaction in what he told them next.

"Well, I don't think he'll have to worry about his next meal."

"What does that mean?" said Frankie, not taking the bait but not keeping the worry completely out of his voice.

"It means your pal is dead," said the agent with a twisted grin.

Betty tried to stifle a gasp. Frankie remained stoic.

"Where can we see the body?" he asked.

The agent's momentary hesitation told Frankie what he needed to know.

"No body?" asked Frankie.

"He's bleeding like a stuck pig so if you are patient I'm sure we can tell you where they take him."

Betty wiped her eyes.

"So you don't know he's dead, but you took pleasure in telling us he was?" she asked. "What kind of person are you?"

The agent didn't answer but if his goal was to unnerve he had gotten only an indirect hit. Later, when they were escorted downtown, Frankie would hold Betty back from striking somebody. All agreed the shock tactic was a mistake.

CHAPTER 75

Willpower is a valuable commodity when sharing a room with a loathsome character like Eddie Doss. Marian didn't have enough and watched on the outside monitor.

He preened so much she wanted to shut off the cameras and smack him.

"Everybody plays his part," Gregory said, putting a hand on her shoulder.

"Look at him," said Marian. "I wonder if it was all worth it."

"It was worth it," said Mackerson, who had followed Gregory into the room. "We took a mad dog off the street today."

"Well," countered Marian, "technically, he's still on the street but I understand your idiotic simile."

"I'd admonish you," said Gregory, "but since you said simile and not analogy I'm going to give you a pass."

Gregory turned to Mackerson and shrugged so deep his shoulders went to the top of his head.

"When they put your boyfriend on a second-floor table you might not act so cute," said Mackerson.

Marian saw no need to deepen the career hole she had already dug.

The room grew silent as the three agreed to stop speaking until it was time to trudge back into the interview room.

Doss had combed his hair and Marian saw him as a rooster. She let her hands unclench, embarrassed to see them balled up.

"I'm getting a little hungry. When do we eat?" asked Doss straight off.

"As soon as you start telling us a story closer to the truth," said Marian.

Doss looked at her with bored indifference. Technically, this was her interview but he played to the two men, believing they had a connection.

"Explain again about the gun," Marian said.

"I'll keep telling the same story because it is true," Doss said. "You guys delivered a gun and told me to protect myself. You said there was a small chance he'd pull a weapon but a chance did exist. I was lucky because he was going for it."

Marian leaned into Doss's personal space. He didn't seem to be affected at first but then moved his head back slightly.

"At your house you said he pulled a gun. Now, are you saying he was merely making a move?"

"What's the difference?" asked Doss. "He had a gun and he was going to use it."

"The difference," explained Marian, "is the first explanation gets you a claim of self-defense. The second one leaves you open to a murder charge."

"What the fuck you talking about murder?" thundered Doss.

"Please watch your language, Mr. Doss," Marian said, pointing her chin at Mackerson. "There is a lady present."

Mackerson turned another shade darker, Gregory stifled a laugh, and Doss looked confused.

"Look, you guys told me to be prepared and I was. It was me or that nut job. I did what you told me. So, I want to get out of here, I want to get something to eat and then I want to see my wife and daughter."

"The first two might happen soon," Marian said, "but your wife and daughter are out of your reach."

"That wasn't the deal," said Doss.

Marian was about to tell him tough luck but when she looked at Mackerson and Gregory they weren't looking back.

Suddenly nauseous she wanted to put her fist through the wall. Or better yet land one on the jaw of either supervisor. Instead, she walked out.

Minutes later Gregory found her reading a file.

"Mackerson knew you wouldn't play ball," he said.

"You sacrificed the safety of a mother and child to capture a man because he gave your boss a swirly when they were kids," she said.

"We both know it is more complicated," said Gregory, who didn't deny her claim out of hand. "Your boy needed to be swept out of office."

"At what price, Robert?"

"Pretty much any price," he said.

"And when Mary Doss comes in with a black eye and her daughter is bruised what do we tell ourselves about the price?"

"It is the business we've chosen," Gregory said.

"Well played," said Marian, and actually meant it. "Is this where you tell me you are going in to take a nap and when you wake up and see the money's on the table you'll know you have a partner?"

"This is where I give you the 'grow the hell up' speech. We don't play this game in short pants."

Gregory was right. She had been beaten and needed to take her ass-whipping like a grown-up.

"So now we live with it?" she said.

"We've always lived with it before," he responded.

"Not like this," she said. "I'm going to pray for the Doss women every day. If anything happens to them I know I'll always be able to drink that memory away. I want to say I did everything in my power to make it work for them but I'd be lying. Robert, if I may be candid, I didn't see it coming. Mackerson played me when he made you the go-between. I might have smelled a rat with him because it is his natural odor. But you masked the scent masterfully."

He was about to respond but she didn't let him. She unclipped her badge and removed her gun, putting one on top of the other. She was so tired and defeated she could not remain another second.

Marian figured somebody would be sent to escort her from her office. She was surprised to find it wasn't true. As she filled a box with personal items her cell phone buzzed. She looked at the number and though it didn't register she accepted it.

"Marian?" said a man's voice.

"Yes?" the agent said.

"This is Frankie."

There was a pause and he added, "Hersh's friend."

She laughed despite herself.

"Hey, Frankie," she said. "I've got no news. This is an active investigation."

She was surprised she still protected the agency but you don't give it up all at one time.

"Coolio," he said. "I'm just calling to give you a heads-up," he said.

"About what?" she asked.

"I was going through Hersh's desk and there was an envelope with my name and a note to call you and read it."

Clearly anxious, Marian waited for him to open the letter.

"Let me see," he said as she could hear the unfolding of the paper.

After a beat, he said, "It says, 'Eddie Doss has a better chance of finding Amelia Earhart and Jimmy Hoffa then he does Mary and Kathy Doss.' "

Marian gasped and Frankie chortled. "I'm guessing that is good news?"

She stared at the phone a long time after hanging up. Eventually she walked back into Gregory's office and picked up her badge and gun.

She smiled at him.

"Short pants indeed," she said.

Desperately wanting another look at the crime scene, she went back to the house.

She double-gloved and after talking to the remaining techs began to move things. She saw a clean spot on a chair and knew where Hersh waited.

"Has anyone touched this chair?" she asked.

A tech looked over and shook his head. "Only clean spot in the place. Nothing was there."

She picked up a cushion and her heart stopped. There was a note.

Putting the cushion back she sat down and maneuvered her hand to grab the envelope before putting it into her purse.

She stayed another 30 minutes but didn't see anything more, so she left.

She hurried to her car and rode a few blocks in case this place was wired for sound and pictures. If the inside had been done she would have heard about it.

She opened the note and began to read.

Marian:

You are reading this because I lost control of the tempo somehow. Otherwise I would have taken this with me when I left.

Eddie Doss was never in danger from me. Even if you guys weren't so clumsy in your setup, I wouldn't have exacted revenge. Despite what my jacket says it isn't my style. I was going to tell him any thoughts he had about harming his wife and daughter should vanish since he wouldn't be able to find them.

Frankie will be calling you with that news later. I am sure you were not consulted about making the Doss girls a pawn in this. Kudos to Mary for pulling it off. Everyone thinks a battered woman has no brains. They believe if she's willing to stay with an abuser she must be stupid. But she's sharp and brave and I used both qualities to get her and Kathy so far away Rand McNally might not recognize their location. They'll have money and protection.

As I write this I don't know how sideways everything got. This could stand as my final words or you may be reading it at my trial.

What matters are the women. If I've overdramatized my situation, then I'll call you from one side or the other. We had some fun and don't think it didn't mean something. In a more trusting world we might have jumped over our problems. Alas, we're not there yet and both of us had jobs to do.

Marian put down the letter and despite the current chaos she couldn't help but be cheered. If this became his last act it was a nifty one.

How do you get two people to disappear so even the federal government can't find them?

It was a money question and too soon to know if Hersh pulled it off. Maybe he figured if they stayed off the grid long enough federal authorities would tire of placating Eddie Doss. He certainly had nothing more to offer.

More impressive was Hersh disappearing. Her phone trilled as she was pondering that move.

"Yes."

"We found him."

Her heart stopped and Gregory seemed to read her mind.

"He's alive but he's hurting."

"Where?"

"He's in a cave up in the hills," said Gregory. "There is blood on the outside and he doesn't seem to be moving around."

"A cave?"

"Yeah," answered Gregory. "A hiker called. Said she saw someone disappear in there and they seemed to be in great pain. She was worried but didn't want to approach him."

"Give me the coordinates," said Marian.

"Just texted them."

"Are you there already?"

"Almost there."

If Marian worried she wouldn't find the spot she was relieved when she saw the huge gathering. There was more law enforcement milling around than she had ever seen. She figured there was a battle on jurisdiction but Robert swung his badge and ended all discussion.

She flashed her credentials and ducked under the rope. Soon she was standing next to her boss and dismayed to see Mackerson. People like Mackerson don't get their brogans dusty unless there was a photo op.

He was like a kid at the opening of an amusement park.

"Any sign of him?" she asked.

"The cave is deeper and wider than we thought," Gregory said. "We don't want to send anybody in before we know how disabled he is and how many weapons he has."

Pleased by the show of caution, Marian was satisfied to wait in silence.

Hersh had done bad things but didn't deserve a legacy as a man who killed the good guys.

Some ambitious underling made sure the bosses had coffee and water. Later, there was a food run.

Content, Marian sat on a rock and enjoyed the sun.

"Please don't embarrass yourself or the agency," Mackerson said as she opened one eye to look at him. "I don't know why I let Gregory talk me into letting you stay. He's putting himself on the line for you."

"Robert is a good man," she said, refusing to rise to the bait.

"Maybe he feels guilty for all the things he screwed you on in this case," Mackerson said with glee.

"Robert did what he had to do. It is hard to be in charge sometimes," she said.

He was clearly frustrated at not being able to get to her.

"Since this will probably be your last case you should enjoy it," he said. "And you might get to see your boyfriend in your favorite pose … horizontally."

Marian blinked a couple of times.

"Sir, that is actually pretty funny," she said. "You should be on the stage."

She paused and said, "And the next one leaves at 5:15 p.m."

"In a way," said Mackerson, totally ignoring her jibe, "this is your fault. If you had brought him in by the rules we'd all be with our families and the government could have saved a lot of money."

"Where is the fun in that"?" she said.

Mackerson would have continued to goad her but Gregory started to talk about timing and strategy. They agreed some action would be needed in the next 60 to 90 minutes.

"He might be dead already," said Gregory. "But no matter, he had to be weak and I'm surprised he hasn't asked for help. He knows what he's facing here."

"You think he goes Cody Jarrett on us?" Marian asked.

" 'Made it, Ma! Top of the world,' " shouted Gregory, slightly giddy from the long day.

Sobered by that, Marian thought about Hersh's family. She didn't dwell on the shame but the grief. She knew Roza was close to death herself. The Grundsteins were in for a long stretch. She looked over to the cave and silently sent out yet another prayer.

CHAPTER 76

I haven't always been truthful but when I say I'm almost done here, take it to the bank.

I don't have the strength to go much longer. Even a person with an overdeveloped superego tires of talking about themselves.

It is good to have self-awareness and I would not have changed a thing. Like *Daredevil* I don't want to regain my sight and risk losing superpowers.

I'll miss so many things but I won't go Woody Allen on you in *Manhattan* and list them all. Trust me, "Tracy's face" won't be one of them but perhaps Louis Armstrong's *Potato Head Blues* makes the cut. And chocolate cake will make the cut. I don't regret indulging at all.

I've passed on a chance to go Woody Allen but I won't miss the opportunity to leave you with Streisand.

Don't tell me not to fly,-
I've simply got to.
If someone takes a spill,
It's me and not you.
Who told you you're allowed
To rain on my parade!
I'll march my band out,
I'll beat my drum,
And if I'm fanned out,
Your turn at bat, sir.
At least I didn't fake it.
Hat, sir, I guess I didn't make it!

CHAPTER 77

As the three agents talked, a deputy walked up.

"Are you Marian Webber?"

"I am."

He handed her a package and excitedly said, "This came out of the cave."

No one moved as they looked at the package.

"Came out how?" asked Gregory.

"It was kind of cool, sir," said the deputy. "We all heard this whirring and we looked at the mouth of the cave and a small robotic device came rolling out and it had this package riding on top."

After being tested by the bomb squad, Marian slowly unwrapped the paper and saw a cell phone and a note that said, "Last testament, enjoy watching."

Trembling she pushed a button and they gathered to watch. His face came up and he seemed to be in good spirits and not a lot of pain. She knew the first might hold but the second surely wouldn't.

By the end, she was laughing and trying not to cry. His performance was vintage and if he had survived this she probably would have killed him.

Or maybe hugged him.

"What a colossal prick," said Mackerson.

"We've got a pretty good confession, though," said Gregory.

Marian snorted. "Robert, do you think he cares about that? He was thumbing his nose at us one last time. He's saying we didn't win but he lost. We didn't catch him in the end, he got himself caught."

"Won't that make for a great eulogy," said Mackerson. "We caught the jerk and we disposed of him."

"A great sound bite, sir," Marian said as she pointed to the news vans gathering. "Why don't you start your press conference now?"

"Missy, this might be a good time to turn in your badge," Mackerson said. "Your career has come to an end."

"What will you tell reporters when asked about the agent who captured the killer?"

"I'll think of something," he said with a sneer.

Marian sneered back.

"And when they asked about Mary and Kathy Doss? When they ask how you lost them? How you made a deal with an abuser and then couldn't locate them?"

Mackerson looked at her and Gregory looked surprised. Marian kept a steady look.

"They've disappeared, guys," she said. "You think Mary made a deal with us and she didn't. She looked in our eyes and in his and it was no contest. She looked at her daughter and thought, 'Whom do I trust her life with?' And we didn't come close to making the cut. She played us."

"You have no idea what you are talking about," said Mackerson with real anger.

He looked over at Gregory for confirmation but he was curling his lip and thinking about the possibility. He punched in a number, waited, but got no answer.

Marian gave him credit for taking it like a pro.

"Son of a gun," Gregory said.

"What?" asked Mackerson.

"They *are* gone."

"How do you know?"

He put his phone on speaker and dialed the number again. After three rings a recorded voice came on.

"You have reached the phone of Mary and Kathy Doss. Please don't leave a message as this phone is now sitting at the edge of a landfill and will soon be covered in garbage. Please do not come looking for us. Thank you for all you did."

Nobody said anything right away and then lost the opportunity when an explosion went off in the cave.

Running toward the sound, the three of them arrived to find smoke pouring out and rubble around the mouth.

"What the hell happened?" Mackerson screamed.

Eventually, when it was apparent no one outside was hurt, it was revealed somebody rolled something into the cave and seconds later there was an explosion. Except no one was taking credit for the pyrotechnics. Officials spent hours but no one came forth.

Diggers removed the rubble and when there was an opening, several went into the cave. They looked green coming out.

"We have a body but it is not in good shape," said the first agent out. He then vomited on his shoes.

The remains were taken to a federal lab, where the coroner announced the subject was probably dead or close to it prior to the bombing. Doing numerous tests and checking dental and medical records he determined the body was Hersh Grundstein.

Marian grieved in private. The part that didn't hope was prepared for this.

Hersh's family grieved in public. The press had a field day but was surprised when no one refuted the charges. The family never asked for privacy.

When Marian showed up at the clinic she wasn't surprised it was business as usual because Hersh would never neglect his kids. She was shocked at the reception she got.

Not only were Betty and Frankie not angry, but they were happy to see her.

Betty reached for a hug and Frankie brought her tea.

"We're keeping busy," Betty said when Marian asked. "Not all the children understand Hersh is gone but most do. Just another shit sandwich they have to chew on."

Susan walked in and climbed in Marian's lap. She recognized the little girl who had done her hair in what now seemed decades ago.

"How are you, Susan?" she said.

"Dead men are heavier than broken hearts," the little girl said.

"We've made Susan our Chandler expert," explained Frankie with a shrug.

The little girl nodded. "I'm neat, clean, shaved, and sober and I don't care who knows it."

She then trotted off to another room, along with Clemenza.

They all stared after her.

"We're worried," said Betty. "We can't seem to get her to acknowledge her pain. She found Hersh's Philip Marlowe books and she hasn't stopped quoting from them. We got her seeing a specialist but it has been a tough case."

"Tougher than a ballerina's big toe," said Frankie, who laughed along with Betty.

"You make that up?" she asked.

"Just now," he said.

"Sweet."

Frankie turned his gaze to Marian and asked if she was calling as a friend or was this business.

"Business?" asked Marian.

"Are you here to see what our involvement is?" he asked.

Thrusting out her palms Marian gave a tired look. She hadn't slept much and it was apparent. It was apparent she was barely keeping it together.

"I'm actually looking for work," she said.

"Did you jump or were you pushed?" asked Betty.

"Why don't we say they made me an offer they told me not to refuse," she told them.

"Those bastards," said Betty.

"Actually, it was pretty generous," said Marian. "After all of this it was a blessing. I was starting to lose myself. I could give Susan a run for her money in the need for professional help."

No one said anything to that.

"I've replayed this so many times and I don't like what I see," Marian finally said. "There were numerous times where I could have prevented this and each time I made the wrong choice."

"Well, aren't we a little full of ourselves," said Frankie.

That shocked Marian into silence.

"Do you really think you are so important it all revolved around you?" he said with no apparent malice. "Hersh made big boy decisions. Don't think he was waiting on you. Or me. Or anyone."

She knew this was his way of releasing her from guilt but she would hold onto a piece. She would accept the weight and someday live with it.

No one thought of keeping this from Roza. They'd pay if she found out on her own.

Frankie and Betty made the trip to the hospital but Frankie did the talking. He did not fudge or withhold a detail.

Roza looked frail when they walked in but stronger when Frankie was done. And she was smiling.

"I'm sorry to bring you the news," said Frankie.

"What news?" asked Roza.

They feared she was fading but Frankie waded in.

"The news about Hersh's death," he said.

"Hersh isn't dead," she said. "He made a promise to me and he never goes back on his word."

Frankie agreed she was right and they left.

"Very sad," said Betty.

"But in a way not," he said.

"In what way?" she asked.

"It is good she still believes," he said. "Roza is so strong. If she were to admit Hersh was gone she'd go right after. At least she's given herself some margin to get some final things done."

"Okay," said Betty. "I like we're seeing this as a glass half full. It makes me feel better."

Betty got in her car to return to the clinic and Frankie hopped on his bike. He was going to dinner with Peter and his grandmother and didn't want to be late.

"I am so sorry for your loss, honey," said Maise Williams as he entered the house. "I don't care what the news people are saying. He was a good man. He helped save my grandson. God will treat him well."

Frankie smiled at the old woman and nodded his head.

"Yes ma'am. I think you are right."

"And how are you doing?" she asked.

"Hanging on," he said.

"Barely."

He smiled again. Frankie was incapable of fooling older women. They had him in their spell.

"I know you won't mind me getting into your business and I'm too old to care anyway," said Maise Williams. "This can't be your excuse."

"Excuse for what?"

"You can't take out your sorrow on the world. This can't be your reason to create mayhem. You have a code and you need to abide by it."

He didn't respond to that but began speaking on another subject.

"For years a guy has a job cleaning up after the elephants and he starts to tire of it and he begins to complain. One day a friend tells him he should just leave. And the guy says, 'What, and quit show business?' "

Betty enjoyed a dinner out with Seth. They didn't talk about Hersh but he was hanging with them anyway. It was Betty who recognized the gloom, so she suggested they go dancing.

She tired of being alone in her room and she wanted to celebrate being with Seth.

She didn't lose her sadness but she did slowly let it slide to the back of her brain.

As they were sitting out a dance, Seth smiled and she smiled back. They held hands and listened to the music.

There was a pause at the end of the record and the DJ began to talk. "We have a request out there," he said as the crowd got quiet. "We are going to take a break from the music we usually play and send out a special cut. This is a bit unusual for us but that is the spice of life."

He then hit a button and the crowd looked at each other as the sound of strings began. Then Tony Bennett began to croon.

The loveliness of Paris seems somehow sadly gay,
The glory that was Rome is of another day,
I've been terribly alone and forgotten in Manhattan,
I'm going home to my city by the Bay.
I left my heart in San Francisco,
High on a hill it calls to me
To be where little cable cars climb halfway to the stars.
The morning fog may chill the air, I don't care.

Seth started to say something but when he turned, Betty was sobbing and her face was white.

"Betty!" he said with alarm. "Are you okay?"

She glanced at him and shook her head no.

"He sang that to me," she said.

"Who sang it to you?" Seth asked and then he knew.

"Holy shit," he said.

That made her smile and stop crying.

"Holy shit indeed, Batman."

CHAPTER 78

Freaked out, Betty called Frankie.

He was surprised but less baffled.

"Coincidence," he said. "I'm not putting it past Hersh to speak from the grave but we need more."

He paused a beat then added, "But it is mind-blowing."

When Hersh didn't appear to them again, the Tony Bennett episode, as Frankie called it, faded and events overtook them. Betty began school. Frankie called Mrs. G and she sent two students who helped during busy times.

The best news was Roza rallied and was able to leave the hospital.

Everyone knew it was temporary but a starving man turns away no meal. She stayed inside most of the day but someone, most often Betty in the late afternoon, would roll her out on the deck.

Roza talked like Hersh was going to walk in the door. No one disputed her because if she needed to believe, no one was going to disabuse her of any notion.

Nobody laughed when Frankie took up yoga. He was at a tipping point and apt to spiral out of control. No person on the planet would benefit if Frankie slipped the leash. There would be no one's grandmother to rein him in.

So yoga helped, as did Betty and the kids. Frankie was doing well, doing it one day at a time.

Marian dropped in and out of their lives. She was a sheriff's deputy out west but called and emailed. She seemed happy and her severance from the bureau went a long way. She testified on numerous cases tied to Hersh. But as they dwindled, so did the interest.

There was always something to occupy interest and many believed the explosion ended the case. The feds were not interested in releasing how many cases Hersh was tied into and that helped taking it off the front pages.

Only Clemenza seemed unaffected. They worried he would be depressed but seemed the same dog. Instead of moping he remained charged, and of course the kids adored him. He was never more than a step from being spoiled and fawned upon.

It was Marian who jump-started them out of their reverie and did it with a phone call to Frankie.

He was working the heavy bag, another of his new hobbies, when the phone rang. Normally he would have sent it to voice mail but when he saw the area code he punched it up.

"How are things in the Badlands?" he said.

"Not so bad," Marian said. "The weather is here, I wish you were beautiful," doing her best Jimmy Buffett.

"We're having a great fall ourselves," he said. "Betty and I are training for a marathon. I think she's going to outrun me."

"Mind and body," she said.

"Amen," he added.

There was a brief silence and Frankie heard an audible sigh.

"That was heavy," he said.

She laughed. "Obvious?"

"My ears are like a dog's," he said.

"This is probably nothing," she started.

"But again, you could have cracked 'Enigma,' " he joked.

"Well, this isn't earth-shattering. Just spooky."

"Just in time for Halloween," he said.

There was another pause before she said, "I'm investigating a death here."

"Uh, huh," he said to get her moving on the conversation.

"We don't get a lot so whenever there is a body we have the time to really look into it."

"Murder?"

"Nobody thinks so. A man was found in the hills and he appeared to be hiking, had a heart attack or was in some kind of distress and not near help. Laid down and died."

"But you suspect foul play," he said.

"Actually, I don't," she said.

"You believe he died like they said?" he asked.

"I do," she agreed.

"So, this is a social call after all," said Frankie.

"Always good to talk to you, Frankie," she said. "But I called to get your reaction. It is probably nothing and maybe I'm using this as an excuse to call."

"I'm always glad to hear from you," he said. "So how can I help?"

"Well," said Marian. "When the coroner finished, his report was sent to me, and like I said, I have no reason to doubt his competence. He's pretty sharp. So, I was packing the files but took a look at the deceased's affects. As somebody who overpacks I was curious what a person takes on a long hike."

Frankie was amused Marian was so bored that she looked for reasons to be suspicious.

"Anything good?" he asked.

"Stuff you would expect. A wallet, with ID, and a few dollars. A small towel, kitchen matches, a Swiss Army knife. An energy bar. I thought you had to be careful what you put in your pocket in case somebody found you stone-cold dead."

"I hear you," Frankie said as he unconsciously put his hand near his own pocket. "It is why I never wear the same pair of underwear."

"TMI, dude," Marian said with a laugh. "Thanks for that image."

"So, a pretty normal guy," said Frankie.

"Way normal," said Marian. "But one thing in his pocket reminded me of you, so I figured I'd call."

"Don't tell me he had a photo of me," joked Frankie.

"No photo of you," she said. "He had a photo of a roller coaster."

Frankie squeezed the phone.

"A roller coaster?" he asked.

"Yeah. And here's the weird part. It was a picture of the roller coaster at the amusement park where you guys go. I think it's called super something."

"Superman," said Frankie, trying to control his voice.

"Yep," Marian said. "How weird that a man dies here and he's got a photo from the town I used to work in. Life can be strange."

Frankie wasn't sure what the protocol was but all of the sudden he did. He had a clear path and there was no doubt.

"Marian," he slowly said. "Do you have the autopsy in front of you?"

"I do," she said. "But I'm telling you there was nothing unusual."

He ignored her. "Can you tell me if the coroner made any mention of the man's hands," he said.

He could hear her rustling the papers. "Let me see, let me see."

Frankie was getting anxious and started to drum his fingers on the desk.

"What are you looking for?" asked Marian.

"A pattern on his palm like a couple of dots. Maybe three but could be two. It would be faint and probably overlooked. Or there was nothing there. That is probably the case."

He heard her draw in her breath.

"Frankie, what is going on?" she asked.

"I don't know for sure," he said. "Did you know this guy?"

"I didn't know him but he was known in the community," she said. "Nothing strange in his background. No record. He was well-liked and active in town."

"How active?" he asked.

"What do you mean?" she responded.

"Did he run bingo? Did he hold public office? A deacon in the church? Those kinds of things."

"I'll try to find out," she said. "You have a hunch about something?"

"Not really," he said. "But the picture is intriguing. Probably nothing more than one of those odd convergences but I need another hobby."

"This will be a financial blow to the students of this town," she said.

"How do you mean?" he asked.

"He provided scholarships for rising seniors," she explained. "Each year he picked a student to sponsor and provided tuition money. He even drove the young man for his college visit. People thought he was a hero."

"Ever any trouble with that?" Frankie asked. "Anyone ever get mad they didn't get the money?"

"Oh, no," she said. "It didn't go to the smartest student or best athlete. I don't think anyone knew how he picked the boys. The only problem ever was the young man who committed suicide two years ago."

"What was that about?" asked Frankie.

"Shocked this town. Good kid, decent athlete, a lot of friends. Then one afternoon his roommate finds the kid hanging from the rafters."

Frankie didn't hear what she said next. It was like an explosion went off in his head. His whole body was numb.

"Can you let me see that autopsy?" he asked.

"Frankie, what is going on?" she demanded.

"Did you ever work sex crimes?" he asked.

"Briefly. I didn't have the stomach for it. Why?"

"Get me the autopsy on the suicide."

Now Marian went numb. She poked the hornet's nest somehow.

"What am I going to find?" she asked.

"Some bad things, I'm afraid. Marian, I'm on the next plane."

"Why?" she demanded.

"Because this was no boating accident."

When Frankie told Betty and Roza they had different reactions. Betty was horrified and wanted to jump on the flight west. She was convinced to stay with the kids after he promised her hourly updates.

Roza couldn't stop smiling and continued to tell Frankie, "I told you so."

When he walked into the terminal, Marian was waiting. She looked tired and scared but thrilled to see him. They made plans to meet in a few hours after he unpacked and took a short nap.

She had some paperwork relating to a B&E and a couple of hours would work perfectly for her.

While they were eating lunch, Marian slid a file over to him. He opened it up, read it and slid it back.

"Could cost me my job," she said. "But in for a penny, in for a pound I guess."

He looked around the diner.

"How did you know about him?" she asked.

"The suicide sent up the flags," he said. "Without that I may have lamented a man who died and applauded his efforts to help kids. You kept using masculine terms to describe the recipients and that set off alarms."

"Nobody will believe it," she said. "I've mentioned this to no one."

He paused his fork in mid-air and said, "Somebody believed it."

"I'm looking at the parents of kids he helped in the past 20 years," she said. "Then I'll go with other family members. I'll look at the kids themselves."

"Unless they have medical expertise I wouldn't bother," he said. "It is possible he did die of a heart attack."

"But you don't think so."

"I don't."

"Because of the hand markings."

"Among other things."

"The roller coaster?" she asked.

He made a pistol with his fingers.

"Tell me."

"I can't right now."

"Then tell me what medical knowledge you need to make it look like natural causes."

"Not detailed as far as being a doctor. More detailed in how to administer a dose and how much to inject."

"And you can't tell me anything about the roller coaster?"

"It was a message," he said.

"To whom?"

"Well, for starters, to me."

"You?"

He nodded his head.

"Who do you know out here?

"That is the mystery," he told her.

"What is the message?"

"Bird lives," he said.

She plowed on with question after question hoping to find a foothold.

"So, you don't know anyone out here?"

He pointed at her.

"I know you."

"Yeah, but…" she said and paused. "Are you saying I am involved in this?

"Maybe."

"Explain."

"I can't and if I did it would sound so strange neither of us would believe it."

"Well, tell me about the markings on his hand."

"There is an urban legend that pedophiles develop the Mark of Cain and it appears as either two or three dots," he said. "Of course, that is just pure unadulterated crap. More likely it is someone marking territory. But the legend served a purpose as an identifier. If you believe the stories, there is a secret society with a goal of ridding the world of people like your victim. I don't know if it exists but sometimes I think Lee Harvey Oswald worked alone."

"So, this society would get rid of people but take ownership also?"

"Yes, but only to let the rest of the group know," he said. "It wasn't for anyone's use except for members of the group. Nobody was gaming for bragging rights."

"But you aren't sure whether this group exists," she said.

"I'd guess they don't but it was good to think so," he said. "Helped some of us sleep better at night."

"Us?"

"Anyone who worked with kids, and more keenly those who worked with kids who had been affected."

Digesting what he said, Marian looked to make sure they were not watched and whispered to him.

"He was dirty, no doubt," she said. "But it is something I'll never prove."

"It is why your guy was murdered," he said. "Because the party who did this knew he'd never be exposed."

"So I'm after another vigilante?" she asked followed by a cruel cackle. "Will I have to fall in love with this one also?"

Waiting a beat, Frankie pondered what to say.

"Maybe not another vigilante," he said.

"Well, what would you call him?"

"I'm not objecting to your description," he said. "I quibble with your math."

Totally confused she scrunched up her face. Then she got it and her eyes grew wide and her mouth dropped open.

"No?" she whispered.

He arched his eyebrows and shrugged.

"Well, trick or treat."

CHAPTER 79

Taking Frankie to the hotel, she told him after doing some research they should meet for dinner. Clearly shaken, she needed some time.

After ordering drinks, she slid another folder his way.

"I called in some favors. No doubt the body in the cave was Hersh. This isn't by a preponderance of evidence; this is 100 percent," she explained. "I so wanted you to be right but it isn't. There are several ways to get a positive ID and they used them all. Unless you believe in reincarnation this was not your boy."

Frankie rubbed his jaw and then clucked his tongue.

"It was good to believe," he said. "But now you've got a copycat and that is harder to explain. There aren't a handful of people who could have done this and your best suspect is sitting two feet from you. And I was 2,000 miles away at the time."

"Could you have talked somebody through this?" she asked.

"And then led you step-by-step to discover it? That would be dumb."

"Yeah, I was just yanking your lariat," she said.

"Still leaves you with a problem," he said.

"Not much of one," she parried. "I'm okay with this going unsolved. I don't need to get burned twice. If we never find out, we still got a bad guy off the street. But I'm sending a warning I don't want this to become a pattern."

"How will you send a message?"

"I just did."

He stopped his glass halfway to his mouth and looked at her.

"Interesting."

"I'm not playing games, Frankie. I like it here and I don't want to revisit my greatest hits. So this far and no farther."

He put his hands up, palms out.

"I'm not saying you did it," she said. "But you're connected; I can feel it in my bones. I don't know how but I just know. This is years of being a cop and a good one."

"This time your bones are misleading you," he said. "But I've received the message and I'm happy to pass it on if the need presents itself. If I was in on this I would not have come here and I would not have said anything on the phone."

"This is a puzzler," she said. "I'm trying to work this out and this time I want no collateral damage."

"Fair deal," he said and put out his hand to shake hers.

"You are a strange man," she said.

"Something we can agree on."

Soon the conversation drifted off the case and onto their lives.

"You miss the bureau?" he asked.

"Sometimes, but it was getting too political," she said. "When Mackerson got a promotion, I wanted to puke but I know how the game is played. Robert was a bit of a disappointment but only because of my own hero worship. I'm here, and living well is the best revenge. I'm less anxious and I like the work. The people are good and the change of scene was welcome. How goes the clinic?

"Well," he answered, "we win some and that carries us through the many losses. Betty gets me through the bad times even if the opposite should be true."

"I miss him so much," she said, apropos of nothing.

"I know the feeling," he agreed.

"He knew how this would end, didn't he?" she asked.

"I don't think so," said Frankie. "Because this is not what he wanted. Saving Mary and Kathy Doss turned into his Waterloo. Do I think he knew it wasn't going to work out well for him? I do. But in the end, he couldn't help himself. He took the risk because he didn't want them to."

"You warned me the first time we met," she said.

He got a bemused look on his face.

"Yeah, me trying to play the tough guy," he said. "When I saw him after your first date I knew he was a goner. I was happy he was happy but he was weaker. You were his kryptonite. Hersh was the most resolute person I knew. He never doubted he was on the side of the angels. He never looked back. But after you he had a sliver of doubt. In his business, it can be enough to upset the balance."

Marian was doing everything not to cry but she wasn't successful. He realized he had gone too far.

"I'm not saying you got him killed," Frankie said. "That was his doing. Plans go awry and Hersh was the best making it up as he went along. But the law of big numbers says you can't get away with it forever. An amateur like Eddie Doss is more dangerous than a field of feds. He is more unpredictable and less likely to do the smart thing."

"For the life of me I can't figure out why we would arm him," said Marian.

"Mackerson had such a hard-on for Hersh, nothing surprises me," said Frankie.

"It was stupid and using a collectable was even stranger," she said.

"What do you mean a collectable?" he asked.

"The gun given to Doss was a Sauer 38H," she said. "I don't know anything about old guns but I'm told it was a pistol used by the Luftwaffe during World War II."

"Wow," he said.

"You want to hear something funny? I thought Hersh had sent the pistol to Doss. Make it look like it was self-defense when he killed him. But Hersh said Doss was never in danger from him and I believe it. I also don't see him owning a vintage pistol. Collecting was not a hobby of his."

"Guns had no appeal for him," agreed Frankie. "I doubt he was carrying when he was killed. I don't believe Doss and in all due respect to our government, I don't believe them. Hersh was proficient in so many black arts. A gun would have gotten in his way."

"So you think we planted something on him?"

"Don't wish to hazard a guess," he said. "But you guys are certainly capable."

"I'm not 'you guys' anymore, Frankie," she said. "I'm happy to put that in the rearview mirror."

Tapping his fork Frankie beat out a rhythm while he thought of what to say. She could tell he was pained. Whatever he was thinking, he was conflicted. He put his thumb and forefinger on the bridge of his nose and squeezed until it made him shut his eyes. When he opened them, his eyes were so clear it scared her. He was going to cross a line.

"A little while ago you warned me about going so far," he said.

She nodded.

"I'm going to return the favor," he said.

"In what way?"

"Much to my surprise, Marian, we've become friends," he started. "I would never have believed I would ever trust you. But it happened and I think you are just a deputy sheriff trying to do good."

"But you are not completely sold."

"Trust but verify," he said wearily.

"If I am not who I claim to be, what do you think I might be doing out here?"

"Like I said, I don't think you are anything except what you claim. I would be a hypocrite if I told you people don't change. But we share a belief and how we deal with that belief is what might separate us."

"And that belief is?" she asked.

He gave her a patronizing smile and said, "The belief Hersh is alive. The belief he set this up and he's somewhere pulling strings. Do we believe it because it could be true or because we want it to be true is up for debate. But no doubt we think it is possible."

She wanted to deny it outright but she would be lying. She heaved a sigh.

"Of course I thought it," she said. "Who wouldn't? But the coroner's report ended it for me. That many tests couldn't be wrong. Even if he fiddled with dental records, there were other tests. You can fault the feds for a lot of things but they are anal. I gave up the ghost yesterday."

He grimaced.

"Well, that is just a lie," he said.

"I beg your pardon."

"You are lying. Like me you're up at night trying to figure out how he could have done it. You don't hold out a lot of hope but you hold out hope of solving this locked room mystery.

She hung her head and grinned. "Guilty."

"Okay. So, we both think it is improbable but possible. And we are going to hang on with all our might."

"So we don't have different beliefs."

"I said we are different in how we hold those beliefs."

"Explain."

"This is going to offend you," he said.

"The barn door was opened a long time ago."

"When you were chasing Hersh, he saw it as a game. The black Taurus was part of the game and even though the office bugs were reprehensible, it was part of the game," he explained. "You thinking you were the good guys was laughable but it allowed you to compete by not worrying about the absolute scum you really were."

"We made some judgments that could be questioned," she said.

He snorted and continued.

"Here is what is not a game. If you are still with the feds and here as a plant to make Hersh show his hand, that will not work out for you or for your organization."

"Are you thinking they shipped me here to be undercover in hopes Hersh was alive and would put his trust in me?"

"Yes."

"Who would come up with a plan so crazy?"

"If I'm right, it would be you," Frankie said.

"Wow. Wow. Wow," she said and started laughing.

It was hard to tell if he was serious.

"I'd give you my word but you wouldn't be satisfied anyway," she began. "Out of curiosity, what are you saying would happen if I was trying to smoke him out?"

He looked out the window and pointed to the hills outside.

"How many holes you figure are on a single mound out there?"

"I don't know," she said. "Hundreds?"

He agreed. "Just enough to fill them with different parts of your body."

"Are you threatening me?"

"Are you still a federal agent?"

"I am not."

"Then I am not threatening you."

CHAPTER 80

As the train moved slowly down the track the man opened his paper and read the headlines. He didn't care for American politics but needed to be aware to fit in. He didn't escape the authorities to get caught in his new country.

He was rich with powerful friends but knew he couldn't be arrogant. Arrogance lost them a war and some had not learned their lesson.

He did enjoy reading about the new president and there were things he liked about Lyndon Johnson. He could impose his will on those inferior to him. The Americans boasted of being a peace-loving country and they had a new leader because the other one was murdered in his car.

He put the paper down and looked out the window. When he turned back he saw a woman coming toward him and he hoped she wouldn't take the empty seat next to him. He didn't like company and he wanted no conversation.

Women made the worst seatmates. They wanted to tell you about their families and the food they were serving and things so boring he sometimes wanted to pull out the gun in his briefcase and end the misery.

She jostled some packages as the train swayed. He thought she was going to lose everything when the engine lurched. But she stayed on her feet and put everything in the overhead. He should have helped but he didn't want to encourage contact.

He didn't mind being thought of as ungentlemanly if it saved him social interaction. She also looked Jewish and sometimes the revulsion involuntarily flared up. This was the wrong place for that to happen.

A minute later she took the aisle seat a row in back and he breathed a sigh of relief. He went back to his paper and the roll of the train first made him drowsy, then put him to sleep. When he awoke, it was dark.

Refreshed he turned to stretch and found the woman in the seat opposite him. To make it worse they were the only two in the car. He wanted to move but then thought it was she who should be taking a different seat.

Why was she here?

Now awake he expected her to start talking but she did not. He grew agitated waiting her out. It was a long ride and he didn't want to be uncomfortable.

"Madam," he said, "perhaps you would be more at ease if we spread out. We are the only ones in this car."

Still, she did not speak. He went from agitated to uneasy and back to agitation. Finally, he rose, picked up his briefcase and walked down the aisle to another seat.

It wasn't long before he felt humiliated at being made to move by a woman who barely acknowledged him. Trying to forget the whole thing he attempted to do some work and then found his pistol missing.

He looked around his seat and the overhead and checked his suit jacket and overcoat. Clenching his jaw, he marched to his original seat. He thanked his luck she was now sleeping and looked around while she dozed. No pistol was found.

Standing with his hands on his hips and totally confused he didn't see her open her eyes. But a few seconds later he deigned to speak with her.

"Madam, I seem to have lost an item when I was sitting here. Did you happen to find it?" he asked.

Surprisingly she answered him.

"What was the item?"

Not wanting to tell her he just shrugged his shoulders.

"Oh, it was nothing important. I'm sure it is in my luggage and I just thought I had packed it with my carry-on things."

She nodded and picked up a book. Clearly she had nothing to say to him and he found himself insulted. Who was she not to talk to him?

He apologized for bothering her and she raised her head to dismiss him and went back to her book. He slunk off and returned to his second seat where he again searched for the gun. He knew the pistol was close and became more confused and angry as the train made its way. The only place he hadn't searched was the woman's bags.

He marched and stood until she looked up from the book.

"What I lost is very valuable and at the risk of being rude, I ask if you have anything of mine?" he asked.

"What did you lose?" she asked.

Seeing no alternative, he said, "I had a pistol in my briefcase. It has sentimental value. So, for a third time, did you find it?"

She shrugged and returned to her reading.

Slumping in the chair across from her he sat, deciding his next move. It wouldn't be prudent to go into her luggage but realized he had little choice. He figured to start with her pocketbook but when he reached for it he heard a click.

It took a moment to realize he'd been handcuffed to the seat and the woman was reading again.

"What is the meaning of this?" he demanded but got no answer.

A few minutes later she walked the length of the car and returned with his briefcase and suitcase. She sat down to read but this time she had his personal papers.

When he protested, she held up a finger. Finishing the document in her hands she placed it back in the case and sat next to him.

"Now, Herr Doktor, we can have the chat you wanted," she said.

"Herr Doktor?" he exclaimed. "You have me confused with someone else."

"Stop," she said. And he did. He looked at her.

"This will go a lot faster if you don't deny the basic facts. I know who and what you are. So please don't insult my intelligence."

Tugging on the handcuffs he tried to intimidate her. Failing that, he taunted her.

"In a few minutes the porter is coming and he'll get the transit police and then I'll make sure you spend a long time in prison. I'm not a man without influence."

She started to giggle and then outright laughed in his face.

"What is so funny?"

"The irony is too good," she said. "You on a train wondering about your future."

Frowning, he became just a little frightened but knew not to show it.

"I have no idea what you are talking about," he said. "If you think I'm somebody else then let us get to the bottom of it."

She reached over into his coat pocket and took out his wallet and looked at his ID. She frowned and he let himself hope this would be over soon.

"Roger Madison?" she asked.

"Yes," he said.

"No," she said.

"What do you mean?" he demanded.

"You are not Roger Madison. You are Geoff von Rickard."

Now he was panicked but he didn't give it up.

"Who?"

"Stop with the charade. If you want to get to the end of this, you can't keep denying everything."

"My name is Roger Madison," he repeated.

She stared down at his ID again and pursed her lips before speaking again.

"And you live in Chester, Pennsylvania."

"I do."

"Have you lived there long?"

He pondered what to say. "Yes, a long time," he said.

"*Sie sind ein Lügner, Arzt,*" she barked.

He pretended not to understand.

"What are you saying?" he whined.

"*Der Krieg ist noch nicht vorbei fur uns noch,*" she said in such a soft voice he didn't know at first whether it was directed at him.

"Please, please, this is a mistake," he said.

"I had hoped to talk in the mother tongue again but I can't have everything," she said. "First, let us dispose of any confusion. You are Geoff von Rickard. You were a doctor in the camps and you disappeared in 1944. You were one of the smarter ones. You figured 17 years of looking over your shoulder was enough."

The smile she gave was pure evil. "The good news, Herr Doktor, is as of this minute you can stop looking. We found you."

"Who are you?" he hissed.

"Does it matter?" she responded. "Why don't you consider me one of those faceless hordes you watched herded off cattle cars. You didn't know our names then so why start now?"

"You are going to be sorry when you find out I'm not who you think I am."

She pulled out a photo. He was startled to see a younger version of himself. He was grinning as he posed underneath a group of prisoners who had been hung.

"Is it supposed to be me?" he said.

She looked at the photo like she mistakenly pulled out the wrong one.

"This isn't you?" she asked.

"I'm an American, not a Nazi," he shouted. "Why do you think I'm this guy?"

Slumping in her seat, she cast her eyes down at the floor.

"So what do I do now?" she asked.

"Well, first, you should unlock me and then an apology would be nice."

Pondering his requests, she reached again into her handbag and this time pulled out his gun.

"I guess I should return this to you also," she said.

"That would be nice. I just want to put this behind me," he said as he put out his shackled hand.

"Well, first, I should apologize. I'm new at this."

He wanted to snatch the gun but she was out of his reach. So he tried to remain patient. But once he was let go then he would be in charge and she would find out what a mistake she had made.

"Thank you," he said. "But I really think you need to unlock me. I'm getting scared and to be honest a little angry."

Reaching over she swung the butt of the gun across his chin. His shocked look gave way to pain and he cried in anguish.

Spitting blood, he saw the gun was back in its upright position with the barrel pointing at his head.

"You bitch," he screamed.

"There it is, there it is!" she said with glee. "I knew we'd see the real you. A sadistic bastard like you wouldn't respond to anything except the real deal. Talk wasn't going to get you to confess but the true colors have come out, Doktor."

"I will kill you," he said.

"Another ironic moment, don't you think?" she asked before squeezing the trigger twice. The first bullet would have been enough but she was a beginner, relatively speaking.

At the next stop she collected her belongings but left the photo on the slumped body.

If she were cautious she would have dropped the gun down a sewer but liked the feel. It was a long time since she had seen a Sauer 38H.

CHAPTER 81

Thrilled to have Betty at the track with her, Roza, if honest, would have preferred to see Hersh getting out of the car. She missed her grandson and a day trackside should be shared with those closest to you.

In the past week Roza had taken a slide downhill. She could no longer see information contained in the past performances and so Betty guided the magnifying glass she now used. The labor-intensive process resulted in Roza playing only the feature.

"I think we're going to get well today," she told Betty.

"Is that good?" asked the teenager.

Pointing to the carpetbag on the chair, Roza said, "It means it might take two of us to carry that out."

Betty wanted to ask if Roza worried about getting robbed and realized how stupid a question that was.

Somewhere on Roza's person was a weapon. Even if you made the mistake of preying on a feeble woman you wouldn't get past grabbing the handle of the bag.

"Well, I'm excited," said Betty.

"Right now you'll have to be patient," Roza said. "We will eat lunch and wait for our race. We can talk and catch up."

Betty figured this might be the day they talked about Hersh. She didn't wait long to find out she was right.

"Do you miss him?" the older woman asked.

"From the time I wake up until I go to sleep," Betty said.

"Do you hear from him?" asked Roza.

Betty looked up sharply.

"I mean, did he leave you any presents or reminders?" said Roza.

"All the time," Betty said. "I'll get something in the mail. It might be money or a joke. One time I got a box of Raymond Chandler books."

Roza looked pleased.

"Anything in the books?"

"Sure. Some were underlined and I think about what he was trying to say. Sometimes I'll find a map and when I follow it there will be something else for me."

Betty grinned, then continued. "One time I got a letter telling me I must go to the track with you at least once. Even from the grave he's guiding me."

Roza nodded.

"Sometimes I think I see him," she said. "I thought I saw him going up an elevator in a building. One day I thought I saw him in a car and twice I swore he was at the track. Once I got up to use the restroom and when I returned someone had circled a horse in a race."

"Did it win?" Betty asked.

"Didn't pick up its feet," laughed Roza. "That is why I figured it was Hersh. A lovely boy, but an awful handicapper. It was one thing I couldn't pass onto him."

Betty chuckled and then grew serious. "I ache when I think I'll see him at work and then remember. But I'm young and I'll get through by remembering what he did for me. But I worry about Frankie. I'll catch him with such a look of sadness."

Roza put her hand to her heart.

"The collateral damage could be devastating. And *entre nous*, I will not accept it. Someone will pay."

Betty had no doubt the threat was real. She pitied the party who had to answer for fallout from Hersh's death. Facing the end only made Roza more dangerous.

"He's so strong in many ways," Betty said. "But this could be a crusher. You know he was out west talking to Marian."

"I did know," said Roza. "He's closing possible loopholes. He wanted to make sure Marian wasn't working some end around."

"Where would he get that idea?" Betty said, arching one eyebrow.

Roza patted Betty's cheek.

"We need to put Frankie on the back burner and find out how you are doing," she said.

"Actually, pretty good," Betty said. "I'm young and in love. I lost a friend but the Dalai Lama said I'll achieve total consciousness on my deathbed, so I've got that going for me."

Roza didn't smile at that.

"Movie quotes won't answer my question," she said. "I can't have you going off the reservation over this. If I can help at all don't hesitate to call."

Betty shocked the older woman when she rose and kissed her full on the lips.

"You'll always be my best girl," Betty told Roza. "I wouldn't ever upset you. When I tell you I'm doing well, I mean it. I'm coping. I don't know whether there will be any PTSD but I don't think so."

Roza touched her upper lip. "It has been a long time since a woman kissed me like that."

Betty's shocked look made Roza give one of her own.

"Why do young people think you are the only ones who ever experimented?" she said. "I've had adventures all over the world."

Betty looked contrite and waved off her friend.

"You're not the type who kisses and tells."

"Wasn't the type," agreed Roza. "But maybe I want my story out there now."

"I'm guessing I won't know the whole story in one afternoon," said Betty.

"Not in many afternoons," the older woman agreed. "But a little will go a long way and hopefully by the end of the day we'll have money to celebrate your knowledge."

Roza allowed Betty to bet the feature and it took her 30 minutes to spread the money through several tellers. Roza believed in numerous betting slips.

The exhilarating feeling of betting money never fades but it is never as acute as when the winnings make a bigger difference.

What never changed was her appreciation for the animals in front of her. Even when she had no money on a race she loved to watch the horses run.

There is something about the outside of a horse that is good for the inside of a man, she believed, along with Winston Churchill.

So when the gates snapped open, she might as well have been by herself. No one could interrupt her joy at what she saw through her binoculars. She was rooting for her selection but she wanted the entire field to run the best race of their lives.

When they turned for home, she put down her field glasses and her eyes were moist. As Roza remained calm, Betty was screaming as their horse took the lead and then shook off all challengers.

They waited for the next race before walking to collect. Meeting at the teller in the middle, Roza had filled her purse and Betty the carpetbag. They drove around to the backside.

On many days the grooms and trainers would have left, but Roza let them know when she was at the track and they waited. It used to be for payoffs but they enjoyed time with her. It didn't escape their notice how happy she was handing out tribute.

They also knew these days were dwindling.

CHAPTER 82

When Maise Williams died in the winter, Frankie wanted to make sure Peter didn't fall through the cracks and into social services. No amount of care by Frankie could overcome that tragedy.

Frankie drew stares at the funeral. How could he not? But not as many as he would have had his motorcycle not been a familiar site in the neighborhood. He stood with Peter at the graveside and they held hands throughout the service.

The little man was holding up but the hard part came after. As they shoveled dirt down the hole, they waited until the casket was covered before walking away.

Before getting to the limo they were intercepted by a man who looked out of place. When he spoke, Frankie knew why.

"Mr. Dolan?" he asked.

Frankie stopped and looked at the man, whose suit cost more than what most people here made in six months.

"Yes," said Frankie.

"I'm Thomas Moreland, Mrs. Williams' lawyer."

Frankie found it hard to believe looking at the man but he had no doubts the man was telling the truth. Mrs. Williams had spent some of the money he gave for legal help.

"Is this the time?" Frankie asked gently.

"I wanted to let you know the papers were signed and processed and just need your signature."

Frankie looked confused and grabbing Peter's hand he walked to the car and motioned for the lawyer to get in.

"This is probably a little more private," said Frankie.

The lawyer sat in the back while Peter sat with the driver, who put the privacy shield up.

"You have me at a disadvantage," said Frankie. "What papers?"

"The papers for you to assume guardianship of Peter," he said.

Rarely surprised, Frankie was stunned.

"It is what you wanted?" asked the lawyer.

Frankie could only move his head in agreement.

"Mrs. Williams drew up the papers and signed them a while back."

"What kind of legal battle do you think there will be over this?" Frankie asked.

The lawyer chortled. "None, sir."

"How could that be?" Frankie asked.

"All parties have agreed," he said.

Frankie wanted to ask how that was possible and then realized how. He knew whose fingerprints were all over this. The talk with the uncle would have been particularly interesting, he thought. No doubt money greased the wheels but there had to be something else to ensure no one tried to change Mrs. Williams' mind.

Shaking hands with the lawyer, Frankie opened the front door and motioned for Peter. He would not do this unless the young boy was behind it 100 percent.

They took a walk back to the graveside and sat on chairs recently filled with mourners.

"Peter, your grandmother says you are to come live with me," said Frankie. "But only if you want it to happen."

Peter hugged the big man, his arms barely reaching halfway around Frankie's waist. The little man and the big man held each other and for the second time in an hour were crying.

The limo took them to Peter's house, where he picked up his stuff. The last thing he grabbed was his grandmother's records.

Peter told Betty and Roza the news and it took the men 10 minutes to get them to stop crying.

Then Peter got everyone tearing up with a simple question.

"Did Mr. Hersh have anything to do with this?"

CHAPTER 83

When Marian got off the night shift she was surprised but not shocked to see her former boss sitting at her desk.

"Robert," she said. "What brings you to the reservation? Is D.C. too hot this time of year?"

"At least pretend to be happy to see me," he said.

"I'm not unhappy," she answered. "Unless you are here to make me unhappy."

"No, no," he said, without convincing her.

"It will be easier if you just come out with it," she said.

He pointed to an interview room.

"What's up?" she said.

"I want to close the book on the investigation," he said.

"How can I help?"

"By signing a declaration you've haven't been contacted by him."

She gaped at him. "This is the second time in a month I've been asked if I've seen a ghost."

Before he could ask she said, "Frankie was here accusing me of working for you to smoke out Hersh."

That raised his eyebrows.

"I'll tell you what I told him. If you think a coroner was wrong in any of the five ways he declared the body to be Hersh, then keep investigating. If you think Eddie Doss was lying about shooting him or our sharpshooter actually missed, then you keep the case open. Otherwise, we should get on with our lives."

Her former boss looked at her a moment and then just nodded his head.

"I can't vouch for Mr. Doss and I have full faith in our sharpshooters. But it might interest you to know that Dr. Scarbath retired right after the case."

The information caught Marian off guard but after processing it she merely shrugged.

"Everyone has to step down sometime," she said.

"So, you don't find the timing curious?" he asked.

"I don't."

Gregory debated about continuing and then dove in.

"What if I told you that Scarbath had a child," he said.

"A lot of people have children," she answered.

"The child was caught up in the whole Catholic church mess," he said.

"What are you saying Robert?"

"Just giving you the facts."

"And I'm going to bite on what you are serving. So, tell me the story."

"It wasn't a priest but it was somebody connected to the church."

"Did they catch him?

"Yes and no."

Marian didn't have to think about what he was saying.

"They found the guy dead?"

"Yes."

"With a confession next to the body?"

"Yes."

"Confession is good for the soul," she said.

"That it is."

"I'm intrigued but I'm thinking coincidence."

"So you'll sign?"

"Give me the paper," she said snappishly. "Could you guys be any more anal?"

"If it is any consolation, Mackerson alternates between being giddy and being scared. I don't think he's sleeping too well."

"Actually, it is consolation," she said.

"Glad I could be the bearer of good news."

She signed the paper and handed it back to him.

"Enjoying being a deputy?" he asked.

"You deal with a lot less assholes at the top," she said with a grin he returned.

"So you don't want your job back?"

"No, Robert, I think I've had enough of the federal government."

"Not even if it came with a raise and an office in the nation's capital?"

"Pass."

"You don't think you're wasted here?"

"What a strange comment for you to make."

"Touché."

"You know I don't blame you. I shouldn't have expected you to act differently. But I never thought you'd work for or with Mackerson."

"You have to grow up and face the facts at some point," he said.

"Not really," she said. "Sad to see you here running errands for him."

"We choose to see things differently," he said.

"I'm as surprised as you are that I'm okay with it."

"You were a good agent," he said.

She grinned at him. "Robert, if we agree on anything it should be I was a great agent."

That made him laugh and they had coffee together and talked fondly of the old days before he left.

Separating on good terms made her happier than it should have but maybe she was growing up. She feared the former and prayed for the latter.

It was some weeks later while making small talk with another deputy, as they waited for the techs to come and collect evidence on the busting of a small meth lab, that she heard the news.

"Well, it isn't a federal bust but this is pretty big for this part of the world," said Percy Milling.

"Your first drug bust?" asked Marian.

"Oh, we've had cocaine and marijuana arrests of course," he said. "Even had a guy with some heroin, but never on this level. It looks like they were shipping out the stuff."

"It is good to do good work," she said.

"You said it," he agreed. "So, are you going back east for the funeral?"

"Hmm," she said barely catching his words. "What funeral?"

"Didn't you work for that Mackerson guy?" Milling asked.

Marian came to full attention.

"You didn't hear?" he asked.

She dumbly shook her head.

"Saw it on the internet this morning before I came out here. I guess you were already on your way. Died in his office of a heart attack."

Marian made several calculations at the same time.

"They sure of the heart attack," she said as a statement and not a question.

"Coroner says so," Milling said. "They are doing an autopsy, though."

"Pro forma," said Marian.

"I guess. Anyway, I guess you're out of that mess anyway."

"You don't know the half of it," she said as she stared down at her ringing phone. She saw the number and hit accept.

"I just heard, Robert," she said.

"Didn't know if you had," he answered.

"When is the funeral?"

"You coming out?"

"Probably not."

"Well, we need to see what the autopsy shows."

"Any doubts?" she asked.

"Not really but the timing is curious and after our talk it is just a bit jarring."

"I can see how it would be. Will you be in charge of the investigation?"

Gregory cleared his throat. "Guilty," he said to her.

"Makes sense," she said.

"I'm not figuring to find anything, but when this happens after you close a big case you have to dot all the Is and cross all the Ts."

"And utter every cliché," she added.

"It will be by the book," he said.

"When you finish, you can run it up the flagpole and see who salutes. But I'm guessing everyone will be saluting no matter what you find."

"I could use you on this one," he said suddenly.

"Whoa, not a chance. I've got a job and even if I didn't I have no urge to put my mouth in the lion's mouth again," she said.

"You've wasted a cliché of your own," he said.

"Robert, you need to be careful. If you find he died of a heart attack there will be people who don't believe you. If you suspect foul play you'll open yourself to a career-damaging backlash."

There was a silence on the phone.

"But look on the bright side," she said. "If he was murdered you'll have a ready-made pool of suspects."

"Whom might be in that pool?" he asked.

"Anyone who ever met the guy," she said.

"Bada boom," he said. "Always a mood lifter to talk to you."

"It is why I take your calls," she said.

CHAPTER 84

Standing at the cemetery it was hard to believe a year had passed. But here they were at the cemetery unveiling Hersh's stone.

Roza was covered in a blanket as she sat in the wheelchair. Sharp mentally, her body was giving up any chance of correcting itself. She talked when addressed but didn't seem interested in starting conversation.

Betty and Seth were the success story. They looked as much in love as they were. With Betty now going to school full-time she didn't come by the clinic every day but spent her free moments with her boyfriend.

Frankie brought Peter because he begged to be included. Even Frankie was surprised how quickly they became a family, with Clemenza the second child.

The dog and the boy were inseparable, with Clemenza laying at the bus stop at the end of the day. The hardest part was giving Peter room. Frankie still worried about him but Peter was now able to take care of himself.

Frankie had to attend a meeting at school after Peter took matters into his own hands when a younger boy was being picked on.

Marian came alone but the others were glad to see her. Betty squeezed her hand and Frankie gave a thumbs-up. It seemed strange to be back here and stranger to be among people who were the closest she had to friends.

Frankie spoke first at the gravesite.

"An old Jewish man is walking across the street when he's hit by a bus. As he lays there the bus driver jumps out and takes off his coat and puts it under the man's head. He says to the Jewish guy, 'Are you comfortable?' and the man shrugs and says, 'I make a living.' "

Betty stepped up next.

"A Jewish grandmother is babysitting when a wave takes her grandson into the middle of the ocean. She starts wailing to God to bring him back and she'll do anything if he does. A second later another wave carries the boy back to shore. The grandmother picks up her grandson, looks at him and then hugs him. Then she looks skyward and says, 'He had a hat.' "

Roza sat and smiled.

"To say goodbye is to die a little," she said. "That is Raymond Chandler from *The Long Goodbye.*"

Marian declined to speak, deeming it a tad hypocritical. So they adjourned to the deli.

"How are things out on the range?" Frankie asked Marian. "When you find a dead guy, does somebody pay the cripple boy who sweeps up the saloon two bits to run and get the sheriff?"

"Seriously," said Betty, "how hard is it to round up a posse?"

"My God, I've stepped onto the set of the *Milton Berle Show,*" said Marian.

It was Roza, who hadn't spoken since they left the cemetery, that brought them back to why they were all here.

"Thank all of you who came near and far for this," she said. "It would have meant a lot to him. My son and daughter-in-law and my granddaughters couldn't make it because it was just too damn hard and I think we know how they feel."

She got a sly smile and added, "But we few, we happy few, we band of brothers; for he today that sheds his blood with me shall be my brother."

Frankie stood up and clapped and took up the cudgel, "And gentlemen in England now abed shall think themselves accursed they were not here and hold their manhoods cheap whiles any speaks who fought with us upon Saint Crispin's day."

They toasted themselves and Frankie said, "Hersh is rolling in his grave knowing we went Willy Shakes on him. That will teach the bastard to leave us."

"Well said," shouted Betty.

The day was remembered for a lot of things and all were glad to be a part. But it would be a bittersweet memory because later Roza pulled

Frankie to the side and whispered, "With Hersh gone I'm going to need your promise."

Those were the last words she ever spoke.

It was Peter who noticed she was sitting at an angle and wasn't following the conversation. He tugged at Frankie's sleeve and his father went pale.

When the EMTs arrived, she was breathing but Frankie figured Sham had a better chance of catching Secretariat then Roza did of living out the week.

He was wrong but not by much. She lived, if you could call it that. She recognized no one and doctors gave the smallest of chances to avoid her vegetative state. They took turns sitting by her bedside and talked like she was going to respond at any minute.

Betty had the idea of playing famous race calls but it didn't rouse her. Mostly they held her hand and listened to the beeps of the machine. Each evening Frankie pledged he would carry out his promise and each morning he delayed another day.

He felt like a coward. One night he felt a hand on his shoulder and looked to see Betty, who had come to take a shift.

"Boy, was I asleep," he said.

"I thought I had two people in a coma in here," said Betty.

While stretching, he saw an envelope on the table. Since he opened her mail he knew this had come while he was napping. While Betty straightened the room and talked to Roza, he went to the window and looked out.

The city was at its best at this time. No traffic and the few people moved at their own pace. In the moonlight, he opened the envelope.

It contained a short message that made Frankie laugh out loud.

"Something funny?" asked Betty.

Frankie wiped a tear and turned to her. "Best joke ever," he said.

EPILOGUE

He crept into the hospital room and looked at the patient, who was clinging onto life with the little she had left. The breathing was shallow and the eyes showed no recognition. At this hour, only the pumps keeping her alive made noise. He looked out the window at the moon and sighed.

He picked up the chair and moved it next to the bed. He held the hand dominated by skin so papery he thought he would tear it if treated too roughly. There was no recognition but he knew somewhere she was there and she would appreciate him being here.

He didn't talk and before long he felt a single tear leak out of his right eye. Then he laughed as he remembered his high school Shakespeare.

If it were done when 'tis done, then 'twere well it were done quickly.

A little something from the Scottish play was little more than macabre now.

He reached into his briefcase and removed a slender book and opened it to page 216, the final page.

"A hundred feet down in the canyon a small coupe was smashed against the side of a huge granite boulder. It was almost upside down, leaning a little. There were three men down there. They had moved the car enough to lift something out.

"Something that had been a man."

He closed the book and smiled. "We've once again finished The Lady in the Lake, *" he said to the sleeping form. "Only this time it is my turn to tell you not to worry, I'm here and everything is going to be okay."*

Her previously lifeless hand squeezed his twice and he smiled.

He lifted himself off the chair and turned off the machine keeping her alive.

Then he walked away.

ABOUT THE AUTHOR

Reid Cherner spent 40 years as a reporter, including 33 years with USA TODAY as a sports writer. His assignments took him from high school games to nine Olympics but he most enjoyed his 19 years covering horse racing. A collector of Bill Bradley memorabilia and $10 bills, he lives in Potomac, Maryland, with his wife, Sara, and their hound dog Huckleberry.